BLOOD ON THE MOTORWAY

PAUL STEPHENSON

HOLLOW STONE

Copyright © 2016 by Paul Stephenson

All rights reserved.

No portion of this book may be reproduced in any form without written permission from the publisher or author, except as permitted by U.S. copyright law.

Current edition published 2023

Published by Hollow Stone Press

Contents

For Ellen, who is the reason you're reading this.

Chapter One
The Beginning and the End

Tom ran his fingers over a cracked wine glass, staring out of the kitchen window, his hands frozen from the bowl of icy water. Had he known the world was about to end he might not have bothered with the washing up.

While Leon sat outside oblivious to the cold, Tom had resorted to putting on every available article of clothing he had. Three pairs of socks and he still couldn't feel his toes. Leon, on the other hand, sat out on the crumbling patio with nothing more than jeans, a T-shirt and a bottle of supermarket own-brand bourbon to fend off the arctic conditions. It made for a ridiculous spectacle, but Tom still half-admired him for it.

Four of them had come to the seaside city of Sunderland some seven years previous, all fresh-faced and innocently prepared for three years of hard work. The plan was to toil earnestly in their mid-level academic institution, then beat a quick exit to the working world. The best part of a decade later, all they had to show for it were perpetual hangovers, short-term memory loss, decimated credit ratings, and piss-poor degrees in irrelevant subjects. Now they were stuck, eternally trying to live the student life on ever decreasing means.

The city itself had proved to have a limitless supply of two things: cheap alcohol and a North Sea breeze that could flatten a man. All you could do once winter came was stock up on the former, crank up the heat and stay indoors.

Unfortunately for Tom and the other residents of the house on Riversdale Terrace, it had been five days since the gas, along with all the other amenities, had been cut off. The house now creaked constantly as it adjusted to the lack of heat, and Tom was concerned the next major event in his life would be dealing with a burst water pipe. There had been portentous rumblings from deep within the walls.

Earlier, Tom had heard Danny banging about against those walls, presumably in an attempt to keep warm. The noise had stopped as abruptly as it had started; Tom guessed his housemate had either given up or knocked himself out.

Their final housemate was a housemate no more. That morning, Adam had collapsed in a sobbing heap after phoning his parents to come and rescue him, then sat on the stairs in silence until they arrived. His father had been so shocked at the conditions his son had been living in, as though he'd walked into some BBC Four documentary on Northern drug dens. They'd left most of Adam's belongings behind in their haste to escape. Tom had taken to house-work to combat the cold, the boredom, and the embarrassment he'd felt when he'd seen the look on Adam's father's face. He'd tidied the communal areas as best he could, then turned his attention to the tower of washing up, a task made near impossible by the lack of hot water.

Throughout all this he'd kept thinking. He needed to get out of this house. This house was where all dreams came to die.

Thinking about how much his life sucked made his head hurt, and the cold water made his hands ache, so he abandoned both tasks.

Since he had arrived in Sunderland he had become a distant echo of his earlier, hungrier self, and nothing at all like the man he'd once thought he would be. All ambition had drained away, eroded by endless nights of excess and days of tedium and daytime television.

He caught sight of Leon again, looking serene on his mouldy plastic sun lounger, dressed in baggy jeans and a faded T-shirt with an ironic vintage computer game logo, just as always. Not that Tom could claim to be any more sartorially developed; his own wardrobe was full of black T-shirts covered with indecipherable heavy metal band names and rude words.

Tom slid open the French doors and entered the terrace.

'Leon?'

'Thomas,' Leon replied, somewhat slurred.

'I thought black guys did better in the heat. Aren't you cold?'

'Fucking frozen.'

'Well come inside then, you berk,' Tom said. 'You'll end up a fucking icicle out here.'

Leon shrugged.

'No, I like it. It's refreshing, and it doesn't smell like feet out here.'

Tom shook his head and turned to go back into the house.

'Have some generic supermarket own-brand bourbon, it helps immensely,' Leon called to him. He offered the half bottle to Tom. Tom turned back, took it and swigged, enjoying the sting as it hit the back of his throat, then the creeping warmth that flowed through him.

He pulled up the chair of crates they had fashioned as a second seat and considered the crumbling exterior of the house. Moss attacked the pipes, and vines had penetrated the brickwork to the extent that the wall now sagged. A month or so ago, they had confronted their landlord over the matter, but he had raised the topic of rent unpaid, and they had beaten a hasty retreat.

'Adam's gone,' Tom said, remembering Leon had missed the action. 'I think he had a bit of a breakdown actually. His dad looked at the house like he'd just walked into Gomorrah before bundling Adam into his Range Rover.'

Leon laughed. 'I don't blame him. Anyway, we don't need his TV now we don't have any electricity.'

'That's true,' Tom replied, taking another deep swig.

Distant storm clouds darkened the night sky, bruising swathes of it a deep purple. They watched them in silence. The buzz from the bourbon diffused the anxiety that had sat in the pit of Tom's stomach all day.

'I think it's time I left too,' he said.

'Maybe you're right,' Leon replied. 'It's stopped being fun, hasn't it?' He motioned for Tom to return the bottle. Overhead an angry rumble issued from the sky.

'It has,' Tom replied.

'Hey, maybe we should do something together.'

'Like what?'

'Well I've spent the day putting together a very vague plan.'

'And here's me thinking you were just getting drunk.' He laughed.

'The two aren't mutually exclusive, you know.'

'So what was the plan?'

'Road trip.'

Tom waited for him to elaborate, but he didn't.

'Road trip?' Tom asked. 'What, around England? That'd be a pretty fucking short trip. Devon and back. We'd be home again in a week.' He took the bottle.

'Beats sitting around in this shithole though, doesn't it?'

He had a point. For the past few weeks, Tom's main source of personal achievement had come from a crossword puzzle which had taken him over a day to complete.

'What do we do on this road trip?' Tom asked.

Leon shrugged. 'I thought I'd leave that part of the plan to you, since you're the brains of the operation.'

'Okay. Why not? Road trip. Makes perfect sense.' He stood, and shivered. 'You coming in for a smoke?'

'Nah,' Leon replied.

Tom went back in. A road trip had merits, he supposed. He could write, get the inspiration for a novel, pick up some freelance work here and there. He sure as shit wasn't doing any writing here. It would make sense for Leon, too. Tom's best friend, since their first day of University, had always struggled with being one of the few black faces in a predominately white northern town, and he'd spoken more than once about wanting to escape. He was an artist, or at least he had been. The painting of Buffy on the wall of Tom's bedroom that had been a Christmas present some years back was probably the last thing his friend had actually painted, but being an art student still served as an admirable chat up line in the pubs and clubs of Sunderland.

He was a good friend though, despite his flaws. Or maybe Leon's flaws just complemented his own. If he was going to leave, he couldn't think of anyone he'd rather do it with.

Tom went back to the lounge and pulled out a little baggie of weed, some skins and tobacco, from a drawer, and set about rolling a joint. He felt the old familiar pang of guilt at not being able to pay the electricity bills, but somehow always managing to find money for weed, then buried it where he normally did.

He lit it, took a deep drag, watched the acrid smoke fill the cold room and thought about leaving. There was nothing tying him here; no work, no family, and few remaining friends. Countless acquaintances maybe, but what good were they? Since the house had fallen into its current state, there wasn't much to separate him from being de facto homeless.

Sinking into the broken sofa, his eyes fell on the dead television, the collection of games consoles, and the towers of DVDs gathering dust. Even his beloved smart phone was now an uncharged brick of useless technology. Maybe the landlord would find all this junk and accept it as rent owed.

A low rumble issued from the sky, barely perceptible at first, but then back it grew louder. Tom took a deep drag of the spliff and walked to the back door. Lights were flickering against the windows so he went back onto the terrace.

Something was wrong. The hairs on his arms stood in rapt attention. Outside, the volume trebled, thunder rolling on and on.

Leon stood up, staring at the storm clouds, mouth agape. Tom looked up. Heavy black clouds covered the sky, spidery arcs of light dancing through them.

'It's warm,' Leon said.

He was right. Tom's permanent goose bumps were gone.

Tom handed Leon the spliff. 'It's not raining either.' Despite the constant rumble and the thick black clouds there was no moisture in the air.

His ears popped. The volume grew again: loud cracking sounds and the sounds of metal expanding and contracting, like old pipes called into action. Tom heard a whistling sound too; although he couldn't tell if it was just in his head. The light show intensified, veins of electricity dancing through the cloud, growing thicker and changing colour.

'Can you hear that?' Leon shouted, but Tom could barely hear him over the din.

As if someone had turned up a dial, pressure filled the air; dropping like a brick on Tom's chest. His legs buckled, everything went dark, and he fell to the ground.

His eyes opened to daylight. A stab of pain rocketed up his left side to greet the day. The rough edges of a dream played at the edge of his memory, something about a weird storm, but then realised he was lying not on his hard bed but on the cold concrete of the terrace. He tried to move, but it hurt. His cheek was wet, his hand too. With a rising panic he brought it up to his eye line, expecting blood.

Drool. That was one less panic, then. His tongue felt like a hard, dry sock, and his ears were ringing. With all the energy he could summon, he dragged himself up, his joints protesting at every small exertion.

Leon slept next to him on the concrete, his chest rising and falling. Tom saw the half-smoked spliff on the floor and picked it up, his hands groping for a lighter, glad it hadn't burnt itself out. He wondered if this was the right response to waking up like this, but his head was a fog of noise and confusion and his nerves were shot to hell.

He lit up, breathing deep and greeting the warm wave of intoxication. The clouds had gone and taken the warmth of the storm with them. The air felt crisp and clean. Purified.

The ground was bone dry. There had been no rain. The only moisture was his own puddle of saliva. He listened for sounds, but aside from birdsong there was nothing.

Leon started to wake, then shot bolt upright, his face full of confusion and fear. 'What the fuck?' he shouted, his voice raspy and hoarse.

'Don't look at me,' Tom said, his own voice husky and cracked. 'I've only just woken up. Spliff?'

Leon stood and took the nearly-dead joint.

'Fucking hell,' was all he could muster. He looked up at the house. 'We should go and see if Danny saw the storm.'

Tom hadn't even thought about their third housemate. Danny barely registered when he stood in front of him. He surfaced from his room only occasionally, generally to plunder the fridge. Since the power died, sightings had become rarer still. Tom had wondered how he was even passing the time now he couldn't play World of Warcraft for eighteen hours a day.

Back in the house, Tom pulled on another jumper, then he and Leon headed up the stairs. They passed Leon's room. Tom glimpsed inside and saw it was immaculate as ever. For one of the laziest people Tom had ever known, Leon was fastidious when it came to his own space. It was the communal areas he didn't give a shit about.

Danny's door was covered in stickers from countless nights out, remnants of a time before he'd discovered massively-multiplayer online games and became a warlock, or whatever the fuck it was.

Tom knocked. No answer. He tried again. He looked at Leon, who shrugged and started pounding on the door with his fists.

'Danny,' he bellowed, 'let us in, you miserable fucker!'

Still no response.

Tom tried the handle. Locked. Danny was the only one in the house who had a lock, the result of smoke-induced paranoia.

'Maybe we should kick it in?' Tom asked.

'Danny, we're going to break down the door!' Leon shouted. They gave it ten seconds or so, then Leon shrugged.

Tom threw his weight against the door. It gave at the first attempt, swinging inward. Before Leon could congratulate him, they saw Danny's body. He lay on the bedroom floor, eyes open in a terrified stare, blood smeared across his face, mouth open in a silent scream.

Leon stepped back. 'Holy fuck!'

They both stared through the doorway for a moment, then entered the room slowly, unable to take their eyes off the contorted corpse. Neither said a word. Danny lay in an awkward position. One leg rested up on the bed, the other tucked behind itself. The blood appeared to have come from his mouth and nose, but other than that Tom could see no visible reason for him to be lying dead on the floor.

'Danny?' Leon asked.

Tom's mind ran through every police procedural show he'd ever seen and wondered how this would look to a homicide detective. The house one step removed from a crack den. The broken door. The dead housemate. His stomach dipped in fear. 'We should call the police.'

'Okay.'

Tom left the room, careful to give the body a wide berth. He looked back at Leon, who was fumbling for a cigarette.

He ran downstairs, his mind racing. Hands shaking, he picked up the house phone and punched in nine-nine-nine, but there was no dial tone. His eyes drifted to the collection of burned-out candles on the mantelpiece. It was a miracle the whole place hadn't burned down in the night.

His mobile phone hadn't worked in days. He tried turning it on to see if it would give him enough juice for one call, but it refused to give him so much as a flicker. Tom flung it against the wall. It didn't even have the good grace to shatter in a satisfying manner, instead falling to the floor with a thud. He remembered the pay phone across the street. He could call the Police from there, if it wasn't already kicked into oblivion by the feral youth of Sunderland. He pulled on his coat and headed for the door.

Halfway down the steps, he stopped.

The smell, burning meat mingled with the heavy stench of petrol, caught at the back of his throat before his eyes could register the devastation before him. Max's Newsagent – good old Max's – was gone, burnt to the ground as though a large fiery thumb had come from the sky and stubbed it out. Corpses lay all over the street. Some were burnt, their limbs curled into themselves from the heat. Some were crushed, entangled in one of several car wrecks that dotted the road. Limbs, torsos and heads were strewn haphazardly in their wake. Some were just dead, lying there oblivious to the carnage that surrounded them.

Dozens of corpses. Old corpses. Young corpses. Bodies, and dead, and bodies again, to the end of the street and beyond. It was more than he could process. Tom stopped, sank onto the step with a thud, and wept.

Chapter Two
Shelter from the Storm

There was something disconcerting about opening her eyes to total darkness. Before Jen could think too much about that, though, there was the pain in her back and neck to contend with. And not knowing where she was. Or what was happening.

What the fuck is going on?

Her heart started to race. She moved a foot, and her shoe made contact with something.

Am I sitting down?

Memories started coming back through the fog of confusion. She'd gone to the cinema with Katie. The big multiplex outside of town rather than the much nicer one in the city centre. Katie had man troubles, as per usual, and the man in question worked at the nice cinema. They had sneaked in some vodka and proceeded to get drunk in a half empty screening room, watching some dreadful schmaltz.

Then, nothing.

'Hello?' she called out.

The room was completely dark. Had she passed out in her seat and been left there by inattentive cinema staff?

She stood, and her back spasmed. She fished out her phone to check the time, feeling around the edge for the button, but it did nothing. Not even a cursory attempt to boot up before dying.

The darkness didn't abate. She felt dizzy and confused. She kept blinking, expecting her eyes to adjust to the gloom, but there was no light. Panic started to flutter like a bewildered butterfly throughout her stomach.

I'm going to murder Katie for leaving me here like this.

She needed light and groped around her pockets for a lighter. She pulled one out with her keys and held it in a now trembling hand.

The little light cut through the dark in a burst, so bright it forced her eyes shut. She tried to stand and tripped over something, then the lighter went out and she fell sideways. She reached out and found hair.

There was someone in the next seat.

Something is very wrong here.

Her flesh crawled, and she pulled her hand away. All she could see was the red afterburn of the light, and she fumbled for the lighter's button.

She took a breath, held the lighter out where her hand had been and hit the button.

Blood, hair, a face. Eyes fixed in wild panic.

Katie.

She screamed and dropped the lighter, her keys with it, then turned and forced her way to the end of the aisle. She pushed past another body, feeling something wet touch her hand. Her gag reflex kicked in, but she fought back the bile and pushed on, past another set of legs, then another. She reached the end and bolted out of the screen.

The doors opened into a light so blinding that she could see no better than inside the screen room, but instinct kicked in and she ran full pelt until she was pushing open the heavy main doors to the cinema and running into the street outside.

Her head swam. She took in a huge lungful of air and started to sob.

Katie.

She looked around. The sun was just coming up, the first rays revealing a world of utter devastation.

Bodies lay everywhere, dead eyes in their dozens staring up at the sky from blood-smeared faces. The car park was full of them. Beyond that dozens more lay dead in the road. The Mexican eatery next door was on fire, and behind the family pub next door a huge torrent of black smoke issued into the sky.

It was too much. She emptied her stomach on the pavement, her vomit splattering just a few inches from the corpses of a couple who had died holding hands. She threw up again, and moved away, careful not to tread her beloved Converse trainers into blood or vomit.

She couldn't process the scene in front of her. It kept going back to that seat, and the sight of her best friend dead. She thought about Katie laughing like a drain on a rollercoaster in Brighton while Jen had clung on for dear life. The same girl who had once knocked a guy out cold with a single punch in a crappy York nightclub because he wouldn't stop pestering Jen.

Gone.

She wiped her eyes with the sleeve of her hoodie and took a deep breath.

The road was a mess of tangled car wrecks and more corpses. There was a twenty-four-hour supermarket on the other side of it, which would mean pay phones.

Daniel. She had to call Daniel.

She picked her way across the road as best she could, fighting off the feeling something was going to jump out at any moment and do to her what it had done to these poor people. Every horror movie she'd ever seen suggested there could be hordes of undead round every corner. Somehow, the disconcerting silence of the scene before her was worse.

As she passed, she chanced a look inside one of the cars. This one hadn't crashed, but there were its inhabitants, dead. The driver's hands were still on the wheel. There was a child seat in the back. Jen turned away. She couldn't look at that.

Once she got off the road, the corpses thinned out. The supermarket lay ahead of her.

Got to get to a phone.

The lights inside Tesco were off, so at first she only saw one body lying down in a puddle of blood. As her eyes adjusted to the internal gloom she saw more. A lady hunched over the till at the cigarette counter. A security guard pitched forward onto his face from his little stool. A large lady shopper dead by a shopping trolley filled with cheap lager, dog food, and ready meals.

Venturing further in, Jen spotted the payphones and ran over. She tried one, but there was no dial tone. So she tried another, then another – all the same. She thought of Daniel. She thought of her Mum and Dad. She wondered if they were trying to ring her right now, staring into useless dead telephones and thinking of her. Or were they gone too?

What in the fuck is going on here?

Tears started to come anew.

So this is what the end of the world looks like.

She felt numb. The large dead lady fixed her with an accusatory stare, and for a moment Jen was convinced she was about to get up.

Pull yourself together. Whatever else, you have to be strong.

The tears stopped. She stood up straight and looked over the rows of corpses dead at their checkouts. One of the till attendants had slumped forward onto the conveyor belt, and before it had finally cut out it had taken half her face away. There was a large red streak across the conveyor as it had looped round again and again before coming to its end. She shuddered.

Picking up a bag, she noted the irony of its emblazoned 'Bag for Life' logo, and headed into the aisles. She might as well stock up while she was here. A calm had descended on her. Probably shock, she knew. She didn't care. She collected a few tins, some pasta, bottled water, a tin opener, and other assorted goods, throwing them absentmindedly into the bag while stepping over corpses. She made her way to the toiletries aisle.

It's the end of the world and I'm looting tampons.

She walked through the make-up section, with its dead perfume girls and mirrors everywhere. She caught sight of herself and saw a dark smear of red across her jeans and hoodie. Her eyes bore the tell-tale panda look of unremoved make up. Her hair was still up from the night before, but now looked like it had been dragged backwards through something thorny. To be fair she doubted even Scarlett Johanssen would be weathering this situation without looking like the bride of Frankenstein. She shrugged, and turned away.

The bag filled, she returned to the cigarette kiosk, ignoring the dead cashier on the counter. Out of habit, she picked up a large pack of her usual cheap and cheerful brand, before remembering she wasn't paying and reaching for the classier ones.

She walked back out into the car park. Her house was on the other side of town, and she had no means of getting there. It didn't seem likely the number six would pull up. Not driving had never been an issue with a functioning bus network and a boyfriend with a car. Now she cursed her teenage self for giving up after ten lessons. She looked around and saw one car stopped in the road with its door ajar and a corpse in the gutter beside it. The driver had gotten out to see something, and then died. Avoiding the body, she got in. She had hoped sitting behind the wheel would bring memories flooding back, but she couldn't think where to even start.

Try turning the key, idiot.

Ten minutes later, she was off, keeping in first gear and driving at a sedate pace. She stalled a few times, but kept going. Soon she was on the ring road, weaving in and out of wrecks, trying her best to leave corpses unblemished with tread marks. She tried the radio, but with her focus on the road she allowed herself only the most cursory of jabs. Nothing. Not even calming radio noise.

She gradually became comfortable with second and then third gear, even picking her way through the wrecks without scraping the sides of the car by the fourth attempt. Half an hour or so later, she turned towards town, towards her house, picking up speed as she went.

It only took a second for it to get away from her. As soon as she clipped the jutting edge of the crashed car, she knew she was in trouble. She was going too fast for the corner. She had no idea what to do as the car swung round, so she panicked, jerking the wheel, hit the brakes and the accelerator at the same time, stabbing at everything with her feet.

The car flipped onto its side, the airbag went off and she slammed into the side door. The air filled with white, chalky, chemical dust, and she struggled to take a breath. As soon as it had started, it was over. The car slid along its side for a moment, screaming metal noises filling Jen's head. Adrenaline pumped through her. She struggled to catch her breath. Her arm screamed pain and her ears were ringing. She tried to move, but her seatbelt was now fixed in a vice-like grip.

The shattered windscreen was still in one piece, but the road outside was at a ninety degree angle. She pulled again at the seatbelt, trying to work the clasp of it. Her arm throbbed. She looked out the rear window.

There were feet approaching. Two pairs at least. Shambling. The panic rose again, and she started to kick at the glass.

Chapter Three
Push the Sky Away

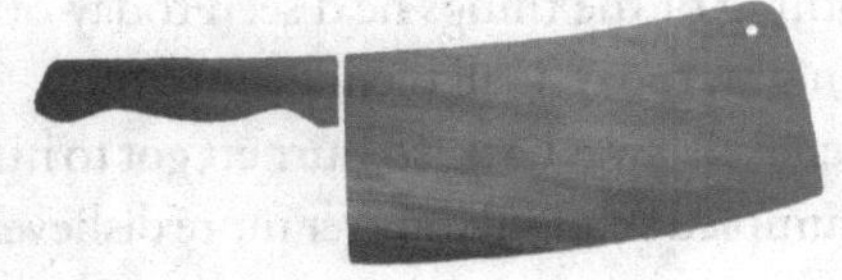

In the glare of the mid-afternoon sun, the doll was hideous. The truck stop was abandoned, walls burnt out and boarded up, the charred contents stacked up by the side. And there, laid in front of the building, the doll.

It looked Victorian, at least that's what the blood-flecked dress suggested to him. Or was it rust of some kind? The hand looked mauled. Some local dog had likely toyed with it before discarding it for some other chew toy. The paint on the face looked mottled and worn, the expression one of panic. From where Detective Burnett stood it was as though the doll was reacting to the scene of carnage behind her, to the charred human leg jutting out of the shrubbery, or the four corpses that lay beyond.

It was irrelevant, unconnected to the scene, but he could not tear his gaze away from the discarded porcelain and focus on the job at hand. He turned to the uniformed officer beside him, who seemed to be struggling to retain her lunch.

He motioned to the doll. 'Bag it.'

The officer seemed pleased with her non-gruesome task and hurried off for an evidence bag. Burnett knelt down so his face was at eye level with the doll.

'What did you see?' he asked it in a low voice. He heard a snigger, but as he looked up everyone looked busy.

Fuck 'em.

This was his fourth straight murder scene in a row, and he'd not slept in well over a day. By comparison, this lot were the new shift. They knew nothing of the things he'd seen today other than hasty rumours. Last night, today, it all blended into one.

Officer Evidence Bag was back, so Burnett got to his feet, his knees popping, his crumpled suit looking ever more dishevelled with every movement.

Fuck this.

He walked over to the pile of bodies. They too were charred, the air still heavy with the stench of burnt hair and flesh. Whoever had set the fire had allowed themselves a little fun with them before lighting the match. All the ankles and hands were tied, and there were multiple stab wounds visible on less charred bits of flesh.

He'd never known a day like it. Four bodies in the bins of a drive-through McDonalds, sprawled amid the rotting food waste, bags over their heads and eyes bulging from suffocation. Four more in an old people's home, at first glance carrying all the hallmarks of a Shipman enthusiast. Not that he could be sure until toxicology came back, of course, but he knew. Five teenagers found butchered in a car parked outside a village, the scene there so grisly that it had taken two hours just count the severed body parts and work out how many victims there were.

Now this. He felt depleted. Like the other scenes, once you got past the barbarity there was little here to suggest much of anything, save that there was at least one sadistic bastard running around North Yorkshire.

Two years since their last murder in the villages. He'd even had to justify his job at the last government-mandated performance review.

Some trumped-up desk-bound Inspector from the County Force asked him if his talents wouldn't be better put to use helping Traffic catch idiot toffs speeding in their high-performance wankermobiles. Now he was looking at either one hell of a spree, or some kind of collective psychotic episode. Maybe he should check the water.

He pointed to a gold bracelet on the ground, smudged with soot, and another officer bagged it. He went around the scene and took notes on a pad, but they were little more than disjointed thoughts. They might as well be haikus for all the good they'd do him. How could anyone make sense of a scene like this?

After another hour the autumnal dusk started creeping in. The evidence had been collected, and his notes ran to six pages of meaningless shit. Someone had put up a tent and there were the first hints of a media presence, kept at bay a hundred yards away.

Burnett growled some goodbyes to the assembled officers, then walked past the reporters and back to his car. He sank into the cool faux-leather seats and tried to collect his thoughts. Clouds started to darken the sky, and Burnett wondered if they were in for a storm. He wondered about the integrity of his crime scenes, then thought 'fuck it' and put the key in the ignition.

His mobile rang. He stared at it for a second, dreading the thought that this might be yet another murder. Some other horrifying tragedy he would be too overwhelmed to deal with.

He hit the green answer button.

'Burnett,' he said, voice catching in his throat.

'Get back here,' barked a voice, his boss. 'We've got him.'

The line went dead.

He drove back through the winding country lanes at a ridiculous speed, wishing he had flashing lights to tell everyone to get the fuck out of his way. He got back to the station as the sky started to bruise.

'Jade, what happened?' he demanded of the desk clerk, as he burst through the doors.

'Got picked up by a uniform.' Her words came out too fast for Burnett to take in. Nothing this exciting had happened in years.

'Covered head-to-toe in blood, he was, just said he wanted to confess.'

'Where is he?' Burnett asked, his head swimming with relief, anger, and sleep-deprived nausea. He never got the chance to put the cuffs on. *He* hadn't caught him.

'Interrogation three,' she said.

Burnett flashed her a quick smile and a 'good work officer' before storming through the doors. He liked Jade. The only other gay in the village. He still remembered their shock at seeing each other in the Pink Pony in York. At least they'd always had someone to share a taxi with back if they struck out.

Chief Inspector Thornton waited for him. 'You've had a busy day,' he growled. 'It's about to get rougher. He's dancing around admitting to the lot, but I want a full and detailed confession, on tape. I want to know who has helped him, why he did it, and have enough to lock him up even if the forensics come back telling me it was Bruce Fucking Forsyth who did it. Got it?'

Burnett nodded.

'Good,' Thornton continued. 'Don't fuck it up.'

With that endorsement ringing in his ears, Burnett opened the door to the interrogation room.

He sat down and looked at the man opposite. If he had to choose a word it would be... *unassuming*. Smallish man. Glasses. Mid-twenties at a guess.

Burnett performed the necessary taped introductions, while the man sat in front of him in silence. He looked eager, happy almost. Burnett felt his stomach sink.

'For the record, can I take your name?' Burnett asked.

'I have many names, Detective. You can call me Shiva. Or Oppenheimer.' The voice was so high and reedy as to be comical.

'I see,' Burnett replied. 'You are the destroyer of worlds are you?'

'You can judge that for yourself.'

The voice was calm, but Burnett was in no mood to rise to the bait.

'Okay. Can you tell me why you are here today?'

'Why? Because I have done some very bad things, Officer. I deserve to be punished.' The prisoner smirked as he said this. It took a mammoth effort on Burnett's part not to reach over and punch the smug bastard right on the nose.

'Bad things? Can you tell me what bad things you have done?'

'Oh, I wouldn't worry about that, Detective. I just didn't want you to die knowing that you hadn't caught me.' He paused for effect. 'I can be quite generous like that.'

'So you think I'm going to die then?'

'Not just you,' the prisoner replied. 'Everyone.'

'I see,' Burnett said. 'What about you?'

'I'm not going to die.'

'Oh. Why?'

'You might call it divine providence, or you might call it the hand of the other team. I call it blind luck.'

Burnett shook his head. He wasn't even sure this was his killer. Perhaps some deluded fool who'd tipped cows' blood over himself in a desperate bid for attention. A waste of his fucking time.

'Well, let's put that aside for a moment, shall we?' Burnett said, conscious of the crowd who would be gathered to watch this on the station CCTV. 'Let's go back to the very bad things you have done.'

'I'm sorry, Officer. I'm not sure we have time,' the prisoner replied, looking at the wall-mounted clock.

Burnett heard a rumble, deep enough to shake the walls. There was a commotion outside the door, angry shouts and people running about.

'Tick tock,' the man said, appraising him with a serene look of expectation. The booming rumble continued, and Burnett felt a sudden sharp pain arc its way across his brain. He looked at the man.

'Wait there, you smug little prick,' he said, and went over to the door. He knocked. Nobody answered. He tried the handle but it wouldn't budge.

He pounded on the door again. His head felt like someone had driven a wedge into it. He blinked to try and focus, but everything swam in front of him. The door opened, but as it did, he lost his footing and fell to the floor. He blinked again, but the world slipped further away.

He was dimly aware of something moving past him, above him, and two words whispered into his ear.

'Told you.'

Chapter Four
Sour Times

Struggling to take in the extent of the carnage, Tom rubbed his eyes free of tears and stood up. Cars piled up in a massive wreck at one end of the road and fires burned in adjacent streets, smoke spewing forth in heavy black torrents. The house next door had a corpse dangling from an upper window. Beyond were houses that had turned to nothing more than ash and rubble.

He fumbled behind him for the door handle. He couldn't stand to see any more, and retreated to the relative safety of his house and its singular corpse.

Upstairs, Leon was still sat in the same chair, chain smoking. He stared at the body on the bed, two fag ends extinguished at his feet and another already lit. He looked up at Tom.

'Did you phone the police?' he asked.

'No,' Tom replied. 'Go look out the window.'

Leon got up, crossed the room and pulled back the curtain. Tom watched his jaw slackening like a cartoon character.

'Whatever has happened, it's bigger than Danny,' he said, and Leon nodded. They stood in silence as Leon surveyed the new world from the window.

'I can't see any movement. Did you see any survivors?' Leon asked. Tom shook his head.

'We can't stay here,' Tom said. 'There are fires everywhere.'

Leon nodded. They both stared at Danny's corpse for a few moments, Tom wondering if it was right that they just leave him there to rot, maybe to burn.

'We have to leave him,' Tom said. Leon looked at him and nodded. They left the room, careful not to disturb the body of their friend. Without a word they went to pack.

Tom closed his door and sat on his bed. Now he was alone, questions buzzed around his head.

How big is this? Is it the whole country? The whole world? Is everyone dead? Are my parents dead? Is there still a government? How did this happen? How the hell am I still alive?

His head swam and nausea gnawed at his stomach. He looked around at his worldly possessions. Useless shit like CDs, trinkets, stacks of music magazines, old video games, and a hundred other things no longer relevant in the world outside that front door. This would be no jaunty adventure. He stuffed as many half-clean clothes as he could find into a rucksack, then a few books, a notepad, and the remainder of his weed and tobacco.

He rolled a cigarette and lit it just as Leon knocked on his door and entered. Tom noted his eyes were as red and puffy as his own felt.

'Can I have one of those?' he asked, and Tom rolled one for him. Together they made their way into the kitchen and dumped their bags on the table.

'So what's the plan?' Leon asked.

In that moment, Tom knew he was somehow now in charge of their combined well-being. On top of everything else, he would have to make the decisions. This was nothing new when it came to his friendship with Leon, whose idea of decision-making was generally restricted to the selection of drinking establishments.

'I dunno. I guess we start by trying to work out what the fuck is going on. We should head into town, at least see if there are any other survivors. If we made it through the night, there must be others.'

Leon nodded his approval, then gave a small chuckle.

'It looks like you got your wish,' he said. When Tom shot back a quizzical look, he continued. 'Only last night you said you wanted to get out of this place. You got your wish. I doubt we'll ever set foot in this house again.'

'Maybe I should lay off the wishes for a bit then, eh?'

They picked up their bags, slung them over their shoulders and headed to the front door.

'Ready?' Tom asked, and Leon nodded.

Tom watched Leon's face as he took in the scene before him. He imagined it looked quite different than it had at window level.

'Fucking hell.'

They made their way down the worn concrete steps and stepped over the bodies that littered the pavements, taking care not to disturb the corpses. The faces all held the same look of wide-eyed accusation and Tom found it impossible not to lock eyes with their dead stares.

The acrid smell of petrol filled the streets, and as they rounded the corner of Riversdale Terrace they came upon its source. A petrol tanker had crashed into the local church, a large gash along one side, its contents spilling into the road. That it hadn't yet been caught by the errant ember of a nearby fire seemed to Tom to be a miracle, albeit one with a limited shelf life.

'Something tells me we should find another route,' Leon said, and Tom nodded his agreement.

They went into the back streets and trudged on in silence. The carpet of bodies thinned here, and they were able to put quick distance between themselves and the tanker.

'Fucking hell,' Leon said. 'We're bloody lucky. If that thing had gone up an hour ago, I reckon it'd have taken our house with it.'

There were no signs of other survivors. They kept their eyes open for movement, but all was quiet. No twitching curtains, nothing.

'We should think about food,' Tom said. 'Water too.' His stomach started to ache. The thought struck him that the most important thing in their lives now, and for the foreseeable future, was finding a way not to starve to death or dehydrate.

Leon's backpack was too heavy. Tom saw him shifting it every few minutes, until it started to affect its owner's mood.

'What are we going to do when we get into town, anyway?' Leon asked, somewhat petulantly. 'Check and see if fucking McDonalds is open?'

'Well, why not, eh?' Tom snapped back. 'If it is, they'll have food.'

'I could go for a box of nuggets, I suppose.'

'I'll tell you now, though, if there are zombies running around the city centre, I'm blaming you.'

'If there are zombies, you can blame me as much as you want, just as long as you don't run faster than me.'

'Deal,' Tom said, smiling.

They were coming up to the city centre now. Smoke billowed into the sky ahead of them. Tom spotted a corner shop with its shutters closed and went to investigate. He gave it a kick, He wasn't hugely surprised when this didn't lead to the shutters retracting and the door springing open.

'Bloody inconsiderate of people not to leave their shops unlocked,' he said, but when he looked at Leon, his friend stared beyond him, his face draining of colour.

Tom turned round, his pulse quickening. Standing in the road, frozen in the same uncertain pose, were three men, and a woman. The middle man carried a large plank of wood, the end smeared with red.

His stomach sank and his knees began to buckle. Their faces were like masks, betraying none of the fear Tom imagined must be plastered over his own. Their uniform tracksuit, gold chain and cygnet ring ensemble would have had Tom crossing the road to avoid them even on a good day. They all seemed to be giant sized.

They stood staring at each other for what seemed an age, Tom feeling his heart pounding in his throat, his bladder suddenly and urgently full.

It was Leon who broke the tension, striding past Tom. 'Hi,' he said, holding out his hand. Leon's ability to charm and disarm had always been extremely useful at parties, especially those he had not been invited to, but Tom wasn't so sure it would have the same impact here and braced for violence. 'I'm Leon, this is Tom.'

The four of them looked taken aback. 'Ow, d'yuh knar what's fucking garn on heya like?' the man with the terrifying death stick said in an almost impenetrable Mackem accent.

'We were hoping you could tell us,' Tom ventured, emboldened by the sudden upsurge in dialogue.

'We woke up after the storm and everything was like this,' Leon confirmed.

'Aye, the storm,' the woman nodded.

These were not the fearsome hoodlums of his imagination, but three teenagers as wary of Leon and himself as they were of them. But they were still carrying a big, bloodied stick.

Without a further word they moved past them, back the way Tom and Leon had just come.

'Um, I wouldn't go that way if I were you,' Tom called after them, thinking of the oil spill, but they carried on as though they hadn't heard him. He stared after them until they were out of sight. Leon fixed Tom with a wry smile.

'How rude!'

'Yeah,' Tom replied. 'Kids today, eh?'

'I honestly thought you were going to faint,' Leon said, laughing.

'Yeah, well I was half expecting zombies. At least we know we're not the only people still alive.'

'Fat lot of good it does us. Let's hope the next people we run into are capable of conversation and not carrying a fucking great big stick?'

'Agreed,' Tom said.

The corpses were more varied the closer they got to the centre. Fewer slippers and dressing gowns, more salmon shirts, cargo pants, and densely gelled hair atop silently screaming faces on the men, skimpy dresses pulled tight over dead flesh and carefully coiffed hair matted with blood for the women.

Tom shuddered. Leon made his way over to the shuttered shop front of a Currys electrical outlet Tom had spent countless hours shuffling around, depressed at the shiny things he couldn't have.

'We need to get in there,' Leon said, sizing up the best possible entrance. 'If this is only local it'll be on the news.'

'And if it's not?' Tom asked.

'Well then there'll be no news and we're completely and utterly fucked.'

Tom couldn't fault the logic. They both started to try to prise their way in.

Twenty minutes later they slumped exhausted to the ground, their efforts to lift the shutter met with immovable metal intransigence.

'Motherfucker,' Leon said. 'Anyone would think they didn't want people to break in.'

The sun was high overhead now. Despite the cold, they had both worked up a considerable sweat. They moved to the back door and tried to force it, but not being master criminals they failed to make the slightest impression on the defences of a shop that had doubtless survived far hardier attempts on its virtue.

Tom bent double, wheezing. 'I'm exhausted,' he said.

'I need a drink,' Leon said in agreement.

Leon pulled out his pouch and rolled a spliff, which they sat and smoked in silence. Tom watched the sky, hoping to see a plane. He sighed. Half the day gone and still nothing made sense.

His muscles burned, his throat was parched. The spliff did nothing to help. All he wanted to do was curl up here in the street and go to sleep.

'Of course,' Leon said, leaping to his feet. 'We could just pop into the completely open nightclub just up the street.'

Tom followed his friend's gaze, shook his head at their combined stupidity, and got to his feet.

Chapter Five
Ashes & Fire

T he windscreen didn't hold out long against Jen's kicks. She glanced back to the approaching feet, two sets of them, but she could see nothing above the ankles. She had no desire to see any higher.

Eventually, the seatbelt gave way to her frantic tugging, and she forced her way out. Without looking back, she ran as fast as she could for the end of the street. Blood flowed down one leg of her jeans and pain shot through one side, but she ignored it as best she could and focused on moving.

A call went up behind her, but she daren't look back. They could be friend or foe, but her fight or flight response was lodged firmly in the latter camp. She ran for five minutes, as flat out as she could, until her leg was numb and her chest swelled with pain. She stopped and bent over, rasping.

Looking around her, she realised she'd nearly made it home. Her heart rose and sank in one fluid movement.

Do you really think Daniel is going to be there in his moth-eaten dressing gown, offering you a cuppa and inviting you to blow off work and watch Jeremy Kyle and Loose Women with him?

She shuddered. She didn't want to go home.

She had to. Had to be sure.

First she had to get there. Dead eyes seemed to fix her with the same blank stare from every vehicle. She ignored them and walked. Her shoulder hurt, her leg hurt more, and her mouth was dry. She thought of the bag of supplies and realised it was still in the back seat of the car.

Bollocks.

She rounded the corner into her street and there it was. 44 St Paul's Terrace. Never had it looked as imposing to her as it did now, the small terraced house she'd lived in with her boyfriend for the last year. She passed the bodies of neighbours who'd come out to the street for a view of the storm and searched for her keys, before remembering she'd dropped them in the cinema.

Fucking great.

Thankfully, Daniel was rubbish at remembering to lock the front window, and after some jiggling, it came loose. She had barely enough room to wriggle her way in.

I'll forgive you for leaving the window open if you could just be alive.

The lounge table showed all the standard detritus of a boys' night in: Pizza boxes, empty lager tins, half a tube of Pringles and an ashtray full of cigarette butts.

Heart in her mouth as she made her way up the stairs, she hardly dared make a sound. All she wanted to hear was a call of, *'Jen, that you?'*

At top of the stairs she walked the final few feet as slowly as she could. Surely, if he was alive he'd have been out to meet her. Or maybe he was out there in the streets somewhere, looking for her? She stared down at his battered trainers, kicked off in the hallway, and knew that wasn't the case. The bedroom door stood closed. She took a deep breath, and turned the handle. The door swung inward.

His body lay slumped against the far wall, eyes open, nose and mouth smeared in thick dried blood. She let out a howl, ran to the body and cradled his lifeless head to her chest, her sobs echoing through the empty house.

She stayed in that position until the daylight had faded, tears streaming down her cheeks until she could cry no more. She finally let go of the body when the light outside became so dim she could no longer make out the blood on his jeans.

Wiping the tears from her face, she rose, and looked out of the window. The distant glow of hundreds of fires filled the sky, smoke and ash drifting through the air.

She flicked a light switch, but nothing happened. She went back to the window. No lights were on anywhere. She went downstairs and fell onto the sofa, staring at the dead television. It was so quiet. She got up and went to the front window. No signs of life in any of the other windows, but she'd seen precious little sign of that before the world ended. The only interactions she'd ever had with her neighbours had been on the rare occasions that she and Daniel had friends round. Invariably, they would come knocking on the door the minute any hijinks passed the midnight hour. She was glad that if Daniel had to die then at least they had too. Then she felt guilty.

How long would it take the fires to make it this far out, she wondered? York, the city that had survived the Vikings, the Romans, and endless Hen Do's, was on fire. The railway station was between her and the town, so until she saw its high-arched roof aflame she was probably safe. It would be her canary down the mine.

She closed the curtains. She was tired, scared and prone to floods of tears whenever she remembered the body of her dead boyfriend in the room above. Her stomach ached.

She didn't want to leave the house. It felt wrong to abandon Daniel. She didn't want to stay, either, with his body in the corner of the bedroom. She couldn't sleep there, that was for damned sure.

Fuck sitting in the dark crying, Jen, be strong. Be practical.

She got up and made herself busy. She found candles, a pen, and a pad of paper. She started scribbling notes on the pad, a cold hard assessment of where she was. She listed all the things she knew, which was not much. She wrote down all the things she had in the house, getting up to check the cupboards to see what food would last out beyond the end of the day. Lastly, she split a page into two halves and wrote 'STAY' in one column and 'GO' in the other. In the stay column she started to scribble.

I know where I am

I know the risks

Few days' worth of food

She stopped there. She started on the go column:

Fires are spreading

Daniel is upstairs

Might find out what's going on

Might find people

She stared at the paper a moment, scrunched it up and threw it against the wall. Daniel used to bemoan the fact that in zombie films nobody ever seemed to think about going to a house in the countryside with a month of supplies and riding it out, or at least he had until he'd seen 28 Weeks Later and how well that plan had worked out.

People. She would need to find people, that much was obvious, but the idea terrified her. Who could she trust? How long would it be before people started to turn on each other for their own survival. She'd need to keep to herself, sustain herself, not get bogged down in other people's problems. She'd need to get moving.

Her mum had always joked that she'd never dealt with being alone well, especially for an only child. She'd moved out at the age of eighteen and moved from house share to living with a boy and back to house share on a cycle for a number of years, never once being on her own for any period of time. Truth was she was never good at having to deal with her own company. She guessed that would have to change.

She picked up the pen again and started a list of everything she might need if she wanted to leave. After scribbling for an hour she ended up with a wish list that would fill a caravan, then added *'caravan'* for good measure. By now the candles were burnt down to their stubby ends, the light fading to the point where she could barely make out her own scrawl. She didn't have even a fraction of what she needed, and didn't need most of what she'd written, but those were problems for tomorrow. Tomorrow she would need to take this grand plan and put it into action.

Looking over the empty pizza boxes she realised she hadn't eaten a thing all day. The milk in the fridge was still okay, so she poured a bowl of cereal and stared at the darkness. She went to the bathroom and examined her head wound, then wiped the mascara mess from her face, washed, and stared into the mirror, the tears welling up in her eyes again. She returned to the lounge, sunk into the sofa and let sleep wash over her.

The house filled with noise, rousing her from sleep. Confusion gripped her as she groped around, eyes adjusting to the orange-tinged darkness. The curtains seemed to be glowing, and the noise coming from outside was disorientating. It took a split second for everything to come back to her.

Is this what it's going to be like every time I wake up from now on?

She got to her feet, ignoring the shot of pain that ran up her leg. She went to the window and pulled back the curtain.

My canary is on fire.

The train station was completely alight now. She didn't have long. A scream rang out, somewhere on her own street. A group of people were working their way down from one end to another, hell-bent on looting whatever they could before the fire claimed the area. They kicked in the first set of doors and two of them rushed in.

There were at least five of them, Jen saw from the light of the fires. Three men, two women. One man stood out as some kind of ringleader, stood in the centre of the road barking orders. He was huge, his top barely covering his massive belly.

Jen's heart thumped hard in her chest. Her stomach knotted in fear. She needed to get out before they came to her door. She didn't know how they'd react to finding her, but she sure as hell wasn't about to find out. Her one hope was to go out the back.

There was no time to grab anything. She ran to the kitchen and snatched a kitchen knife and tucked it into her belt.

She could hear voices outside her door now, rough and harsh.

She fumbled with the back door key with trembling hands. At the other end of the house someone was trying the front door handle, then kicking the door. The key in her hand turned and she was out. The front door splintered behind her. She hoped they wouldn't see her scaling the back wall. No time to work the garage door now.

The heat of the fire hit her like she'd walked into a solid barrier. Beyond the brickwork the houses were aflame, fire engulfing everything, spitting little pieces of orange shrapnel all around. It robbed the air and she struggled to breathe.

She looked behind her. There was no choice. Broken glass covered the top of the wall, embedded in cement, but she managed to scramble to her feet without cutting herself and launched herself into the alleyway below. She landed on the hot tarmac of the passage that now separated her from some fresh hell. She looked around. She could hear voices in her home, but she doubted they'd follow her out here, even if they had seen her.

To her right was nothing but heat haze and smoke. To her left, she could make out houses not yet burning, but the fire seemed to be spreading that way faster than she could run.

'Oh, give me a fucking break!' she shouted.

She started to run. The knife in her belt dug into her thigh, so she pulled it out and dropped it, then sped past the flames with all the energy she could muster, hoping against hope she hadn't heard someone leaping over the back gate behind her.

Chapter Six
Board up the House

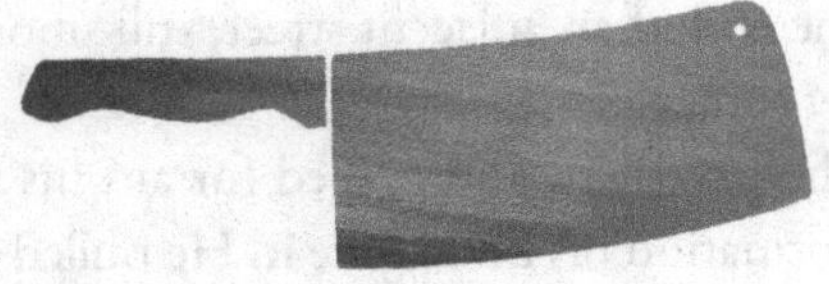

Burnett grasped at the floor in front of him, his hand finding nothing but worn linoleum. He fought against the ache in his bones to push himself up, and prised his eyes open.

He blinked, but it did nothing to remove the corpses that lay everywhere. His head swam at the sight of them. Each one wore the same vacant expression. Blood smeared around the nose and mouth. There was no sign of struggle; most of them must have dropped where they stood.

The station house was dark and silent. He forced himself up and stumbled through the corridors, taking care not to step on his old colleagues. Anger overwhelmed his fear. Whoever that man was, he must have done this. Some kind of gas, perhaps, but why had Burnett survived while his other colleagues hadn't?

Burnett pictured the grin on the bastard's face as he had turned away – those self-satisfied eyes. He had to get out. He pushed his way through the heavy doors that separated the reception from the station house. Jade's body lay on the floor behind the desk.

'Aww, fuck.' In the absence of any other sound, his voice echoed around the small room. He went over to her body and put his hand on her shoulder. He checked her pulse, to be sure. 'Sorry, lass,' he said, turned away and strode out though the heavy blue door.

The thrilling first inhalation of fresh air blinded Burnett at first to the bodies. They dotted the once idyllic streets of this market town, like some hideous performance art. It took a few moments to take it in, from the dead bodies laid where they had fallen, to the upturned car with its attendant streak of dark blood, to the burnt out houses that marked the end of an adjacent street, still smouldering in the bright morning sun.

He fell to the pavement and gasped for air, his body rebelling against the information his brain gave it. He pulled out his mobile phone, but it was nothing more than a lifeless black mirror. He headed back inside and found a radio console. He tried scanning the frequencies but the machine was dead. He picked up a microphone and hammered the buttons anyway.

'Hello? Anyone?' he said. Nothing but silence. Nothing worked.

He went through into the station house. It was dark; the little light there was came from two windows at the far end. The man who did this might still be here. His flesh crawled at the thought.

'Hello?' he called again, louder now.

Silence.

From somewhere inside the station house, a creak. Burnett froze. It sounded like it might have come from above him, but he couldn't be sure. The smell of death was already in the air, so he found a dish rag and tied it round his face, for all the good it did. Now all he could smell was mildew. He went to the booking board, and tried to find the booking slip for his man, but found they had all been burnt. He found one that could have been his, but he couldn't be sure. All that remained was the name of the arresting officer, one PC Tana. He didn't know the name.

Burnett looked round, wondering which of these poor dead souls was Tana.

Maybe if he could find the dead officer, he could find their notebook, get some more details. But he didn't much fancy rifling through every corpse in the station. Christ, who was to say they were even still in the building?

Another sound rang out, a distant floorboard creak. It definitely came from upstairs. He made his way to the stairwell. As he moved up the steps he heard the sound of movement again. His heart leapt into his mouth and it occurred to him he didn't have a weapon. He searched himself for anything to use, but he wasn't carrying so much as a pen.

He opened the door. The large room was much darker than downstairs, but he could still see the bodies, dozens of them.

'Hello?' a voice called out.

'Hello?' Burnett replied.

'Who's there?'

'DI Burnett.'

'Oh thank fuck for that,' the voice said. Burnett couldn't work out where in the gloom it came from, but the voice sounded out of place here. He tried to place the accent but couldn't.

'And you are?'

'Oh, sorry, sir, it's Tony. Tony Tana.'

Burnett couldn't help but let out a chuckle.

'Of course you are,' he murmured to himself. 'Where are you, Officer?' he called out.

'Over here,' came the reply. 'I'm a bit stuck.'

Burnett made his way over, tripping on a few bodies as he went, one of which made a dull crack that turned his stomach.

'Over here,' the voice came again, closer now. Burnett could make out a mass on the floor that seemed to be the source of it. He fished around in his pocket for a lighter, held it in front of him and clicked, his last thought before he did so that he had walked straight into a trap. Instead what he saw was a gruesomely absurd scene.

'Hi,' said PC Tana. His embarrassed grin poked out from underneath three bodies that had fallen on top of him, pinning him to the floor.

'Hi,' Burnett said. 'You seem to be in a bit of a pickle there.'

'Yeah, I can't seem to get the leverage to, well, can you give me a hand?'

Burnett heaved the first body off and then the second, which turned out to be his beloved Chief Inspector. Burnett fought back the urge to salute and helped the living man to his feet. He was a big man, Burnett saw. He recognised him, but then he was not the type of man you'd forget, with his rugby player build, unruly afro and beaming smile. He winced as Burnett pulled him to his feet. He must have been six feet.

'You all right?' Burnett asked.

'Fuck me,' Tana replied. 'Pins and fucking needles like you wouldn't believe, sir.'

'Just call me Burnett, Tana.'

'Right you are,' Tana said. He looked around the gloom. 'So, what the fuck's going on?'

'Your guess is as good as mine, but if I had to hazard one I'd say it's the end of the world. What happened to you?'

'Oh fuck, I have no idea. I was talking to the Chief about the collar I made, then there was a commotion and everyone went to the windows. Someone shouted to close the blinds and there was a loud buzzing noise in my head. I must have passed out. I woke up about an hour ago in the dark, covered in the brass.

'At first I reckoned it had to be that sick fucker I brought in, so I figured I should keep schtum, but I tried to move my legs and realised I couldn't shake these three for love nor money. Then you came along. I was certain you were going to be him.'

'Your sick fucker,' Burnett said. 'He was my sick fucker too. I was interviewing him when it happened, he told me what was coming. I'm not convinced he wasn't behind this.'

'What, all that God of Hellfire, day of judgement bollocks? I got an earful of that in the car on the way to the station. Unsettling stuff.'

'How did you arrest him?'

'I'd love to tell you it was some skill on my part but he walked out in front of my car. Covered in blood, wearing a sign around his neck. It said 'I am a murderer' so I nicked him. He didn't resist at all. I've been hearing about all the bodies that have been turning up the last few days, so I hauled him back to the station.'

'Where did you pick him up?'

'Uh, round by the war memorial I think, on Briggs Street? Right by the Methodist church.'

'What, exactly, did he say in the car?'

'Christ, he wouldn't shut up. Ranting on – calm though – about the end of the world, how he was a messenger from God. Started talking about the people he'd killed. If I'd had a partner out there with me, I might have gotten it all down, but you know what this place is like, budget cuts and all.'

'Anything else?' Burnett asked.

'Just, you know, nutter stuff.' He paused for a second. 'Wait, where is he? Is he still in the station?'

'He wasn't here when I woke up.'

'Do you think he's still out there?'

'I do.'

'And?'

'I'm going to go out and find that fucker, and we're going to make sure he isn't doing any more of the Lord's work.'

'How are we gonna do that?'

'We're not. I am. Go and find your family, do whatever it is you need to do.'

'I'll stick with you, if it's all the same.'

Burnett frowned. He had spent the last few years avoiding every attempt to partner him up with every Tom, Dick, and Harry. He had no intention of taking a partner on now.

They made their way out of the building. As soon as they were outside, Tana stood dumbstruck and stared at the carnage. Burnett gave him a minute.

'I'm going to walk the village, see what I can find,' he said.

They walked in silence for a few minutes, the constant discovery of bodies numbing them as they went. Tana stayed in step with him.

'So, Tana, what's your story?'

'You mean, how did a cockney end up working as a bobby in rural North Yorkshire?'

'Yeah.'

'I came up here to play rugby. I'm Samoan, or at least my family is. They moved here when I was a kid. London. I came up here to play for Leeds Rhinos; did that for about five years, but my knee went and I couldn't get my fitness back up. So the Police seemed like a good fit for me. I joined the West Yorkshire force at first, got transferred here a few months back. What about you?'

'Me?' Burnett replied. 'Not much to tell. I was from London too. I met someone and followed them here. They left, I stayed.'

Tana seemed to sense that he shouldn't push further, which Burnett appreciated.

There were no signs of life in Cottingthorpe. They crossed into the centre of the village, but there was nothing there. Burnett surveyed the scene. Duck ponds. Churches. Milk Vans. Corpses everywhere. A damn nice place to live, yesterday.

He looked back at the duck pond. One body in particular caught his eye. All the other bodies lay where they had fallen, on pavements, against cars, in bushes. One figure alone stood out, sat upright on a bench, overlooking the duck pond. He motioned to Tana. They started to cross the open ground between them.

At first he wondered if this might be their killer, but as he drew closer he saw that the man's figure was held upright, the rigid pole of a broom handle wedged down the man's coat, tape holding it to the bench. He was alive though, his back rising in fitful breaths.

Burnett lowered his weapon as he rounded the bench. He had to fight back the urge to gag at the sight before him.

The man clung to life, his shallow breaths and distant eyes a result of the sheer willpower required to try and hold in the intestines that spilled out of his stomach.

He seemed to sense their arrival, although he made no effort to look their way.

'Help,' he said in a small voice. Burnett looked around him. There was no help. Not anymore.

'Fuck,' he said. He covered the man's mouth and nose and put him out of his misery, the muffles of his dying breaths carrying around the empty park.

Burnett looked to Tana once the man had finished struggling, expecting some kind of protest, but his attention lay elsewhere.

'Detective,' Tana said, and pointed to the ground. Burnett's eyes followed his partner's gaze to the grass in front of them, where a hewn section of the dead man's guts spelled out rough words:

Too Late

Chapter Seven
Stuck Between Stations

The nightclub was the source of many of the bodies that now littered the streets. The closer they got to the gaping outer doors, the denser they became. It must have been quite the crowd.

'Well I don't know about you but I could go for a drink right now,' Leon said, looking up at the darkening sky. They had spent the day entirely fruitlessly.

'I don't know,' Tom replied. 'I'm not sure it's safe.'

'Looks to me like everyone came outside and died,' Leon said, stepping over the bodies. 'So I don't see why not. And besides, I'm fucking thirsty.'

Tom nodded. They started to pick their way through the rare patches of ground not covered by dead club-goers, slowly progressing to the double doors, which had been flung open. The corridor beyond was thick with corpses. Tom imagined the scene as rumours of the storm circulated through the busy club and everyone strained to see what the fuss was about. Most of them would have barely seen the sky before the storm claimed them.

Leon stopped at the doors. There was no way through. 'We'll have to go over them,' he said.

Tom looked at his friend and nodded. They were too thirsty not to try. He put one foot onto a corpse and put his weight down, slowly. There was a sharp crack, and he had fight to keep down the rising bile. He put his hand out to steady himself and stepped forward. Another crack rang out.

It was slow going, and as they made their way into the dark corridor they stumbled more than once, each time their outstretched hands finding cold, dead flesh.

Tom couldn't see a thing, the dusky early-evening light of the outside world completely gone now. The darkness pressed in around him. All he could hear was his own rattled breath and the crunch of bones, and soon the panic overwhelmed him. He scrabbled forward, wanting desperately to be free of this.

He heard Leon retching behind him.

There was a solid door in front of him. He groped for a handle, sure the way would be barred, but the cool metal handle turned and the door swung open.

The bodies ended, and Tom found his feet back on solid floor. It was still pitch black.

'Let's find the bar,' Tom said, his voice echoing around the cavernous room.

'Good idea,' Leon replied. 'Although...'

'What?'

'It's just... who closed those doors?'

It clicked with him an instant too late.

There was a high, shrieking scream. Something slammed into his stomach, hard, and Tom crumpled. He fell to the ground, aware of sounds and movement around him. He was winded, curled up into a ball on the floor, half expecting his attacker to follow up their initial volley with a flurry of kicks. There was a shout and a crash.

'Tom?' Leon called out.

'Here,' Tom replied, as best he could.

'Stay the fuck there,' Leon shouted.

'Leon?' he tried to say, but the word got lost somewhere in his chest. A hand clamped onto his shirt and pulled him up.

'You okay?' Leon asked.

'Don't hurt me.' It was another voice. Terrified and urgent.

'We're not going to hurt you, you silly prick,' Leon said.

Tom had no idea what was going on. He flicked a lighter, illuminating the scene. Leon stood, brandishing a long bit of wood, which Tom assumed was the same one which had swung at his own stomach. Standing across from him was a wiry bespectacled man, clad in what passed for fashionable garb amongst the townie types Tom associated with this particular nightclub. His salmon pink shirt was smeared in dirt and blood. The man's eyes flitted between Tom and Leon, red raw from crying.

'Hey,' Tom said, struggling to his feet. 'We're not here to hurt you; we're looking for something to drink, okay?'

The man nodded, just before the flame on Leon's lighter gave out and darkness filled the room again.

'Hang on,' the man said, and a few moments later a candle light flickered a few feet away, then another. 'I stubbed them out when I heard you coming.'

'Why?'

'I don't know.'

'Probably wise,' Tom said.

The candlelight showed the rough outline of the bar. Tom went over and opened a now-defunct fridge and removed three bottles. He opened them and passed both men a beer. The look of relief on the face of the bespectacled man confirmed what Tom had suspected. Despite walloping Tom in the stomach, this man was as far from a threat to them as the beer in his hand.

Tom drank deep, savouring the harshness of the bubbles on his dry throat.

'I'm sorry I hit you,' the man said. 'I just, well, I have no idea what's going on, and I didn't know what to do.' He struggled to keep his voice even.

'It's okay,' Leon said, placing a hand on the man's shoulder.

The man smiled weakly and continued. 'It was so confusing. I was here. Pretty drunk. I was dancing with a girl and I remember thinking she seemed to be into me, so the night wasn't a complete write off. Then everyone was shouting.

'Something was going on by the doors and everyone tried to get out. I thought maybe someone had pulled out a knife or something. But there was this buzzing sound, and people were pressing around me. I remember seeing the girl, she had a nosebleed I think. She passed out.'

He started to weep openly now, gesturing with his hands to try to articulate the moans and sobs into some kind of narrative. Tom got the general gist. He'd passed out while still in the club, and came to in the dark surrounded by bodies. For some reason, probably shock, he'd moved the corpses from the nightclub into the corridor, which explained the red carpet they'd had to climb over to get in.

It struck Tom he'd been pretty fortunate. He'd woken up to this new world in his own home, next to someone still alive. Not alone, surrounded by bodies. He could only imagine what this man had gone through.

All those faces.

They sat in the bar for a while, drinking the still-cool beers. They finally got a name out of the man: Olly, a trainee estate agent. Or, he had been. Now he was a shivering wreck suffering from shock.

'So,' Tom said. 'What now?'

Leon shrugged in response. Olly looked at him blankly.

'I don't much fancy staying here,' Leon said.

'Agreed,' Tom said. 'I still want to know what the fuck is going on. But we should stay here tonight.'

'You reckon we can lock this place up?' Leon asked.

'Let's give it a go.'

It didn't take them long to get the doors closed and bolted, once they'd moved a couple of obstinate bodies. They returned to the bar to nurse another drink.

No matter which way Tom ran it in his head the never-ending unknowns made choosing a course of action nigh on impossible. As they drank, he and Leon ran through endless arguments on the merits of staying put, of getting out, of moving on or settling in somewhere. They got no closer to a conclusion.

Olly sat and stared at his drink. He wasn't in any mental position to be able to leave this building, not until he was clear of the shock. Tom knew nothing about how to treat shock, but was reasonably sure letting it run its course was not the wisest of moves.

What time was it? Tom felt exhausted. He eyed up one of the booths as a potential place to sleep.

A huge boom rocked the building. They leapt to their feet. The blackened windows shook in their frames. The candlelight flickered.

'What the fuck was that?' Leon asked.

Tom ran for the stairwell; there must be actual functioning windows somewhere. Leon and Olly followed. Olly hadn't cleared this part of the building of bodies, and all three of them trampled over corpses in their haste. Behind the top bar was a door, beyond that an office.

They piled in and got to the window in time to see the tail end of a huge fireball mushrooming against the night sky. Olly let out a scream.

'It's okay,' Leon said. 'It's not a nuclear bomb. It's the tanker we passed earlier.'

They stood in silence, watching, mesmerised.

'Well I guess our house has gone,' Tom said.

'I won't ever be going back for my box of vintage SNES games,' Leon said.

'There goes my collection of Buffy comics too,' Tom replied.

'Worse still, think of Danny's porn stash,' Leon said.

Tom chuckled, and looked down at the street.

'Oh shit,' he said.

'What?'

Tom pulled them both back from the window. In the street below them, their attention also fixed on the fireball, stood a large group. They were a motley looking bunch, numbering twenty or so. They were right outside the nightclub.

As the fireball finally faded, voices filtered up from the street, thick with Mackem accents.

'We need to get out of here,' Tom hissed to Leon and Olly.

'Why?' Olly asked, a look of panic on his face.

'Because that lot are going to want to get in here for the booze, and those doors aren't going to last long. I don't much fancy being here when they come in.'

'I'm sure it'll be fine,' Olly said. 'Why would they want to hurt us?'

'Weren't you the one who hit me with a plank of wood?'

'Who knows?' Leon interrupted. 'Let's not find out, eh?'

'I'm not going anywhere,' Olly said.

'Fine by me,' Leon mumbled.

Tom grasped Olly. 'If you stay here, they will get in. I don't know what will happen, but I can't imagine for one second it'll be pleasant for you.'

Olly shook off his hand. 'I'm staying. I'll be fine.'

'Suit yourself.'

He followed Leon, who had found another staircase, this time leading to the roof. The two of them bounded up the stairs, followed by Olly. At the top was a heavy fire escape door, which Leon opened. On the far side of the roof was their escape: a rickety looking ladder that made Tom's heart sink to look at. He looked back at Olly.

'Last chance.'

'I'll be fine.'

'Good luck,' Leon said.

They both gave him as much of a smile as they could muster and closed the door behind them. They crossed the roof as low as possible, the voices of the mob below clearer now. Leon motioned Tom over to the fire escape.

It took Tom every ounce of effort to look over the edge of the roof to the street three floors below. He got down onto his front and gripped the edge so hard he thought the stone might come away in his hands. He wasn't about to let his lifelong aversion to heights actually kill him.

The crowd below were now focused on the same electrical store he and Leon had tried to break into, but the shutters held, just as they had before. Tom couldn't help but feel a little vindicated that their feeble attempts had not been bested by the mob. The voices were louder now, but Tom couldn't make out much, save for the occasional barked order which seemed to emanate from one particularly large skin-headed man. Then came the call they were expecting.

'Oi, what about Ziggy's?'

That was all it took. The mob turned its attention to the club below them. They started to clear the corridor of bodies. It wouldn't be long now. Tom turned to Leon.

'Okay, so we wait for them to go in, and we make our way down, yeah?' He whispered.

Leon nodded. They watched the mob below go about their task.

'Shit!' Leon hissed. 'We left our bags downstairs in the bar.'

He was right. What little possessions they had were gone, including the jumpers and thick clothing they would need if they were going to make it through the night outdoors.

'Fuck,' agreed Tom. 'We can't go back now, we'll have to figure something out.'

Below them the doors gave way with an almighty crack. The mob had made short work of them as expected. Tom looked down as they poured into the nightclub, hoping they wouldn't think to leave sentries outside. He gave them too much credit though, the whole mob were inside the building in seconds, leaving nobody outside.

They were down the fire escape in less than a minute, Tom's stomach lurching with every step. They got to the bottom, cast around for a direction and hit out westward, or what Tom assumed westward to be. They were less than twenty metres away when the shriek which wrought the air told them whatever hiding place Olly had opted for had not been a wise one. Without looking back, they ran into the cold dark night.

Chapter Eight
Marching to the Heartbeats

Jen kept running, past the point she thought her lungs might burst, until she could no longer feel the heat at her back. There were no footsteps behind her. She stuck to the back alleys, not wanting to chance what might be happening on the streets.

She slowed to a walk, her ears straining for any sound above the distant crackle of fire, but all she could hear was her own gasping breath and feet on the pavement.

She ran out of steam and stopped, trying to catch her breath. She sat by someone's back gate and risked a look back. There was nothing behind her. She was far from the fire now; it provided little more than a red tinge to the breaking dawn.

A body lay nearby, a lighter protruding from its hand. She went over to it and searched the pockets for the accompanying cigarette packet. She lit up and stuffed the half-full packet back into her pocket. Her head swam with a hit of nicotine and unwanted thoughts.

What the fuck do I do now? My home is gone. My city is gone.

It wouldn't be long until the fires caught up with her. For a split second, the thought occurred to her that maybe that wouldn't be such a bad thing, after all. Her body ached so much that the thought of moving filled her with more dread than the abstract concept of burning to death. She sat there for hours, watching the sun creep over the horizon, hazy over the heat of the fires.

The fires never came. They seemed to find their natural edge and moved no further in her direction. In the daylight the alleyway regained a sense of normalcy, her corpse friend the only sign of something out of the ordinary.

From somewhere, she found the resolve to stand, and in doing so seemed to shake off her fugue state. She stretched her limbs out, each one of her joints popping as she did so.

She looked around. Going back the way she had come was not an option, but beyond that she had no real idea where she was, the streets leading off the alleyway unfamiliar in their bland suburban anonymity. She weighed up her options.

Try not to pick a way filled with murderous mobs, deadly fires, or dragons.

She stepped out of the back alley and into a street. There were no signs of the chaos she'd seen, but she immediately felt watched. What there *was* plenty of was bodies. The first two she came to was an elderly couple in matching dressing gowns who made Jen's heart pang for her parents.

There were survivors out there, she knew that much, and out here on the open streets she had a definite sense of eyes on her, the sensation sending her hair into attention overdrive. She didn't want to look afraid for her audience, so kept her pace to a brisk walk. She wanted to break into a run, to get the hell away, but she doubted she could manage even a hundred metres without collapsing.

She was halfway down the street when she heard a small quiet voice.

'Hey, psst,' it said, and Jen's eyes darted to the source. Huddled in a gap between two houses was a scruffy looking girl, her clothes grubby and her dark hair bushy and unkempt. Jen looked around but saw nobody else. She looked at the girl again, who beckoned her, her finger to her lips.

'Come here,' she hissed. Jen hesitated. The girl beckoned again, terrified.

Jen started towards her. As she moved, a loud crack rang out above. A window shattered, scattering glass. Another crack, and this time Jen felt something whoosh past. The girl had turned and ducked into an alley between two houses. Jen turned on her heels and sprinted after her, as another crack rang out and something thudded off the hood of a nearby car. She hoped they didn't work out how to aim.

She felt exposed as she dived between the two buildings. She fell to the ground, arm skidding along the concrete and leaving a bloody stripe up her coat sleeve. She got up and saw the girl dart through a gate at the end of the alleyway. She followed, and found herself in a messy back yard, scattered with old toys and plastic gnomes.

'What the fuck was that?' Jen asked her.

'There's a boy in one of the houses across the street, he's been taking pot-shots at me with a crossbow,' she said, voice full of fear.

'What the hell for?'

'It's that loser, Rich, from number 28. He bought it a few months back on the internet, but his parents confiscated it from him. I guess he got it back.'

'You know this little shit?' Jen asked, sizing the girl up again. She guessed she couldn't be more than fifteen.

'We go to school together,' she said. 'Or, we did.' The girl's eyes glazed over and Jen felt a sudden urge to gather the girl up and run away with her.

The walls around the terrace were high, and there was no back gate to the garden other than the one they'd come through, back into the firing range.

'Shit,' she said, under her breath. 'What's your name?' she asked, still looking around for options.

'I'm Mira,' the girl replied.

'I'm Jen.' They shook hands.

An odd look crossed the girl's face. 'Sorry,' she said, and backed away.

Jen's heart sank. The gate burst open, and at the same time the back door to the house she'd paid no attention to opened. Two boys, only children themselves, appeared. They stood either side of her, weapons pointing at her head. One, baby-faced, dead-eyed and terrifying, held a crossbow in front of a smirking face. The other, an older boy with a mop of black hair, maybe a tad older than Mira, had what Jen hoped was nothing stronger than an air rifle pointed at her back. He had the good grace to look embarrassed by his actions, but not enough to lower the weapon.

Jen turned to Mira, whose face looked to be experiencing every emotion known to teenage girl-kind. 'So much for the sisterhood,' she said, anger starting to replace fear. She turned to the grinning one. 'What do you want?'

'Your stuff,' the boy said. His voice was cold.

'I don't have any stuff,' Jen replied.

She couldn't help it, she felt more affronted than anything else. The two boys exchanged unsure glances.

'We want your stuff,' the grinning boy affirmed.

Jen shrugged.

'Doesn't change the fact that I don't have anything.'

'Search her,' the younger boy barked at Mira, who shot him a look like she'd been asked to do her homework. Jen fought back a laugh. The girl huffed and came over.

Jen held her arms out. Mira patted her down half-heartedly.

'She's not got nothing,' she said.

'See,' Jen said. 'Maybe next time you run your little trap you might want to see if your quarry is actually carrying something worth stealing, eh?'

'Thanks for the advice,' the boy said.

Jen noticed he didn't lower his weapon.

'Can I go now then?' she asked.

'Not yet,' said the younger boy. Her stomach turned. She looked into those eyes again. This was no child. This was a predator.

'I've got nothing you want,' she said, trying to keep the fear out of her voice. The finger on the crossbow tightened.

'Rich!' Mira cried, but the boy carried on staring straight at Jen. She fixed the stare right back.

'Let's go in the house, shall we?'

If I go in that house, I don't think I'll be coming out again.

She moved. There was no other choice. Her eyes never left the crossbow. Its aim never wavered from her throat. Once they were inside, the demeanour of the boy Mira had called Rich changed. Immediately he was more at ease, laughing and letting his guard down. This was his house, he felt safe here in his domain.

He strode over to the table. There were empty beer cans, a half-drunk bottle of peach schnapps, and dozens of packs of cigarettes, all half empty. Rich picked up a beer and opened it, then sank into a chair. The other boy and Mira both looked like they wanted to run out as fast as she did. She glanced around at the walls, covered in pictures of Rich in less psychotic times, with doting parents smiling and laughing and posing. What they would make of this scene? Would they recoil in horror at their little angel's actions, or have their worst fears confirmed?

'Where are your parents?' she asked.

None of the children replied, but their reactions spoke volumes. Mira's eyes filled with tears, the older boy looked at his feet, and Rich smiled an unsettling smile.

Rich held up the crossbow again, waving it generally in Jen's direction, her heart giving a little involuntary leap every time its trajectory passed over her. Rich saw a slight flinch and gave an appreciative little half smile.

I really don't like this little prick.

'Mira, chuck us a cig,' he shouted.

Mira threw him a packet and fumbled for a lighter. Jen saw the terror in the young girl's face and forgave her. She looked at the other boy, who stood silent, holding the air rifle close to his chest. Bigger than the younger boy, but every bit as terrified as Mira. Jen could understand that, but noted him as the wild card.

'What about you, you got any cigs?' Rich asked her.

'No,' she lied.

'I think I'll check for myself,' he replied, the smirk back on his face. The other boy and Mira both stared at their shoes. Rich got up from his chair and moved towards her.

He sidled up to her, and she looked into his eyes.

'Let me check you over,' he said, his free arm caressing her side, moving upwards. He cupped her breast. His face was a few inches below hers, and he moved the point of the crossbow bolt under her chin, the steel cold against her skin. Then he moved the crossbow down. The smirk remained. He didn't fear her. That was his mistake.

She whipped her head forward with as much force as she could muster. Even with the height difference, she managed to connect her forehead with the bridge of his nose, and watched his expression change as he fell. She swung her left fist hard into his cheek. He slammed into an expensive-looking dresser, the side of his head cracking against the wood. He fell to the ground.

She remembered the other two, and wheeled round in anticipation of an attack, but they both stood dumbfounded.

They stared at each other a moment. She picked up the crossbow. She had no idea how to use it, but figured it was better off in her hands. She looked back at the body on the floor. Had she killed a child?

She turned and headed for the back door.

'Wait!' Mira called out behind her.

'What?' Jen said, turning back.

'Take me with you?' she asked.

Jen's heart broke again.

'Can you drive?' Jen had no idea where the question came from. It appeared fully formed in her mouth, but it was a good one. Mira's face dropped and Jen guessed the answer was no.

'I can drive,' the other boy said, the first time he had spoken. His voice was deeper than she'd imagined. She turned to him, the crossbow aim following her gaze, which made him drop the gun and put both hands in the air. Without the weapon she saw them both as they were: scared shitless teenagers who had fallen in with the wrong boy. Kids, trying to make sense of the end of the world.

She sighed.

'Come on then,' she said. She turned and headed for the door.

Out in the street she felt the weight of what had happened in there, what might have happened to her, and her knees almost buckled. The sun was out now, the smoke from the fires mingling with the few clouds and leaving an ashen hue to the sky. She took a breath and strode out, looking behind her to see her new charges running from the house.

Chapter Nine
Dead Melodies

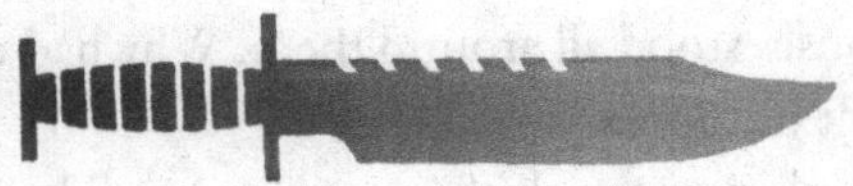

Tom slept on a curved concrete ramp in Sunderland's skate park. At least, he tried to. The combination of cold concrete, the noise of the park's nocturnal wildlife, and adrenaline still coursing through his veins ensured any sleep he got was fleeting at best.

The sun rose over Mowbray Park, highlighting the famous lion statues. Tom sat up, every joint protesting as he did so. Morning light struggled to break through the smoke of the fires punctuating the skyline. Dotted around the park were corpses of the tramps who'd used to take refuge here every night despite the best efforts of the Council.

His stomach ached. He looked at Leon, who stirred in the ramp of the next half pipe. The dark rings under his eyes suggested sleep had not been his companion, either. Tom felt dreadful, the gnawing pain in his stomach complementing the headache jackhammering his skull.

'Urgh,' was all he could say.

Leon didn't respond. Tom stood and stretched, but a pain jolted his stomach. He bent over.

'You alright?' Leon asked. Tom struggled to stand upright and nodded.

'Just need to walk it off.'

They left the skate ramps and headed for the edge of the park. Tom rued the alcohol they'd drunk in the nightclub, its diuretic properties not the best choice for someone already dehydrated. Neither of them had eaten in over a day. Leon looked as bad as Tom felt.

He also stank: a nauseating mix of sweat, beer, and fear. He longed for a warm bed and a warmer shower. It occurred to him that empty houses stood all around them. Why had they chosen to spend the night outdoors?

A distant explosion shook the morning air. They stopped by a bench and watched as a pillar of smoke arced into the morning skyline.

'We need to get out of the city, I think,' Leon said.

'Yeah,' Tom replied.

'I don't think it's safe.'

Tom nodded, the pain in his head making it hard to focus.

He needed to sit down.

As if to prove his friend's point, a battered old Fiat Punto careened around the corner of the street that backed onto the park, its engine buzzing.

'Down!' hissed Leon, but the car was gone before Tom could even process the order. 'Tom, get down!' Leon barked again.

There were other voices, but Tom couldn't place them. His head swam, and his vision went fuzzy. People shaped blurs followed the car's path, running. Tom couldn't move.

'Fucking bitch!' a voice exclaimed. It sounded male, angry, and local.

Tom stood, struggling to stay upright. He stared at his feet, the only things that didn't seem to be spinning.

'What the fuck do we do now?' another voice shouted.

'We find another car,' came the reply. A third voice? Tom squinted in their direction, trying to make them out.

'Guys! Just let it go, yeah?' This one sounded different from the others, a note of panic floating around it. 'I don't think we need–'

'Shut up.'

Tom had lost track of the voices now, and willed himself to move, to stop standing there, but his body refused to obey the order. His heart pounded, and he tasted bile at the back of his throat.

'What the fuck is that?'

They'd discovered him.

Hands pulled him down, but he fought them off, and he stumbled forward. He managed to look up, but could make out nothing more than abstract shapes, colours, and stars shooting past him. He grabbed hold of something, a hedge, perhaps, and promptly vomited all over it.

It felt like he was purging his own soul. It hurt him deep inside. He fell, and all went dark.

His head was an abrasive mess of noise and light when he awoke. There were people all around him. Hands jostled him. Was he in a fight? He didn't remember being in a fight.

He tried to swing his fist, but his arm felt leaden. He gave it all the effort he could.

'Argh, fuck's sake,' a voice said nearby. Tom chalked that one up as a victory.

'Fucking get off me,' he managed to say, or noises somewhere in that general direction.

His head pounded and his stomach hurt. He burst into tears, which he hadn't meant to do. He couldn't make out what was happening, but there were definitely hands on him. He fought them weakly, and felt himself slam into something.

He started to crawl. He was on the ground. He deduced this meant he could escape. He looked up through bleary eyes and made out legs, lots of legs.

The world went dark again.

His eyes forced themselves open. To his relief, all was silent, and he was in a bed. His whole body ached, and his first conscious breath came out as a rasp.

'Welcome back, Frodo,' Leon said from the chair beside his bed. 'The Dark Lord is no more. The ring is destroyed, and we are back in Rivendell.'

'Fuck off, Leon,' Tom said, with some effort. 'Where am I?'

'A house. You passed out. Actually that's not quite right. You pulled off a full exorcist, threw up, collapsed, started convulsing, started fighting yourself, and fell over. You were a one man Jim Carrey movie.'

'What?' was all Tom could manage.

'Your little piece of performance art was enough to convince those guys we shouldn't be beaten to death.'

Tom sat up, his head still throbbing, but some sense of equilibrium returning to him. 'Who were they? And where are they?'

His throat felt like sandpaper, and Leon handed him a glass of water, which he gulped down.

'Drug dealers,' Leon replied. 'But, you know, okay ones. Some girl had stolen their car not knowing they had stashed it full of pills and weed. They were not best pleased. Luckily for you, one of them was also a med student, said you were suffering from shock, dehydration, or exhaustion. Possibly all three. They helped me get you in here, and went on their merry way.'

'Did they have any news?'

'Not about the storm. They said a big crowd had come down from the estates the first night and went fucking berserk. Looting, raping, and pillaging. Even they'd hidden and waited for it to pass.'

'Wait,' Tom said. 'First night? How long have I been out?'

'A day, more or less. It's morning again. Yesterday was quiet though. No mobs. I guess they moved on in another direction.'

'Where are we?' Tom looked around the room, which was sparsely decorated, but somehow opulent.

'Not far from where you passed out. The door was unlocked. No bodies inside, I guess the inhabitants were in the street watching. We should be safe here until we decide what to do.'

Tom nodded. He tried to get out of the bed, unsuccessfully at first

'Any food?'

'I'll see what I can do.'

'No, it's okay. Thanks for sticking with me and helping me out.' He swung his legs out of bed, at which point he became aware of his own nakedness. They both exchanged a momentary glance of discomfort.

'Here, try these on.' Leon chucked some clothes his way, oversized boxer shorts, jeans, and an ironed plain T-shirt.

The bathroom suggested a single male inhabitant to the house: single toothbrush, lots of male grooming products. Nothing to suggest the permanent presence of a woman. As Tom cleaned his face and stole the dead man's toothpaste for a finger brushing, he wondered who it might have been, whose house they were playing magpie in. Affluent, he guessed; the clothes were stylish and the grooming products spoke of fashion consciousness. Fashion. Another thing that would be dead and buried in this new world. Functionality was the name of the game now. So, it wasn't all bad. No more fashion magazines. No more celebrities. No more reality television.

He left the bathroom feeling much better, Leon passing him on his way out with a magazine in hand, closing the door after him with a grin. Tom made his way downstairs.

The ground floor was no less tasteful than the first, and Tom wondered if he and Leon might not stay there, wait this whole thing out and see what happened. They could go out for food and hope to Christ nobody ever came knocking on the door.

The kitchen was well appointed, although the floor was wet from the defrosted freezer. There was still no electricity. He paddled through it in bare feet and opened the fridge. The milk hadn't yet turned, so he downed half of it, reasoning this might be the last chance he had for proper milk for a while. He searched the cupboards for cereals to accompany the remainder.

He took his bowl of Shreddies, drenched in milk and sugar, and sat at the breakfast bar, feeling a twinge of happiness for the first time since the storm. Was it too soon for that? Did feeling happy to be eating Shreddies make him a bad person? He was halfway through the bowl when he caught sight of the man watching him from the lounge out of the corner of his eye.

Tom jumped, spilling the milk over the counter.

Their eyes met. A smart man, his eyes staring at Tom through stylish glasses; he made no reaction when Tom noticed him. He moved a gun into his lap, and Tom's heart sank.

'Hello,' Tom said.

'Hello,' the man replied, a menacing half smile creeping over his face. He was tough looking, in his forties by Tom's estimation. His stylish jumper betrayed the outline of a well-maintained physique.

'We're in your house, aren't we?' Tom offered, and the man nodded.

Leon came bounding down the stairs, also dressed in the clothes of the man with the gun. He too didn't notice him at first.

'Ah, mint, breakfast,' he said. 'I can't believe how nice it is to be wearing clean clothes.'

'Um,' was all Tom could say, before the other man spoke up.

'Well I wouldn't get too comfortable in them.'

Leon jumped and issued a tiny yelp. He span round in the direction of the sofa. He took in the sight before him, and when he saw the gun his hands shot up above his head.

'What the...'

'My thoughts entirely,' the man said in a low voice. 'You two scruffy little cunts want to tell me what you're doing in my house?'

'I, um,' spluttered Leon.

'I passed out. I was sick. My friend brought me here.'

'You just thought you'd break into my house?

'I, we...' stammered Leon.

'Yes,' Tom said. 'Sorry, but we thought it was empty.'

'And you don't know who I am?' the man asked.

'No?' Tom and Leon answered in unison. Why would they know him?

'Okay,' the man said, and stood, putting his gun into a holster in his jacket. Tom relaxed as the gun disappeared from view. The man fixed them with a cold look.

'Don't get too fucking comfortable, you pricks. I'm putting the gun away because I've decided you two are about as threatening as a fucking pot plant.' He moved to the breakfast bar opposite Tom and motioned for Leon to join them.

'Look, we're sorry, and we'll get out of here as soon...' started Tom, but the man held his hand up to silence him and Tom obliged.

'I don't want to hear it. The whole world's gone fucking mad and if we're all going to have to start explaining ourselves and apologising for every decision we make then we're not going to get anywhere. You do what you have to survive, yeah?'

Tom and Leon nodded their vigorous agreement to his rhetorical question.

'Do you have any idea what's going on?' Leon asked.

'Big storm kills almost everyone. There's no radio, no news, no government, no help. By the looks of it, it's taken roughly a day for people to start going off the fucking deep end.'

'It's not just a local thing?' Tom asked.

The man shook his head. 'Who knows? I've been trying all military frequencies and there's nothing.'

'You're military?' Tom asked, surprised at how comforting that notion was to a lifelong pacifist.

'In a way.' The man left it there.

So that was it. This was the end. Tom thought about his parents, whether they were still alive. He'd not even tried to phone. A wave of guilt and sadness washed over him, but the man snapped him out of it.

'So, are you two going to clean up my fucking house, or what?'

They stared at him. He broke out in a wide grin.

'Don't be fucking dense. We're not staying here. None of us.'

'What do you mean?' Leon asked.

'We're going to start to put the pieces back together. Sound good to you?'

Tom felt relief wash over him, smiled, and nodded.

Chapter Ten
Bring it on Home

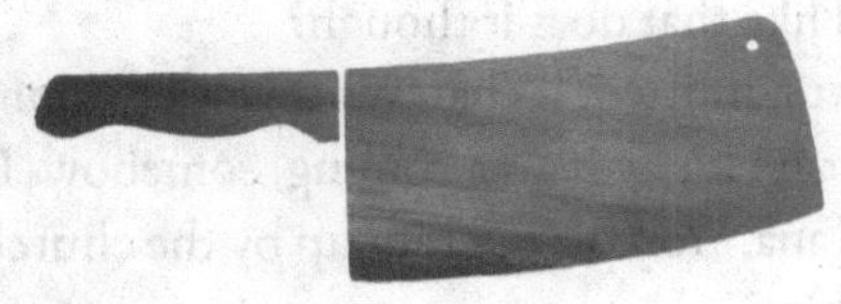

Burnett stared at the mutilated corpse.

He's still out there.

A shiver ran down his back. He left the man on the bench. There were no forensics to collect. This was no crime scene to investigate. There was only a killer to find, and Burnett intended to do exactly that.

He walked back to the station house, Tana following behind. Burnett looked at his companion, who seemed to have shrunk somehow, his eyes dazed and fixed on the ground in front of him. They entered the building.

'Short of driving around the place looking for an obvious and blatant serial killer there isn't much to go on,' Tana said, exasperated.

'I'll find him,' Burnett replied.

'How?'

'I'll find him as soon as he decides to be found, and not a minute sooner, but I can't sit about and wait.'

Tana nodded.

'Do you think all this is down to him?' he asked, gesticulating around at their new world.

Burnett shrugged. He was trying to find an arrest record, anything written down, but he knew any report would be stuck in the computer that sat dead on the front desk.

'What do you reckon it is?' Tana asked, pacing now.

'No idea. It could be it's a local thing, like a chemical leak or something. He could have arranged something like that.'

'Doesn't feel like that does it though?'

'No,' Burnett admitted. 'Whatever this was, I don't think it was man made, but he knew it was coming, somehow. He's involved.' He turned to Tana. 'You picked him up by the church. Did you get a name out of him?'

'No. Asked, but nothing given, so I put him in the back of the car and brought him back.'

'Okay, well let's go to where you picked him up,' Burnett said.

Tana nodded, but Burnett could see reticence on the man's face.

'Yeah, of course,' Tana said, 'but don't you think we've got bigger things to be looking at?'

'By all means, you go deal with the end of the world,' Burnett replied. 'Just take me there first.'

Tana frowned.

'There's a fucking lunatic running around disembowelling people for fun,' Burnett continued. 'The end of the world doesn't seem to have made him pause for even a second, so I'd say stopping him is priority number one. We'll figure out the rest of it afterwards.'

'Okay.'

They broke into the firearms locker, such as it was, took a few handguns and two shotguns, and made their way out to the parking lot. Armed with all the keys they could find, they managed to unlock one of the high-speed pursuit cars, but it wouldn't start. It wasn't until they tried one of the battered pool cars that they had any joy.

'Weird,' Burnett said, as they climbed in.

Tana took the driver's seat. 'Electrics,' he said, as he gathered his huge frame in enough to get behind the wheel. 'Whatever did this, it's fried every circuit-board. Any modern car that relies on an internal computer will be completely useless now.'

'Great,' Burnett said. What he needed right now was less obstacles in his way.

Tana took the opportunity of the short drive to the church to regale Burnett with his many theories. 'Have to be something pretty spectacular to fry the electrics like that. I mean, the emergency lights were out in the station, you notice that? They're supposed to come on come hell or high water, but nothing. I reckon it was those scientists in Switzerland or wherever, you know, where they were shooting atoms or whatever at each other?'

'I'm pretty sure it won't have been that,' Burnett said, but Tana had already moved on.

'Or, it could be some kind of terrorist plot. Like an electronic bomb or something. An...'

'EMP,' Burnett said.

'Right! Or it could be the Government. Or...'

Burnett blocked him out. This was why he didn't have partners. He'd never been in possession of a sparkling wit or gregarious nature, and as the years had rolled on social interaction seemed to be a trick he was getting worse at. Where long ago he'd suffered homophobic taunts and chants, now nobody even knew that much about him, or took the time to find out. Coming out in a rural Police force in the mid-nineties, especially when he'd not had any choice in the matter, that wasn't much fun. These days it wouldn't even be much of a deal.

Over the intervening years he'd begun to resent others for their ability to be jovial, witty, and warm. He'd gone from being the station poof who'd cheated on his beautiful wife with a rent boy in Hull, to the weird detective nobody talked to. After a few more years, even the resentment had eroded and now he just didn't give a shit.

All he wanted to do was solve puzzles, and he had a job where he could do that. If he'd been more outgoing chances were he would have been promoted out of the only job he wanted by now, so *c'est la vie*.

Soon they were pulling up in front of the church. Burnett checked his gun.

'This is it?' he asked Tana.

'Yep.'

'Let's take a look.'

The air was still, the only sound the occasional chirrup in the trees. There were no bodies here, and for a moment it was as though nothing had happened to this sleepy hamlet. Burnett scanned the buildings, but there was nothing out of the ordinary.

Across the road was a bakery. Tana went over to it. 'I don't know about you, but I'm fucking starving,' he called to Burnett.

'Be my guest,' Burnett replied.

Tana tried the door. Locked. A swift kick later, it gave way. Burnett wouldn't want to be on the receiving end of one of those barges.

The church itself was as austere and imposing as most village churches tended to be. Burnett had been inside this one a few times, for the funerals of people whose deaths he'd been investigating, to provide the liaison between the police and the family, but more often than not he'd been trying to work out who in the room had done the deed.

So why had their man chosen this place to give himself up? He didn't know much about him, but he knew enough to know there'd be some kind of symbolism to it. Tana had said the man was full of religious rhetoric, had this been his church?

He needed to go inside, but Tana was right, he needed something to eat first. Tana emerged from the bakery laden with pastried goods and cans of fizzy pop, a big grin across his face.

'I guess this'll all go off in the next few days, so we might as well load up while we can.'

The two of them sat on a bench and started devouring pasties. The coke was still cold. They ate in silence for a few minutes. The sausage rolls were good, and Burnett managed to push their killer to the back of his mind for a while.

'We've got to go in there, haven't we?' Tana asked.

'Yep,' Burnett replied.

'You religious?' Tana asked.

Burnett shook his head.

'Me neither. I hate churches. My school was dead religious, I seemed to spend half my life listening to some priest or another prattling on and on about my sins, or someone else's sins.'

'Sounds about right,' Burnett said.

'Fuck me I've got killer indigestion now,' Tana said, throwing half a pasty into the bin from the other side of the bench. He smiled at Burnett. 'Worth it though.'

He started to wonder if Tana had a point. If this was the end of the world, why the hell was he still turning up for work? But he knew the answer to that already.

'Come on, let's check it out.'

The large oak doors were sealed shut, the stained glass and gloomy interior giving nothing away. Burnett tried the cast iron knocker, neither expecting nor receiving a response. Tana had gone round the side, and after a few moments he returned, munching away at a second Cornish pasty.

'Locked up solid,' he said.

'I thought churches stayed open,' Burnett said.

'What, like a twenty-four hour Tesco?'

'I suppose.'

'Don't think it works like that. They'd be full of homeless and the like,' Tana said.

'Well they wouldn't want to give shelter to the needy, would they?' Burnett replied, half under his breath.

'I'm sensing a lack of partiality for the church there, Detective Inspector.'

'How keenly observational of you.'

They worked round the building once more, and found a door which couldn't withstand their combined foot power.

The air inside the church was putrid. Tana retched, his mouth still full of pasty.

'Fuck me,' he said, spitting out a mouthful of pasty before retching again.

'You need to go outside?'

'No, I'll be okay.'

'Here,' Burnett said, handing Tana a cigarette.

'What's this, old Detective trick?'

'Used to be,' Burnett replied, lighting one himself. 'You can't smoke at a crime scene anymore.'

'I won't tell if you won't.'

They moved into the main hall, and both stopped in their tracks. Even in the dull light from the stained glass windows the sight before them was more than they could register. A crudely erected crucifix hung, upside down, from the roof. The naked body of the priest hung from hammered nails, his genitals mutilated, his throat cut. Blood pooled on the floor alongside the corpses of two altar boys, their faces disfigured and throats cut, bodies posed in mock worship of the crucified figure.

'Jesus,' Tana said.

'Do you think he's trying to make a point?' Burnett asked.

Tana didn't reply. They stared at the scene for a moment, until a thud came from behind them, making them both jump and pull their weapons.

They scanned the room, but nothing moved.

The bang came again, a hollow thud of something hitting wood. Burnett motioned Tana to move forward, and they moved towards the sound, guns raised.

Another bang. It was coming from inside the altar.

He lifted the heavy bible and hymn books, pulled off the white sheet and opened the lid, revealing the bound and gagged figure of another man, dressed in priest's robes.

They lifted him out. His eyes and mouth had been taped, and he recoiled from their first touch. Tana spoke to him in the reassuring patter of a beat bobby.

Once they had him on the floor they pulled the tape from the man's eyes and mouth. As soon as they did the priest uttered a howl of abject sorrow, so loud that Burnett's first instinct was to cover the man's mouth again.

'Let's get him out of here,' Tana said. Together they carried him past the scene of ruination and out into the daylight.

The man moaned at the sight of the crucifix. By the time they got him outside he was so wracked by sobs, all they could do was lay him out on the grass, where he curled up into a ball and continued to sob.

Tana ran over to the bakery and came back with a bottle of water, helped the man into a sitting position, and urged him to take a drink.

'Thank you,' the priest said, when the sobbing passed. He took another deep gulp of water.

'Try not to move too much,' Tana said.

Burnett checked the man over. There didn't seem to be any obvious injuries.

'Can you tell me what happened?' Burnett asked.

Tana shot him a look, but he ignored it.

'He was a madman,' the priest began, but seemed to be unable to go any further.

Burnett looked into the man's eyes and saw the distant stare of someone who had long since left the state of shock behind and moved onto something much worse.

'He's not going to be able to tell us much,' Burnett said, turning away from the priest and trying to keep the exasperation out of his voice.

'We need to help him,' Tana said.

'He's beyond our help,' Burnett replied.

'What the fuck are you talking about?' Tana asked. 'Show some fucking compassion!'

'What? What exactly is it you think we can do for him? Take him to a hospital? Nurse him back to health ourselves? Bring him three square meals a day until he's feeling better?'

'If that's what it takes!'

'No, what we need to do is find the sick mother fucker who did that in there, and stop him from doing it to anyone else.'

'For Christ's sake, he probably doesn't even know the world has ended!' Tana shouted. 'We can't just leave him here.'

'Sorry,' the man said in a quiet voice. 'The world has what now?'

They took the priest and led him into the bakery, where they could sit him down and go through what they knew, which they realised through the act of recounting, was very little indeed. The priest seemed to be growing in strength with every minute, aided by the energy from a not-quite-stale sandwich and a can of sugary drink. He listened to their tale. When Tana drew to a close they sat in silence. When the priest spoke, it was in the calm even tones Burnett remembered from his own school priest.

'I will tell you what I know about this man you are looking for, but I also want to urge you to look away from the path you are heading down.'

'You think we should continue to let him run around killing the few people who survived the apocalypse?' Burnett asked.

The priest mulled that over for a second.

'Why don't you tell us your name first?' Tana asked.

'I am Father Leonard.'

'Okay, Leonard, what can you tell us?' Burnett asked.

'It's Father Leonard,' the priest replied, and shot Burnett a look before continuing. 'A man came to see us a few days ago. A student, he said. He told us he was not a man of God, but that he'd seen something that had made him question his lack of faith. I don't know what it was, because Father Connelly took him away to talk to him at greater length.' He shifted in his seat, and arched his back. 'Excuse me, my muscles are cramping up.'

'I'll see if I can find some paracetamol,' Tana said.

'Thank you.'

'Carry on,' Burnett said.

'As I say, Father Connelly took him into another room to talk to him. The young man was upset. After their talk he had left in a hurry, and Father Connelly would only say that he was a troubled young man.

'The young man came back the next day, and as soon as he walked in the door I could see there was something not, how do I put this?' He paused. 'Not altogether the same person came in. He walked with purpose. We were planning the fayre I believe, and we had Mrs Wilson there and a few of the boys from the choir.

'When Father Connelly stood up to greet the young man he pushed him aside, and that's when I saw he had a carving knife in his hands. He...'

The priest paused for a second and took in a deep breath, steeling himself to continue with the story.

'Before any of us could react he had stabbed Mrs Wilson, in the chest. He picked up Marcus, one of our choirboys, round the throat, and pinned him to the wall.'

Tana returned with some painkillers, and the father washed them down. He fixed Burnett with a stare.

'I am not a violent man, Detective, but I don't believe the Lord will condemn me. I picked up one of the heavy candlesticks and swung it at the man's head, but alas he read my intentions and blocked my blow. He struck me, and at that point I must have passed out.

'I woke up unable to move, my hands and feet bound, my eyes and mouth gagged, and all I could hear was screaming. Wailing. It went on and on. I couldn't identify who it belonged to, but soon it were gone. Then came the silence, which was worse.

'At one point I thought I was going delirious because it felt like there was some kind of pressure or something, and my head felt like it was going to split in two, and I could see stars, and I passed out. When I woke up I was still in the box. I started to resign myself to the fact that I would die there, and I made my peace with my Lord.

'Then you both came.' He looked at them in turn. 'Thank you, both of you.'

Burnett nodded.

'Now, please,' the priest continued, 'for the love of all that is holy, do either of you have a spare cigarette?'

Tana fished out a battered pack from his back pocket, and lit one for the priest, who took in a hungry gulp.

They sat in silence as he smoked.

'So what do we do now?' Tana asked, once the Priest had stubbed it out.

'I'm going to find the man who did this,' Burnett replied.

'You two must do as you see fit, of course,' the priest said. 'But I believe you would put your skills to better use by helping to rebuild after everything that has happened. "Whoever has two tunics is to share with him who has none, and whoever has food is to do likewise." You could be of great service as a man of authority.'

'Don't quote your book to me, Father,' Burnett said. 'It's not my book. And anyway, "he that doeth wrong shall receive for the wrong which he hath done, and there is no respect of persons".'

'Interesting that you say it is not your book, Detective, and yet you can quote it at will. People out there will be lost, confused, and they will need order and hope to guide them through the next dark days and weeks. They will, in short, need you, Detective.'

'Well I'm afraid they're going to have to get along without me,' Burnett replied. 'I am going to find this man, and I am going to stop him. If you're so convinced we need a new messiah, Father, perhaps that's something better suited to your job description?'

The priest looked wounded by his words, and Burnett felt a stab of guilt.

'Yes, well. What about you, young man?' The priest turned to Tana.

The other policeman had been sat in silent contemplation as both men had spoken, and he looked at each in turn.

'I'm with the Father,' he said. 'If you need me, I'll be there, but if this is the end of the world, of civilisation as we know it, someone needs to help the survivors. We need to regroup, and we need to rebuild. I'm sorry, Detective.'

'Fine,' Burnett said, relieved and disappointed at the same time. 'What are you going to do?'

'I guess we need to find some kind of refuge we can use and start to gather supplies,' Tana said. 'We'll need food, blankets, medicine, and somewhere to operate from.'

'Excellent,' the priest replied, his face breaking out in a smile for the first time.

Tana stood and gave Burnett a guilty look.

'You be careful,' Burnett said to both men. 'What you are planning is going to be exactly the sort of place he'd want to hit.'

'We'll take a few of the guns,' Tana said.

Burnett nodded. The priest looked to argue for a second but thought better of it. Burnett and Tana stood in front of each other for a moment, until Tana stuck out a hand. Burnett shook it.

'You know where we are,' he said. 'Good luck.'

Tana started to walk away, then turned round. 'You get that fucker.'

Burnett nodded. 'Good luck to you as well.'

Burnett left the bakery and got into the car, but didn't start it. He stared at the broken bakery door, and contemplated his next move.

Chapter Eleven
How We Land

'S am! Watch where you're fucking going,' Jen said, making him jerk the wheel. The car swerved and took out the wing mirror of a parked Mercedes. It had been two hours in the cramped car before she'd discovered the boy's name. It had taken her considerably less time to realise he'd less than truthful when he'd declared his ability to drive.

Four hours into their drive around the suburbs and their carnage-strewn streets and they'd not made it more than a few miles. To be fair to the boy, he'd not had the easiest of tasks. The roads were strewn with bodies and they'd yet to see a single one that didn't have a wreck of some kind blocking their way. Finding their way out was like negotiating a maze, and Jen felt like they were never more than twenty seconds from an ambush.

Crossing the bridge had been the hardest part. The car climbed the pavement, scraping down the side of the bridge. Her new driver sucked air between his teeth in exasperation.

If Sam hadn't been a great driver to begin with, he was definitely getting better, although his insistence that he drove while smoking a spliff 'to ease his nerves' had done little to ease her own.

The plan was to head to the Designer Outlet for some good old-fashioned looting, then find somewhere safe to hide out and find out what was going on. That the prospect of looting had provoked such unabashed enthusiasm in her new travelling companions was by the by. They needed supplies. It wasn't unlikely they were the only survivors to have the same idea, Jen knew. They might be driving towards terrible peril.

'Oh for fuck's sake, give me a drag on that,' she said, and took the spliff off the now grinning boy.

'Go Jen!' came the voice from the back seat.

Stupid, she knew, but her nerves were shot and she needed to calm down. She took a drag and closed her eyes, preferring not to watch the endless parade of bodies and coffin cars as they passed.

'We're nearly there,' Sam said, pulling off the main road. 'At this rate we'll be there in twenty minutes.'

'Wait,' Jen said, 'pull over.'

'What's the matter?'

'It's getting dark,' Jen said. 'I don't like the idea of going in there when it's dark. We'll have no idea who's in there, and we won't be able to see for shit. I don't want to spend an hour scrambling around trying to find a sleeping bag, only to find out I'm in the fucking teapot shop.'

'I don't think I want to be murdered today,' Mira said.

'Fair point. What do we do instead, sleep in the car?' Sam asked.

'I'm sure I saw a pub back there,' Mira said.

'I could definitely use a drink,' Jen agreed.

The front door swayed open.

'What do you reckon?' Sam asked. 'If there were people in here they'd have locked up, right?'

'Stay close and stay quiet,' Jen replied. They moved through the bar. Only a few corpses remained, most having opted to view the storm from the pavement outside. Enough remained to ensure a fetid stench had filled the room. Jen locked the doors.

They checked the whole building for other survivors. Jen's heart remained in her throat with every door she pushed open.

Confident they were alone, they made their way back down to the bar.

'We'll sleep down here tonight,' Jen said.

'What?' Sam asked.

'Do you want to be trapped upstairs if there's a fire? Or if someone tries to break in? Better we're together down here.'

'If someone breaks in we'll be no safer down here than upstairs. Chances are we'll die a little bit sooner,' Sam replied. 'At least if we are upstairs we get to sleep in a bed, and who knows how often that's going to happen. Besides, we can keep watch out of the windows.'

'Fine,' she said.

She walked behind the bar, grabbed two bottles of wine from a fridge and a glass and made her way upstairs.

The wine was enough to take the edge off the impending sense of doom, but not enough to see off her reservations. She stared at the door of her bedroom, and ran over how she might get away from these two without them noticing. It was the end of the world and she'd been burdened with looking after two teenagers she hadn't even met that morning. How had that happened? She could leave now, walk out the door. They'd be okay, and if they weren't, what the hell did it have to do with her? She never asked for this. She never asked for any of this.

She awoke to bright sunlight streaming in through thin curtains, and for the briefest moment she thought she must be on holiday. By the time she'd turned over to see if Daniel was next to her, she'd already remembered he wouldn't be. She fought back the urge to scream into her pillow and wondered if every morning from now on would be the same, reliving her loss every time she woke.

She forced herself to sit up and get back into the same dirty clothes she'd worn yesterday.

A sound outside snapped her mind into focus. She went over to the window. Four men stood on the road, sizing up the B&B. All four of them looked as though they could either be the sweetest guys in the world, or complete lunatics.

They were talking to each other, but Jen couldn't hear it. The discussion looked heated.

Mira and Sam entered her room, Sam pulling on his top as he came in.

'Did you see?' asked Mira.

'Yeah, how long have they been there?'

'Dunno,' said Sam. 'At least five minutes.'

They watched as discreetly as they could. The men walked back to a beaten up Land Rover, got in and drove off.

The three of them exhaled in unison.

'Thank fuck,' Sam added for good measure.

'So,' Mira said. 'Do we get our shit together and go shopping?'

'I suppose so,' Jen replied.

She noticed an odd glance between the two of them, an embarrassed half smile as they both tried to go through the door at the same time. She didn't much like what it signified, nor the blush on Sam's cheeks when Mira smiled at him.

York's huge Designer Outlet was one of Jen's least favourite places at the best of times. Her idea of hell was an afternoon trawling the discount versions of shops she hated for twenty per cent off a top she didn't even like, crammed into windowless box units alongside thousands of people for whom 'personal space' was not a high priority. In the morning light of a post-apocalyptic day, however, it took on a whole new level of menace.

'I don't suppose it matters if we park in the disabled bays any-more,' Sam said, pulling up to the front entrance. The car park was empty; the shops had been long closed before the storm had arrived. The large doors had been smashed in, however, and who could tell what lay on the other side of them?

'Looks empty,' said Mira.

'There's a fair bit of smoke on the far side,' Sam said, pointing to the other end of the building, where the beige stone walls bore the black stains of a fire, the windows shattered in the heat. 'We don't want to get caught in there if there's a fire.'

Jen puffed out a deep breath and looked over her two wards. 'We're not going to know anything until we get in there,' she said. 'Remember what we're looking for?'

'Warm clothes, blankets, tents, camping equipment, mini stoves,' Sam and Mira said in terse unison.

'Good,' Jen replied. 'I swear, if either of you come back with a basketball hoop or an Xbox you'll be carrying it along the road hoping some other idiot picks you up.'

'Does that go for the driver too?' asked Sam.

'Shut up.'

'So does the broken door count as good luck or a bad omen?' Mira asked.

Jen shrugged and stepped through the broken door into the dark. Her eyes adjusted to the interior gloom, but that only lasted another ten or so metres until the light ran out completely.

'Add torches to the list as well,' she said.

Those stores in the light were not much use to them, all trendy boutique fashion stores whose stock would not fare well under apocalypse scenarios. That didn't stop her and Mira picking up a few tops and dresses somewhat mournfully while Sam stood in the doorway looking incredulous. He disappeared for a moment and returned with a shopping trolley (which, fortunately, didn't need a nominal cash deposit). Because the centre had already been closed when the storm came, the stores and hallways were absent of corpses and clear for free-wheeling trolley action.

They delved into the dark, their every footfall echoing off the walls, and Jen tried to recall where the camping store was. Some stores were already looted, but aside from some empty shelves and knocked-over display cases there was little real damage. She did notice a jeweller's, its glass cases smashed and empty, and wondered why anyone would take the time to loot necklaces at a time like this. She supposed some kind of currency would have to continue in this new world. Why not gold?

'Over here,' Mira called out.

Jen stumbled towards the voice, now immersed in total darkness, until a light cut through the air in front of her, blinding her.

'You found the torches?' she asked.

'Oil lamps, actually,' Mira replied. 'Even better though...' She shone the light to the sign above her, which read 'Mirkwood Camping Supplies.'

'Clever girl,' Jen said.

They went, guided by Mira's torch, through the beaten down door and into the dark of the store. It had already seen some looting, but most of the stock remained. Soon they were ferrying armfuls of stuff to the shopping trolley outside.

'Why do these camping stores always try and make some tedious fucking link to Tolkien?' Jen asked, but Mira and Sam looked at her blankly. 'Never mind,' she said.

Soon they had three large tents, enough sleeping bags for them to use three apiece, and camping stoves galore. Jen dumped armfuls of what looked like packets of astronaut food into the trolley when a huge clatter down the hallway froze her to the spot.

'Lights off,' she hissed

Mira extinguished the flame. From far down the corridor a distant whoop reverberated off the walls.

'Get back in the shop and find somewhere to hide,' Jen whispered.

She watched their shadows melt back into the dark. She could make out more than one voice now, moving closer. She had to draw attention away from Sam and Mira. The door she could do nothing about but a stocked trolley would be a red flag.

The voices were getting closer. She had maybe twenty seconds before they would walk right into her. She eased the trolley down the corridor, away from the voices, cursing the weight of it. She built up some momentum and parked the trolley off the main thoroughfare, then turned and headed back towards the camping store, hoping the dark would give her cover.

The voices had stopped now. The corridor was silent. Had they heard her?

'I want some new sweet sneaks,' came a voice.

Jen almost fell back. It was no more than ten metres from her.

'Yeah, well, wait,' came another voice, deeper and more commanding than its counterpart.

'Gonna steal me some shit!' replied the other man in a sing-song voice. Both voices carried heavy Yorkshire tones.

She crouched down and tried to melt into the wall. The two men stopped, right outside the camping store.

She moved back to the trolley, and lifted out one of the small stoves. She looked down the corridor away from them, and with all her might swung the bottle and threw it as far as she could.

The weight of the stove carried it an impressive distance. It clattered to the floor with a metallic thunk, the sound echoing like an explosion through the silent corridor. Someone rushed past her, another lagging behind him whispering, 'John, John!'

'Oi!' called the first man, presumably John. They moved round the corner.

Jen started to run back to the camping store. She only made it a step or two before she ran straight into another person, whose hand came up quick as a flash and grabbed her by the throat.

'And where do you think you're going?' the man asked, his voice deep and raspy, his hot breath in her face, making her flesh crawl.

'Hoi, lads,' he called out. Somewhere down the corridor came a reply and the sound of returning footfall. 'You two must be the dumbest fucking idiots around,' he laughed. 'You hear something being thrown and you follow the sound of the thing they've thrown? What are you, fucking seals at the Sea Life centre? I bet if I threw a stick down this corridor right now one of you would come back with it in your mouth.'

She started to gasp, the panic, the lack of air, and the terror mixing together in her chest as his grip tightened around her throat.

'Stop,' she tried to say, but it came out as half a rasp.

He didn't seem to care. He held her with the same disinterested air she'd seen in her father when he'd come back from shooting with a brace of pheasants dangling by their necks. She hated this man even more than she'd hated her father in that moment.

'Hey, fuck you,' John replied, full of false bravado and fear.

The other man turned to her, only the outline of his face visible in the gloom.

'So who are you then?' he asked, letting go of her throat enough to let her answer.

'Jennifer,' she gasped.

'Well, hello, Jennifer. Is this your shopping trolley full of carefully looted camping supplies?'

She nodded. 'Yes.'

'So why were you hiding, Jennifer?'

'Trying to stay safe,' she replied.

'You alone?' he asked.

She nodded again. 'So can I go?' she asked, trying to sound as defiant as she could.

'I haven't decided yet,' he replied.

'Come on, Lundy,' one of the other men chimed in. 'Let's take her stuff and go, yeah?'

'You don't mind if we take your stuff, do you, Jennifer?' asked Lundy.

She could hear the sneer she couldn't see in the dark. 'Be my guest,' she said.

'Let's go, lads,' Lundy said, and he released his grip. She fell to the floor, gasping.

The trolley issued a dull squeak as they wheeled it down the corridor.

She let out a sigh of relief but stayed where she was. After a few seconds all she could hear was her own rasping breath

'That was close,' Mira's voice appeared behind her.

'Wait,' she said. 'They're not–'

'I'm not a complete fucking idiot,' came Lundy's voice, not two feet behind her.

'–gone yet,' Jen finished.

'So,' Lundy said. Jen felt his hand on her shoulder. 'You lied.'

Something rushed past her. There was an almighty crack, a thud, and his grasp was gone. Jen felt a small, delicate hand on her wrist.

'Run,' Mira said.

They rounded a corner and into brightness. Jen looked at her cohorts, both of whom were running as fast as they could with filled holdalls over their shoulders. Sam carried a cricket bat in one hand, a red smear across its front. She didn't stop, and dared not look back.

Back in the real world, the brightness made them stop. Jen held her hand up to the sky, trying to blot out the blinding light. Air rustled the perfectly sculpted trees.

Sam stumbled under the weight of the holdall, so Jen took it off him and Mira helped him to his feet. The weight nearly took her shoulder off, the handles rubbing deep grooves in her skin. An angry cry came from behind them, but Sam already had the car keys out and in a flash they were in the car, pulling away.

Two large skinhead men charged out toward them.

'Gun!' screamed Mira from the back seat.

One of the men raised his arm. Gunshots popped behind them, as Sam swung the car around a corner.

'Holy fuck!' Sam shouted, swinging around another corner at inadvisable speed. He drove with the cricket bat wedged between his legs, the blood-stained end sticking out, a grin beaming from ear to ear.

'What the hell happened?' Jen asked.

'While you were distracting them we figured the trolley was a goner,' Mira said from the back seat, 'so we found some bags and started filling them with stuff. Sam grabbed the bat in case one of them went for you.'

'When they left, I saw one of them double back. I could see his silhouette beside you,' Sam said. 'Mira went to go and make herself known and, as soon as he talked, I wound myself up with a pretty epic hit. Clocked him right in the temple.'

Jen stared at them both, their faces filled with glee, and she felt an intense wave of pride.

'You saved me, both of you,' she said. 'Thank you.'

'No worries,' Sam said, his neck turning a deep crimson.

They rode in silence for a few minutes. Adrenaline coursed through her body.

'So,' Jen said, pulling the holdall up onto her knees and opening the long zip. 'What did we get?'

'Fuck knows,' Mira replied. 'We were trying to grab stuff without making any noise. Figured some of it would be halfway useful.'

'No, good work,' Jen replied. 'Let's get some distance between us and the gunfire before we investigate properly, yeah?'

'Agreed,' Sam said. 'But we need to stop soon, because I am fucking hungry.'

'Me too,' said Mira. As the adrenalin started to ebb out of her system, Jen's stomach started to ache.

'Shit,' she said. 'When did we last eat?'

'Um,' Mira replied, and shrugged.

'We need to start looking after ourselves more,' Jen said. 'If we come across arseholes like them after not eating for two days or not sleeping, we'll be next to useless.'

'Yeah, but where are we going to eat?' Sam asked. 'It's not like I can rock up to McDonald's drive-through.'

'Eww,' Mira said, her face pinching up. 'As if we would eat there anyway.'

'Oh, Mira, enough with the tortured vegetarian routine!' Sam shouted, only half in jest.

'Fuck you, Sam.'

'Wait,' Jen said, 'Mira, you're vegetarian?' Mira nodded.

'Six years now.'

'Um, that's great, but...' Jen said, trying to phrase her next line without sounding patronising but failing. 'We have to think about survival now. We're going to have to eat when we can, what we can.'

'Yeah,' Sam said. 'The good people at Quorn aren't going to continue to produce their line of frozen and tasteless meat substitutes in the face of the end of the world, are they?'

'Oh yeah?' Mira replied. 'Do you think you'll be killing a lot of animals by hand; do you, Sam? Know a lot about how to skin a carcass, preserve meat, that kind of thing? My guess is we're all vegetarians now. And, I'll have you know that Quorn mini-kievs are excellent.'

They sat in silence for a moment. Maybe Mira was right. Where would they get their food once the shelves were full of rotten produce? She thought again about escaping to the countryside.

A small farmhouse maybe. Grow our own food, raise chickens, and wait for the world to return to normal. If it ever will.

'I'm not eating any fucking meat, and that's the end of it,' Mira said, finally.

'Fine,' Jen replied, too lost in her own thoughts to argue.

'I guess we'd better make use of as much food on the shelves as we can before it goes off,' Sam said. 'I mean, after that we're down to tins and shit, yeah?'

'I suppose so,' Jen said.

Fuck. There's so much I haven't figured out.

Chapter Twelve
A Wolf at the Door

An hour after they met Baxter, they met his men. It turned out he was the leader of a civilian military contractor group, which Tom assumed correctly was polite speak for a bunch of mercenaries. They had recently come back from Afghanistan and had been on a celebratory night out when the storm hit. Somehow, ten had survived the storm, and once they'd buried their fallen comrades, they'd decided to take action. Between them they had decided that, in the midst of great tragedy, there was opportunity.

The men had turned up at Baxter's house, and soon Tom and Leon had realised they were not their kind of people. All the men were big, alpha-male types, ex-squaddies with the necks and military tattoos to prove it. The two fey student types were soon the butt of many puerile jokes, and after an hour of dick jokes and casual misogyny, Leon turned to Tom and spoke in a hush tone.

'Let's go.'

'You think?'

'I don't get a great vibe from them. Do you?'

'No, but I think we're safest with them.'

Leon shook his head. 'I dunno. I think we should go.'

Tom nodded. 'Okay, if you want to.'
As they made their way to the door Baxter spotted them.
'Oi,' he called. 'Where do you two think you're going?'
'Out for a fag,' Tom replied.
'I don't think so,' Baxter said. 'You can smoke on the bus.'
Tom and Leon looked at each other.
'What bus?' they asked in unison.

Tom, Leon, and a few others already rounded up by Baxter's men were herded on board the second minibus of three. Military jeeps completed the convoy at either end. They set off, collecting anyone who crossed their paths. So far everyone had come of their own accord, glad at the sight of armed men in the chaos of the new world. Tom knew how they felt, but after a few hours under the control of Baxter's men, he didn't share their optimism. What Baxter's end game was, Tom had no idea, but he was in no rush to find out.

'What are we going to do?' he asked Leon, the first time their two handlers left them alone. Their driver was a wiry ball of nervous energy, his companion, a man with arms seemingly carved out of oak. The latter carried a baseball bat that had roughly the same IQ as its owner, judging by the quality of his conversation. He seemed to prefer the bat to the large machine gun resting on the dash of the minibus.

Leon shook his head in response.

There were five passengers in their bus now: Tom, Leon, two teenage lads whose eyes never left the floor, and a young woman who stared forward, grasping a carrier bag to her chest that probably contained her entire worldly possessions. Tom and Leon didn't even have that much, their bags left in Baxter's house.

The side door of the bus was flung open and Oak ushered two more people in, both women flashing nervous smiles. The wiry driver and Oak got back in the front seats and, without a word, they were moving again. The new passengers exchanged looks with the others, the nature of their new predicament dawning on them.

'Where we going?' Oak asked, his voice a thick cockney.

'I dinnae know,' the wiry man answered in an equally thick Geordie voice. 'Follow Baxter, that's all I know.'

They drove for hours, searching Sunderland for easy prey. They got their first demonstration of Baxter's propensity for violence when they had their first refusal. A man said he had to go and search for his family and received a swift baseball bat to the knees, before being set upon with a flurry of kicks. They left him by the side of the road, a broken and bloody mess, left for dead for having the temerity to walk round the wrong corner at the wrong time.

After that, Baxter and his men dropped any niceties when picking people up. Tom couldn't for the life of him think what they planned to do with them. By now Baxter had to be carrying at least twenty people in the three buses.

They carried on in the same way for hours, driving around and collecting people, although their own minibus didn't get any fuller. There was total silence on the bus aside from a few coughs and wheezes, and the occasional sob. The convoy crawled along at a slow pace, its path blocked by wreckage, which they snaked around as best they could.

Out of his window Tom watched the endless parade of carnage, so much death that it numbed his senses. Cars burned out, houses reduced to smouldering ruins and a never ending slew of bodies. That Tom was already so immune to the sight of them turned his stomach more than their twisted faces did, so he closed his eyes and rested his head against the window.

He must have fallen asleep because when his eyes reopened the sun had turned an ominous red and was receding over the tops of the houses. The convoy had ground to a halt.

Oak and Wiry both jumped out of the minibus together. Tom blinked himself back to consciousness and looked around to see what was going on. Baxter and his men had found a middle aged couple walking along the side of the road. Perhaps they'd even had the misfortune of flagging the convoy down. Tom couldn't hear anything but the body language was plain enough. The man had pulled the woman behind him, and his hands were out, pleading. Baxter and his men had surrounded their prey.

The rest of the minibus's inhabitants moved forward to watch. The man fell backwards with a shove, and one of Baxter's men grabbed the woman by the throat, pulling her away. She clawed at the man's face and he dropped her. Oak raised his bat.

A crack rang out as the wood connected with the woman's face, the force of the swing knocking her backwards. Her body collapsed against a wall, broken and dead.

At this the man let out a howl, a sound of utter desolation which wrought the air. A loud pop cut it off, as Baxter drew his gun and shot the man in the face. The man's body fell backwards, as dead as his partner.

'Ohgodohgodohgodohgod,' the woman behind Tom started to chant. Beside him Leon retched. Panicked cries issued around him as Oak and Wiry made their way back to the bus. It dawned on Tom they'd missed the best chance they might have had to get away. He looked at Leon, his friend's ashen face staring back in utter disbelief. He looked back at the crumpled bodies on the street, then at Baxter getting back into his jeep. Oak and Wiry were back now, Oak's bat smeared red.

'You see that?' Oak asked, turning to his captives. 'Let that be a lesson to all you cunts.'

They started moving again, silent, save for the sound of gentle sobbing.

When the convoy finally pulled to a stop, night had long since fallen. The prisoners on the bus had not managed any sleep. They stared out of the windows at the total darkness outside, but when the convoy pulled up as one they looked around to see what fate awaited them.

In the moonlight Tom saw what looked to be a motorway service station. Had they made it as far as Scotch Corner? Memories came back of his first drive to the north east, when his Dad had sat opposite him over a stale motorway service meal and told him flat out that he didn't plan on ever venturing that far north again. He'd kept his promise too. He'd have given anything for his father to be here now, though. He'd know what to do.

Baxter's men were exiting their vehicles now. Oak got out to join them. Tom had hoped they might get a chance to make a run for it, but Oak turned to Wiry and grunted at him to stay and watch them. Baxter held court with his men, gesticulating this way and that. He sent some of the men to extract fuel from the dead petrol station, while others were ushered into the main hall.

Next to the service station was the outline of a budget hotel. Oak returned, yanking open the side door. 'Out,' he barked.

Tom followed the other prisoners off the bus and soon they formed one large group with the other captives, standing in the dark together, shivering with cold and fear. Tom and Leon hardly dared exchange glances.

In front of them stood Baxter, flanked by two of his cronies, each scanning the crowd for trouble like it was second nature to them.

Tom remembered they were dealing with trained killers. What hope did he and Leon have?

'Now,' Baxter said. 'You probably think me a monster. That's fine. Maybe I am. But someone needs to take charge. I have worked in some of the shittest holes this world has to offer, and I've learnt one thing. Leadership is not about making friends. It's about being in control. Some of you will not like me being in control, but there's nothing you can do about it. So we're going to keep moving, keep finding survivors, and we will rebuild this country.

'For too long this country has laboured under the illusion of freedom. You know what freedom really is? It's a fucking lie. Democracy, human rights, all horseshit. If we're going to get through this, you need to learn that. And trust me, you will learn.'

Nervous glances went amongst the crowd. Tom heard Leon mutter something under his breath. Baxter continued.

'We're going to stay here tonight. I know you're tired. We don't know if the water will be working, but if it is, take a shower, take a bath. We will try and sort out some food for you.

'But, and I cannot stress this enough, don't think about running. If any of you try to leave, or you give me or my men any trouble, I promise you you'll regret it for the brief time you can call the rest of your life.'

He stopped and stared at the crowd, as though daring them to challenge him. When no response came, he turned and headed to the building.

Baxter's men jostled the crowd, ushering them toward the Travelodge. They shuffled in line, through the big double doors and into total darkness.

'We'll stick together,' Leon said.

Tom nodded, then remembered Leon couldn't see him. 'Okay,' he replied.

The air was thick with the smell of death, putrid and dank, and the mutterings from their fellow captives were like a ripple of fear on top of the stench.

'I've got keys,' came a voice ahead of them. A small light flickered on the ceiling, and Tom had a key thrust into his hand. He looked at it in the dim candlelight, room 205. He wondered how the hell he was even going to find it.

They were past Baxter's men now, making their way along a corridor, the crush of people not so heavy now.

'Leon?' Tom asked.

'I'm here, buddy,' came a voice behind him.

'Any idea where your room is?'

'It started with a two, so I'm guessing the second floor.'

'Me too.'

Doors opened and closed around them. Murmurs of panic ran through the crowd and the occasional stumble made the crowd lurch back and forth. Someone called out they had found the stairs and they headed upwards.

On the second floor they spent an interminable amount of time trying keys in doors until Leon happened across a correct combination of lock and key.

The room was lit by the thinnest glimmer of moonlight, but after the pitch black of the corridors it was enough. It was a small room. There was one double bed, which they both sank onto. Together they stayed like this – inert, silent, for hours – until finally Tom forced himself up. He looked around.

'No minibar,' he said.

Leon sat up. 'Fuck. I really could drink an entire set of miniature bottles of assorted spirits right now.' He got off the bed and stood up, took a step and immediately stumbled against something.

'What happened?' Tom asked.

Leon bent down and lifted up a suitcase with a grunt.

'Shit,' Tom said. 'There was someone staying here.'

'Where are they now?' Leon asked.

'Restaurant? Bar, maybe?' Tom replied.

Leon moved round the bed. 'Or,' he said, moving to the bath-room door. He tried the handle but the door remained shut.

'I'm not sure I want to see what's on the other side of that door,' Tom said.

'Me neither,' Leon replied. 'But I'm also not sure I can sleep in here without knowing. Besides, we might want to at least try to wash at some point.'

He kicked at the door, but it didn't give. On the third attempt there was a crack, and the door flew open. The bathroom was pitch black and filled with a smell of decay so severe it made them both retch, and step backwards.

Leon fished around in his pocket and removed his lighter. 'Fucking hell, that smell.'

Tom pulled his sleeve up to cover his mouth, but it had negligible impact. Leon moved into the bathroom, retching again, and hit the lighter. It flared up bright against the dark.

The light danced across the surface of the water in the tub, dark and blood tinged. The bloated corpse had tilted a little, so one dead eye stared accusingly at them. One bloated arm pierced the surface, black and swollen.

'Jesus,' Tom said under his breath, backing out of the bathroom.

Leon followed, pulling the door closed behind him. 'You can have the bathroom first mate,' he said.

'I think I'll give it a miss. Jesus, that fucking smell.'

'I know what'll sort it out,' Leon said, and started fishing things out of his pockets. Rizlas, tobacco, and a tiny ball of cling film.

'Fuck man, you've had weed on you this whole time?'

'Yeah,' Leon said. 'You can thank me later. But first, you can make yourself useful.'

'Oh yeah?'

Leon pushed the suitcase over to him. 'If I'm not mistaken, that was a fella rotting in our bathtub, so maybe we should see if there's anything useful in his suitcase. Then, maybe we take this spliff and go have a look to see if your room is a little bit less corpsey.'

Tom nodded, and pulled open the suitcase. There was a bag of toiletries, so he pulled out the deodorant and gave the place a quick spray. Clothes, a dead laptop, nothing of much use. He looked at the clothes. Business stuff, gym stuff, but it was clean, which was more than he could say for his own sweat-soaked attire. He closed the suitcase.

He pulled the key out of his pocket, emblazoned with the number 205. 'What number room is this?' he asked.

Leon lit the spliff and pulled his own key out. 'Um, 213.'

'Okay, so mine must be reasonably easy to find.'

As they navigated the corridor by lighter flame they heard the occasional noise seep out under the closed doors, usually muffled sobs, and the wheels of their dead man's suitcase trundling along the corridor.

A loud crash came from somewhere, maybe the floor below, but it was enough for them to freeze in their spot. Leon let the light go out, but no further noise came.

Tom's room was a mirror of the previous, except this had two single beds and no corpse in the bath. Being on the other side of the building, however, there was less moonlight to see by. Tom threw open the curtains.

'Shit, look at the sky,' he said. He'd never seen the stars stand out so vividly. 'No light pollution.'

'Maybe this is nature's way of stopping us from destroying her,' Leon said.

'Well if that were the case she could've taken the likes of Baxter too,' Tom replied. He looked at his friend. 'Leon, what the fuck are we going to do?'

'We're going to get the fuck away from that lunatic,' Leon replied, handing the spliff to Tom.

Tom pulled on it, feeling the tension seep out of his body as the first tendrils of smoke worked their way into his lungs.

Leon opened the suitcase and tipped the toiletries bag out onto the bed. He went through them, picking out the nail clippers. 'I don't think they'd do much damage,' he said. 'Fuck, there's nothing useful here. So how do we get out of here?'

'Beats me,' Tom replied. 'Maybe we could make a run for it. Late at night, Baxter's men will be tired too. Maybe we can slip out undetected.'

'These are mercenaries, fresh back from a warzone. You have to imagine they're pretty well drilled in controlling an area like this.'

'Maybe we wait and see if anyone else has a go, see what happens.'

Leon nodded his agreement. 'In the meantime, let's check the water.'

Turning the taps brought about a sudden shudder in the pipes, but no water. A moment later it spluttered through. The shower was dead and the water ice cold, They took turns to strip down to their underwear and wash themselves with tiny flannels and complimentary soaps. Tom could still smell the accumulated sweat and filth on himself, but felt marginally more refreshed.

Back in the main room, Leon had sorted through the clothes in the dead man's suitcase. As Tom came back in, his friend held up a suit.

'Very dapper,' Tom said.

'Yeah, but I don't know if I fancy trying to make a daring escape across woodland in a tailored suit,' Leon replied.

'James Bond manages it.'

'Yes, but neither of us are James Bond.'

'Fair point.'

Leon put the suit down and fished out tracksuit bottoms, T-shirts, and jumpers.

'Good job this guy is a gym nut,' Tom said, pulling out the dead man's membership card from his pair of tracksuit bottoms. 'Sorry, *was* a gym nut.'

'Shame he was the same size as most of Baxter's goons,' Leon said, looking at the over-sized jumper sleeves which engulfed his hands.

'At least we'll be warm.'

They both lay on the beds, Tom's thoughts drifting to several daring escape scenarios, some involving him somehow rescuing the entire group from their dastardly captor. He was somewhere in the netherworld between thought and dreams when the sound of machine gun fire brought him back to earth.

They both ran to the window. About two hundred metres from the building lay a splayed corpse, half of its head missing. Tom recognised the clothes from one of the boys on their minibus.

'What happened?' he asked.

'He ran, he got shot,' Leon replied. He turned and kicked the bed in frustration. He hobbled a bit, conjured a raft of expletives, and sat down on the bed.

'Well now we know,' Tom said.

'Yeah, great, so we know we're fucked. Wonderful. I feel all positive and warm with the glow of knowledge.'

Tom lay back on the bed, his head swimming. Maybe if they hid out in the room, the convoy might leave without them? Unlikely. Baxter was bound to do a head count.

'Well, I'm going to have a shit,' Leon said. He stumbled off to the bathroom, making sure it was still empty with a brief flicker of the lighter before pulling the door closed behind him. Tom lay back down and closed his eyes.

A loud crash brought him back again, this time close by. A scream, another loud bang and the sounds of splintering wood. Someone was kicking in the doors.

Leon reappeared from the bathroom. They both stood by the door, eyes fixed on it as they awaited the inevitable pounding.

It never came. What they heard was far worse.

After a few minutes they recognised the sounds for what they were, the anguished cries of a woman in pain. Once Tom realised what was happening his stomach turned and he retched, except there was nothing to bring up. He watched as Leon instinctively went to the door, but pulled his hand back from the handle. Leon looked to him, but Tom could only look to the floor.

The silence was horrifying, punctuated only by the occasional scream or sob. Tom felt wretched, every thought in his head telling him to go to help the woman, to do something, anything. But he couldn't move. Tears rolled down his cheek long after her cries died out and they heard footsteps retreating down the hallway.

He felt like a coward.

He *was* a fucking coward.

The fact he was too terrified, too ashamed, to even bring himself to go and offer even a fraction of help to someone in need, that cut him even deeper. In his shame and misery he buried his face into the pillow and began to weep, wanting the nightmare to end.

Chapter Thirteen
Death Letter Blues

Burnett looked out across the moors. Bathed in the early evening sun, the chill of the autumnal air bit into his arms. He didn't care. He'd driven around for two whole days looking for a ghost, and found nothing. A few potential punters for Tana and the Priest, some unsavoury behaviour, and two corpses that dated from after the storm, but nothing with the hallmarks of his man.

He wondered how they were getting on back at the sanctuary, and batted away the suspicions that his killer was there now, laying waste to them all. He'd head back there, probably, but he wasn't in any rush. Tana could look after himself, and they had guns. For now he wanted to stare out at the Moors.

A lifetime ago he would drive out here with his wife, and they would sit and look out at the bleak majesty of the Moors. She would dance for him, twirling and spinning and singing ever so slightly off key about Cathy coming home. He had loved those moments. This was before he ruined her life, or maybe it wasn't. Maybe he'd ruined her life the moment he walked into it. He couldn't help what happened, any more than he could make the sun set with his hands, but he understood how hurt she had been. It had been ten long years since he'd had the courage to admit to himself who he really was, and nine since he'd reached the point where he could no longer keep it from her. One foolish night in Hull had forced his hand, and he'd had to break it to her over a call from a police station, rather than how he'd wanted to do it. But there wasn't a good way to tell someone you loved that you were living a lie and forcing them to share it. She'd walked away from him and he'd never seen her again without a solicitor present.

He guessed she'd be dead now, judging by the devastation he'd seen over the last few days. Driving around Yorkshire he'd seen thousands of bodies, and only a handful of survivors. The entire infrastructure of the country was dead, that much was clear. The electrical network was down. The phone lines were too, and there'd been no sign of police, government, or military in the last forty-eight hours. As a veteran of the police, someone who'd been through more than one emergency planning session in his time, he knew that if it took over forty-eight hours, they weren't coming. There were no knights in shining armour-plated vehicles coming to save the day. They were on their own.

As much as he hated to admit it, the priest had a point. Burnett was wasting his time here, chasing ghosts. There was no point trailing the bogeyman all over the place, especially when there wasn't even a trail. He'd admitted as much to Tana – they'd find the bastard when he wanted to be found. That might mean more deaths along the way, but he couldn't be responsible for every body that fell.

He took another lungful of clean country air and let the cold breeze wash over him. He loved this place, even if he'd never been able to fulfil the role of Heathcliff. Come to think of it, Heathcliff was an absolute bastard to Cathy. Elaine should have seen it coming, really.

After he'd filled up on regrets and recriminations he walked back to the car and got back in. He had no idea what to do now. He wouldn't fit in back at the sanctuary. Not enough of a people-person for that gig. He could waste months chasing a killer down a rabbit hole, or he could go full-on lone wolf, and strike out on his own. None of the above sounded much fun to him.

He thought of Elaine again. Maybe he should go and see if she was alright, if she had survived the storm. The scenario entered his mind of turning up at her door to find her alive and well. She'd start screaming at him about how he'd ruined her life. She'd probably hit him with something. Seemed a waste of his efforts.

Turning back onto the main road again, he headed back toward Cottingthorpe. The sky darkened. The wrecks and bodies were hard enough to navigate in the day, so he resolved to stop at the next opportunity. Out here on the open roads there was little to distract him, and Burnett began to realise how tired he was. His eyelids felt heavy, his concentration waned, and the car started to pull over to the grass beside the road, threatening to tip into the verge. Burnett's attention snapped back into place.

He cursed. The adrenaline of almost crashing would sustain him for a few minutes, but he needed to get off the road. As the skies darkened, he had no frame of reference outside the glare of his own headlights. He couldn't see if there were farmhouses, or anywhere to hang his hat. All he could see was the road.

A corner came up and Burnett eased off the pedal to allow for it, but he couldn't see beyond the curve. He was going too fast when the deer appeared in the road before him, and swerved as hard as he could to avoid it. He was only partially successful. The driver's side of the front bumper clipped the hind of the startled animal, sending it careening out of sight.

The car hit the grass verge of the roadside. It flipped, and Burnett tried in vain to regain control as it flew through the air and into a field. It connected with the ground in an angry jolt of metal and earth. Burnett tossed around in his seat, his brain registering pain from several places at once and responding with a clear, calm message to its owner that he was about to die.

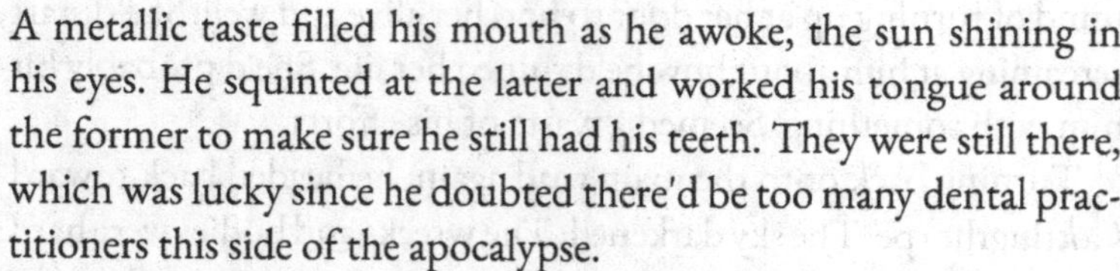

A metallic taste filled his mouth as he awoke, the sun shining in his eyes. He squinted at the latter and worked his tongue around the former to make sure he still had his teeth. They were still there, which was lucky since he doubted there'd be too many dental practitioners this side of the apocalypse.

He was still strapped into the driver's seat of the car, held in place above the passenger side by a thin strip of seatbelt. The car had flipped onto its side, and below him he could see the other side of the car was in a lot worse shape, all concertinaed up and mangled.

Lucky.

He started to move his legs and arms to check how well that luck held up. His arms seemed fine, if a little bruised, but as he moved his right leg something wasn't right. Eyes adjusting to the sunlight streaming in through the broken windshield, he looked down. The trouser clung to his leg, matted with blood. He moved his hand down as far as the seatbelt would allow, but all he discovered was that touching it hurt. He'd need to get out of his trousers to check what the hell was going on down there.

His fingers worked the seatbelt clasp. He was careful to hold onto the little handle above the window so as to stop himself falling down to the other side of the car, but it wouldn't budge. He adjusted his weight a little, hoping it would give him the slack to release the catch, but it still refused to yield.

After a few minutes it began to dawn on him he was stuck. He continued his attempts to open the clasp, and started to yank the other end of the belt, but that wouldn't give, either. He looked around for something to cut the belt. His gun was gone. He reached as far forward as the belt allowed and tried to gather up some of the broken glass to cut through the belt, but it was safety glass, and had no impact on the fabric, no matter how hard he rubbed.

He had no idea how long he tried to force the button, but it felt like hours. The sun shone straight through the windshield, unmoved by his efforts. He cursed and adjusted himself. Sitting in the same position for an age made his bones ache. The thin strip of synthetic fibres that seemed to be his new nemesis didn't help much, digging their way into his chest. He thought about the killer, and what he would think if he saw Burnett now, bested by a seatbelt.

The sun moved out of his eye line. He stopped struggling, and stared through the broken glass to the field outside for hours, punctuated only by the occasional burst of mania as he wrestled with his prison to no avail.

His stomach started to ache and his mouth was dry.

He was going to die here in this car. The realisation arrived with an unnerving but welcome sense of calm. He started to drift off to sleep, wondering whether he would wake again in the morning.

When he did wake, it was to the same bright sunshine that greeted him the day before. He tried to stretch his limbs again, and as a reflex tried the clasp again, knowing full well it wouldn't work. This time it did. The belt retracted back into the door and Burnett fell the short distance to the floor, slamming into the broken glass and twisted metal with a shriek and a wail, and hot, fiery pain.

He lay there for a moment, his right leg still on the driver's side, held up by the handbrake. Burnett shifted, and saw a deep gash had cut through the skin on his shin. It was an ugly wound, but the blood had dried over and started to heal. Not so bad.

More pressing now was the need for water. He felt weak and nauseous and knew he needed to rehydrate soon. After some tricky manoeuvring he climbed out of the broken windscreen, his body aching with every movement. He managed to get his feet into the field to stand up. He looked around, dismayed to see nothing other than endless miles of rolling fields, cut through with the road he'd come off.

He leaned on the cut leg. It hurt like a bastard, but he could walk on it. He looked at the car. If he hadn't climbed out of it himself he'd never have believed anyone could. He would have to proceed on foot and hope for a farmhouse, or a stream, or anything.

He cricked his neck, shook out his legs, and started to walk.

Chapter Fourteen
Black or Blue

Tom flitted between sleep, nightmares, and staring into the dark until the first light of dawn crept through the curtains. He looked across the room at Leon, his skin a pallid grey, his eyes fixed forward and red.

'Morning,' Tom said.

Leon didn't reply, but blinked himself out of his state and stood. He went over to the window, outside which last night's body still lay. Tom joined him, fighting back the urge to open the window and head out to a certain death. He couldn't see any point in doing anything else. If this was the world now, if last night was some measure of the life they had ahead of them, was there any point in sticking around? Did he want to be party to humanity's final descent into savagery? But the window was suicide-proof. It wouldn't open more than a crack.

Foiled again.

Sounds returned to the hotel as people in the other rooms roused themselves. Tom's stomach growled, but the idea of food turned his stomach. Knocking sounds and conversation came from outside. In anticipation, Tom and Leon made their way to the door and stood, waiting.

The knock came to their door and Tom opened it. It was Oak. Tom felt utter revulsion at the sight of him. He wanted to leap forward and break the man in front of him.

'Morning campers,' Oak said. 'Breakfast is served downstairs.' He moved to the next door.

Was he the one?

Oak make his way down the corridor. Tom looked at the other rooms, wondering which one held last night's victim. The corridor offered no answers, only confused and broken people leaving their rooms and trudging down the corridors.

'Move it along,' Oak called behind him.

Tom and Leon joined the others. A man ushered out them of the hotel, and Tom wondered if they were going straight back onto the buses. Instead they were herded into the main service station and its huge open plan restaurant area. At one time serviced by four separate fast food outlets, it was now serviced by three tables upon which the contents of the adjacent WH Smiths lay scattered.

Baxter and the majority of his men had had first pick. They sat on two tables together, munching their way through the pick of the sandwiches and giant chocolate bars.

The prisoners stood together, unsure.

'Well go on then!' Baxter called out to his captives, and they trudged forward to the table. At the sound his voice a surge of anger flowed through Tom again, but this ebbed away into sullen helplessness. Tears welled up, but he wiped them away with his sleeve.

People started to pick through the remaining stale sandwiches. Tom joined them. He found a Cornish pasty and some crisps, and a small bottle of warm orange juice. He and Leon took their offerings to a table and sat in silence as they ate. The only sounds came from the top tables, where Baxter's men laughed loudly.

Having finished his paltry breakfast, Leon pulled out his tobacco pouch and started to roll two cigarettes for them, and surreptitiously sprinkled a little weed into each. 'Might as well numb the pain a little, eh?'

Tom said nothing, and scanned the tables. He wanted to see if the victim of last night's attack was there with them. He didn't know who he was looking for, and the thousand-yard stares on his fellow prisoners meant it could have been any one of them.

Then he saw her. Alone on a table, hair not covering her face enough to hide a fresh bruise, a young woman sipped an orange juice. She stared at the table like she was trying to burn a hole in it with her mind.

Tom's own shame and self-loathing were nothing compared to what this woman had gone through. A fresh sting of guilt burned in the pit of his stomach.

'You coming?' Leon asked.

Tom nodded. They headed to the doors.

'Where are you going?' one of Baxter's men asked. It was Wiry, but if he recognised Tom and Leon from the minibus his eyes showed no sign of it. They may as well have been cattle to him.

'Smoke,' Leon said.

'Fine,' he said after a moment. He leant in. 'You try and make a run for it, you won't get far.'

They headed out into the fresh air. Tom revelled for a second as a cold blast of morning air hit his face. He lit up. The smoke hit the back of his throat and he allowed himself to imagine he was still in his previous life. He wanted to go back, back to hanging out with his friends, watching television, drinking, and smoking. Back to having no purpose, being able to lose weeks to the newest computer game. All he had now were a woman's muffled cries reverberating around his head.

'Oh for fuck's sake,' Leon said.

'What?'

'Up there.'

He pointed up. A sniper lay on the roof of the adjacent building, his rifle pointed at them. The man gave a little wave at them.

'Jesus,' Tom said.

'We need to get out of here somehow.'

'I don't disagree, but how?'

'I dunno, maybe if we can get everyone to rush them all at once, most of us might make it out?'

'We'd walk out straight into sniper fire,' Tom said. 'Besides, I don't like your chances of turning a load of terrified and bewildered hostages into a group formidable enough to face down a load of trained mercenaries.'

Leon nodded. They smoked in silence for a few minutes and put out the joints on the concrete floor. Neither made any move to return indoors.

'Why are they doing this?' Leon asked.

'Maybe this is all they know. They've spent the last God knows how many years repressing the fuck out of people in the name of democracy and now they think this is how you do things. You have to say it's working for them, too.'

'Where are the real army? The government? If we all survived, and Baxter and his men survived, surely somewhere some bit of government did too?'

'Maybe,' Tom said.

The doors opened and out came some of Baxter's men.

'You boys smoke?' one of them called out. They nodded. 'Well get in there and help yourself to some tabs before they all run out.'

They made their way in, as everyone was on their way out the door, all clutching cigarettes and lighters. In the WH Smiths the cigarette counter stood decimated. Tom and Leon helped themselves to a few packets each and some tobacco pouches.

'Wonder how long it'll be before we start running out of tobacco?' Leon said.

'I'm more worried about when we run out of food,' Tom replied.

'I reckon Baxter's the key,' Leon said in a low voice. Tom nodded.

'Agreed.'

'If we could get him away from the rest of his group.'

'We'd need to get the sniper down from the roof as well,' Tom said. 'Without that our chances go from slim to fucked.'

The hall was nearly empty. The only other person in the room was the woman sat alone at her table. She looked up, sensing his gaze, and he tried to convey his guilt, remorse, solidarity and everything else in a weak smile, but she looked away.

'Fuck's sake, can you say Stockholm syndrome?' Leon said, looking the other direction.

Tom followed his gaze. Outside the smokers from Baxter's men and the hostages were milling together like they were on a collective fag break from reality, laughing and joking together.

Tom looked back to the woman at the table.

'Do you think we should say something?' he asked Leon.

'Say what, exactly?'

'I don't know.'

'Well, you should probably try to figure that out before you go over there.'

Tom nodded.

'Fuck, Tom, what are we going to do?'

Tom had no answer. He was still watching the woman sat alone. She wiped a tear away with her sleeve.

Oak walked over to her table, leaned over to whisper something to her. She turned to the huge man, her face full of hatred, and spat in his face.

Tom was halfway to her table when the mercenary's fist slammed into the woman's chest. All thought abandoned him as he leapt at the huge man and swung his fist. It connected with the bigger man's ear, sending a righteous flash of pain up Tom's arm.

The man stumbled, confused, but that barely lasted long enough for Tom to congratulate himself for a job well done before Oak bore down on him, face filled with rage.

When the punch came it connected with Tom's chest, driving all the air from his lungs. Something snapped somewhere inside. He flew backwards and smashed against the floor.

Everything hurt, all at once. He managed to draw a breath and open his eyes in time to see a thick leg pulling back to deliver a blow to his head, but something rushed past him and sent his aggressor sprawling.

Leon!

He could kiss his friend, had he the energy to do anything other than wheeze.

His moment of triumph was short lived. Baxter's men arrived, and Tom saw Leon fall to the floor, blood spurting from his nose. Tom took a heavy blow to his back, sending a surge of pain across his body. Something struck his head, and everything went black.

He awoke to the curious sensation of sliding sideways, which registered before the searing pain in his head, back, and ribs. His eyes stubbornly wouldn't open. They felt sealed. He raised his fingers to them and felt some kind of dried crust, which he rubbed away. The sliding motion came to an abrupt end as he bumped into something.

He blinked, his vision blurred. As the world came into focus he realised he was in some kind of container. A van? The back was empty aside from himself and someone else. He blinked again. It was Leon. He looked terrible, his face bruised and swollen, his leg in some kind of rudimentary splint. A strap around his wrist prevented him from sliding around. He stared away from Tom, his face contorting with pain at every movement of the van.

'Leon,' Tom said, the words hurting on their way out of his throat. His friend looked over at him. 'What the fuck happened?'

'What the fuck happened? I'd pretty much say *you* happened.'

'Are you okay?'

'Not really, no. I have a broken ankle, probably a couple of broken ribs and no doctor to treat them, no hospital to go to, so there's a pretty good chance I'll die from a relatively minor wound. Oh, and my face feels like the meat in Rocky Balboa's freezer after a training session.'

'Shit,' Tom tried to interject.

'Oh, I'm not finished,' Leon said. 'I was dumped, broken ankle and all, in the back of a van, presumably being driven by a drunken blind mule. All because you had to go and be the hero.'

Silence fell. Tom felt a sinking feeling. 'What happened?'

'No idea. Someone stamped on my leg and I blacked out too. I came too as they were putting us in the back of the van, there was a lot of shouting and noise. To be honest I thought you might be dead. They closed the door and we started moving. I would have presumed they were taking us away to kill us, except they didn't seem too shy about killing in front of people before.'

'I'm so sorry.'

'Yeah, well, I can't be too pissed off with you for doing what I didn't have the balls to do. Besides, it was pretty funny trying to watch you fight with all the skills of a four-year-old.' He motioned to Tom's face. 'And it's not like you got off scot-free.'

'Is it bad?' Tom asked.

'You'd better hope it's true chicks dig scars.'

Tom raised his hands to his face. The moment fingers met flesh deep rivulets of pain opened up. It felt like great chasms had opened up across his skin. He groaned. His hand moved to the back of his head, which seemed the source of a lot of his pain. It was a mess of matted hair, blood and more pain.

'I'm going to really, really kill those fuckers,' he said, almost believing it as he said it.

'Well you'll get your last chance soon enough,' Leon said, 'I reckon Baxter's going to kill us sooner rather than later.'

'At least we've got something to look forward to.'

The van went round a corner and Tom let himself slide across the floor to Leon, watching his friend's face contort with pain as he tried to hold his mangled leg in place.

'Any thoughts?' Tom asked.

'On how we survive?'

Tom nodded.

'I thought, seeing as my leg is pretty much fucked I might tear it off and use it to bludgeon to death the next person who opens that door.'

'Well if you do, don't forget to use the shoe end.'

Leon laughed, then winced in pain.

'You know,' Tom said, 'I always thought that all those hours of playing *Resident Evil*, watching zombie films, and box set after box set of *Buffy the Vampire Slayer* meant that, come the apocalypse, I'd be one of the ones who had it sorted. That it wasn't wasted time, because one day all my bullshit survival knowledge might come in useful. But look at us now.'

He glanced over at his friend. His eyes were closed. Tom worried for a moment that he'd gone unconscious, or into shock or something. Thankfully Leon soon uttered a gentle snore.

He waited for something to happen, but nothing did. On and on the lorry rolled, pitching and yawing. Tom sailed on, until he too sank into sleep.

Chapter Fifteen
Such Hawks, Such Hounds

Having pilfered so much camping gear, Jen, Mira, and Sam decided to try a night out in the woods. They left York behind and headed north, stopping off for a quick raid on a sandwich shop. They drove for most of the afternoon, munching on stale sandwiches that Jen hoped they wouldn't regret within the next few hours, until the urban sprawl gave way to rolling fields. They passed a farmer's gate and backed up, took a turn onto the grass, and headed out of sight of the road.

Jen hadn't been to a festival for a few years, but the tent-building muscle memory was pretty well honed, and soon they had two tents up. She looked at her companions.

'So do I need to build another tent?' She asked them.

Sam stuttered for a moment and Mira looked at the ground.

'We, um...'

'That's what I thought. Fine. But here's the deal. No sex.'

Mira flashed a look of indignation.

'But...'

'No, Mira. Listen to me. You two can do what the hell you like, I'm not your mother and I'm not about to tell you you're too young. What I will tell you, though, is there's not a fucking chance in hell I'm going to let Mira get pregnant. Not now.'

Mira looked down again.

'I mean it. Either you both agree to keep it in your pants or I'm building another tent.'

'What do you want us to say?' Mira said.

'I want you to make me a promise and I want you to know, to understand, that if you break this promise and make me not trust you, I will leave and you will be on your own to do whatever the hell you want. Okay?'

Sam nodded. 'We promise,' he said.

'Good. Mira?' Jen said.

Mira nodded.

'Let's eat.'

They ate a second round of stale sandwiches with a side order of uncomfortable silence. Jen felt bad, only half of what she had said was true. She didn't think they were ready. In fact, she was already starting to panic about what might happen should their young love turn sour. It had bugged her so much over the preceding hours it made her head throb.

'These aren't bad,' Sam said, breaking the silence through a mouthful of sandwich.

'Yeah, we're going to have to learn to fend for ourselves a bit better though.'

'Might as well use all the food out there first,' Mira said.

'True.'

'I haven't slept in a tent for years,' Sam said. 'My mum and dad used to take me all the time. I used to hate it. We'd spend the whole time arguing and sitting out in the rain. Then we'd go home again. I never understood why we did it at the time but, looking back, I think we were so skint it was all we could afford. They were determined to give me a holiday.'

He stopped, and Jen saw his eyes welling up. She wished she had something profound to say. Mira squeezed his hand.

'This is my first time camping,' the young girl said. 'I've always wanted to go to Glastonbury, but I guess that won't happen now.'

'We could go if you want but I doubt the line-up will be any good this year,' Sam said, laughing.

'I never did Glasto, but I've done my fair share of festivals over the years,' Jen said.

'Oh yeah, which ones?'

'Leeds, Reading, V, T, Download, Latitude. Loads.'

'Wow, you must have seen some great bands,' Mira said.

'I did, yeah.' She thought of Daniel. 'That's where I met my boyfriend. We were the only ones who turned up to see some nobody band on the bottom of the bill in some tent at Leeds, we'd both read some blog about them and went to check them out. We stood and watched this dreadful emo band playing their hearts out to the two of us. We both felt like if we left the band would burst into tears, so we stayed for the whole set and on the way out he was in fits of giggles. We got talking. Two weeks later, he left Essex and moved to York to be with me.'

'How long were you together?' Sam asked.

'Four years,' Jen said. The thought of him, back in their bedroom, came unbidden into her mind and she couldn't help but burst into tears.

Mira dashed over to her and held her as the tears turned into sobs. The tears dried up and she wiped her face on her sleeve.

'So what do we do tomorrow?' Sam asked, looking a tad uncomfortable at the sudden appearance of crying women.

'I don't know,' Jen said.

They sat up until the darkness around them was total. The night was overcast and there was no light from anywhere. Jen had never known darkness like it. Mira looked terrified, and when they turned in to their tents, Jen was glad and only slightly jealous that Mira would have some company in the dark.

Sleep didn't come easily. The woods were teaming with sounds, and her head swam with thoughts and fears, half-baked survival notions bumping up against Daniel's dead body in her mind's eye. The night was bitterly cold, even inside three increasingly restrictive sleeping bags she couldn't shake the bitter frost of the night air.

She awoke to a tent filled with bright morning light. Her three sleeping bags were like a furnace now, albeit a not unpleasant one. Mira and Sam were moving about outside, and for a moment she allowed herself a brief moment of relaxation, before the swirling questions returned and she tried to work out what to do next.

She rose, had a festival shower with baby wipes, dressed into random bits of camping clothes purloined from the shopping village, and exited the tent. Sam was already up and out of his tent.

'Morning,' she said.

'Morning,' Sam replied. 'Glad you're up. We've been thinking.'

'Okay.'

'Let's never camp again, yeah?'

Jen laughed and nodded.

They got back on the road much less burdened with camping gear than before. They salvaged the things they might need and didn't even bother to take down the tents. With all the empty houses out there, the chances of them actually needing to sleep in tents seemed remote, a ludicrous folly. They were in the countryside now, and felt safer than they had in York. They hadn't seen another survivor since the shopping centre, and after a day in the country they felt more at ease with their surroundings.

A few hours later, they pulled up into a tiny hamlet. There weren't many bodies, save for the odd ones dotted about by their front doors. The whole hamlet ran to two roads and a local shop.

'I like the ones who had the good grace to go outside when the storm came,' Sam said as they parked up. 'It means they left their door open behind them, and it means their house is stinky-corpse-free.'

'Very empathetic, Sam,' Mira said.

'Oh, so you don't want to go in and see if we can get some food?'

They entered the first house, stepping over the old man's corpse outside. It was empty.

'Maybe one of us should stay by the door,' Jen said. 'We don't want any other survivors in the area thinking we're looters or anything.'

Sam nodded and moved to the door.

'Even though that's exactly what we are, right?'

'Yeah, but we're nice looters.'

The house bore the hallmarks of an old man living alone. It seemed sad, somehow, that the man was lying outside, rather than in his home. The place was drab but tidy. 'Tinned food jackpot!' Mira called from the kitchen. She found a large shopping bag and started to fill it.

'Grab some plates, cutlery, and a tin opener,' Jen said. Family photographs and beige tones covered the living room walls. 'Make sure you don't do anything to wreck the place.'

'Why?' Sam asked from the doorway.

Jen motioned to the photos lining the shelves. 'Family. Could be some of them have survived and are coming to look for him. Don't want them coming in and feeling like their old Dad's house was violated by looters.'

Sam nodded. 'I'd say this place is pretty dead,' he said. 'No sign of anyone.'

'Let's not stick around,' Jen said. The house had an odd vibe, and she didn't feel like staying to investigate it.

'We've got enough food here for a few days anyway,' Mira said, emerging from the kitchen with two full bags.

Back in the car, Sam started regaling them with his knowledge of human decomposition from biology lessons, and the probable outcome of having endless dead bodies decomposing together. His vivid description of cholera-ridden streets was enough to make Jen never want to head to a city again.

'We should find a nice little cottage in the country, like a country house or something,' Mira said.

Jen nodded, but she wondered where. Anywhere too desirable and they wouldn't be alone for long, and once they staked out territory they'd have to either defend it or leave it. Would they stand a chance against anyone wanting to take their home, should they ever be able to make one?

They drove around for the rest of the day, Jen stalling for time, putting off any eventuality where she might have to commit to a decision.

As evening fell they pulled into the car park of an empty bed and breakfast, where they found a well-stocked larder and a freezer full of defrosted but edible meat. Jen spent the best two hours since the storm coaxing a gas cooker to life and cooking a roast dinner with all the trimmings while Mira and Sam got up to god-knew-what in one of the bedrooms. She wasn't sure if she trusted them, and remembered back to their age. When she'd had her first proper boyfriend and taken that step, would anyone have been able to stop her?

The meal itself was delicious, Mira feasting on the plentiful veg while Jen and Sam devoured a huge joint of beef. Together they got merrily drunk in the moonlight streaming through the windows. They were tremendous company, her two charges. Funny and sweet and naive; they had already developed the shared interior monologue only available in the throes of young love, but were sensitive enough to her own loneliness not to be showy about it.

She stumbled to her room for the evening, wondering if they might stay here for a while, maybe see if they could weather the worst of it here. Surely, some kind of normalcy would come about in the coming weeks? Some kind of authority must be out there right now trying to lift the country up off its knees. If they could wait here until they managed it, that wouldn't be so bad.

Deep down she knew this to be wishful thinking. There was no government now. If there had been, they'd have seen it. It wasn't a big country. No, they needed to keep mobile, keep moving until they could figure it out. Get too comfortable out here and the new world would punish them for their complacency. At the very least if they were going to stop somewhere, it'd have to be a damn sight further off the beaten track than a B&B on a major road.

They got back on the road the next morning, in a new car whose petrol tank showed as half full. They drove for hours, meandering around villages and towns trying to look for signs of life without alerting anyone to their presence.

Nothing fits yet.

Lunchtime came and went. Sam ran into a newsagents and came out laden down with unhealthy snacks that had expiry dates so far into the future as to be a warning, which they wolfed down before they moved on again.

Soon time started to drag, and Jen's patience wore thin. Several attempts at conversation went nowhere, and Jen started to itch for some time by herself, or company more capable of adult conversation.

'So bored,' came a call from the back of the car.

'I think we got it the first dozen times you told us,' Jen replied. 'Perhaps at the next place we stop we should pick you up some crayons and paper, since you seem determined to act like an infant.'

I've become my mother.

Mira responded with a sucking sound through her two front teeth, another noise Jen had become all too familiar with over the course of the day. They rode on in uncomfortable silence until they reached a village that had an altogether different vibe to the others they had cruised through.

'No bodies,' Sam said.

Jen nodded. Unlike everywhere else, the streets were completely clear of corpses. 'Slow down,' she said.

'Either no one was outside when the storm came,' Sam said, 'or someone has been clearing up.'

'Pull up here.'

They came to a halt in the heart of the village. Jen peered around the houses and the row of shops for any signs of activity. It was eerily quiet, and Jen felt the first rumblings of unease.

She got out of the car. A fox crossed the street in front of them.

'Seems dead,' Sam said, getting out his side.

There was movement in one of the windows. Jen caught it out of the corner of her eye, but when she looked to see what it was there was nothing there. She had a sinking feeling. More movement, on the periphery of her vision. Her heart pounded.

'Guys,' she whispered.

Mira gasped.

Jen wheeled round. In the window next to her was the face of an old woman, staring at them, a blank look on her wrinkled face.

'Holy shit!' Sam exclaimed.

'What do we do?' Mira asked.

'Back in the car,' Jen said, and they backed towards the car, eyes casting around.

Jen pulled her door open.

'Jen,' Sam hissed.

She whirled around. In the road behind her a man stood, hands held out in front of him. 'Stop right there,' she called out, holding her car keys out in some kind of futile threat. The man was in his late fifties or so, dressed in the type of clothes Jen associated with people who either watched or presented Top Gear, which hardly endeared him to her.

'We aren't going to hurt you,' he called out. 'As long as you're not here to hurt us.'

Behind them a door opened. Jen whirled round. A little old lady appeared in the doorway, her face a picture of wrinkled kindness.

'It's okay,' she said. 'You're safe.'

They were using their local post office as a central hub. They were lucky to still have one; Jen had been under the impression they'd been sold off years ago, but here was the epitome of a local store. A local shop for local people. Now Jen and her companions crammed into it with a dozen other survivors.

They referred to it as 'the retirement village of the apocalypse'. There were twelve of them, all pensioners, or as near as made no odds. The youngest of them was Nigel, the man who had attempted to greet them before, and he was well past fifty. Once they established Nigel wasn't an axe murderer, and the residents had established Jen and her charges weren't ASBO hoodlums looking to cause havoc, the two groups warmed to each other pretty quickly.

Nigel seemed to be the face of the group, and its most enthusiastic member, but it was Joan, the old lady at the window, who seemed to be in charge. Once the other inhabitants of the village had come out to greet them the names flew past in a blur of enthusiastic grins and wrinkled handshakes. More than once Jen had to turn down a cup of tea held out by shaking hands.

Bloody tea. I could murder a coffee and all I get offered is sodding tea.

'You three look like you've had a rough time of it,' Nigel said, his face shiny and red from smiling.

'It's been mad,' Sam replied. He looked more at ease than he had done since Jen had met him, and when he saw the drinks fridge his eyes lit up. 'Irn Bru!'

'Help yourself,' Nigel said.

'I've been dying for some Irn Bru for days,' Sam said, scrambling to open the fridge. He took out three cans and thrust two into Jen and Mira's hands, not for one second considering either of them might not share his predilection for Scottish teeth-rotting fizzy pop. Jen opened the can and took a sip. She hadn't drunk it in years, and childhood memories burst into her mind as soon as it hit her taste buds: long summer days in fields covered in wispy dandelions, stolen kisses with cute and not-so-cute boys, arguing the merits of pop music made by blonde twins and American boy bands with her girlfriends.

I should drink this more often.

'...so we got out of there as fast as we could.' Sam continued to tell their tale of woe.

Jen wanted to return to the fields of wispy dandelions, but the second sip tasted of crap pop.

'We've been driving around ever since, trying to work out what we're going to do. Mostly we've been looking for people who don't want to rob us or kill us or anything.'

There were mutters of 'oh my' and 'gracious' from the gentle folk around them.

'How did you find each other?' Joan asked. She watched them with a dispassionate eye, Jen noticed, not quite so sold on their appearance as the others. Jen couldn't blame her.

Mira and Sam exchanged a guilty look, unsure whether they now had to tell their tale of highway robbery, but Jen spoke first.

'I found them in a house together, their parents were, well, you know. So I took them with me. York wasn't safe anymore, so...'

She tailed off.

'You did a good thing,' Nigel said, putting his hand on her shoulder.

Jen shrugged it off a little more blatantly than she had intended, and Nigel's face fell. An awkward moment passed between them, unnoticed by everyone else.

'So how about you?' Jen asked. 'Forgive me, but this was the last thing we expected to come across when we came into the village.'

'Not much to tell,' Nigel said. 'We're all from the area. When the storm happened people seemed to come here to check what was going on. We decided to stick together in one place, cleaned up the village and whatnot. There was,' he paused, 'a little unpleasantness, but that's behind us now.'

'Do you know what's happened?' Mira asked, speaking for the first time. 'I mean, out there? The storm?'

'Not really, no,' Joan replied. 'Some of us have theories, but nothing concrete. We know it killed most things electrical, and there's been no TV or radio since.'

'Actually,' Nigel said. 'Jeremy has an old wind up radio and he thought he heard some French voices on it, but none of us speak French.'

'I think it might have been Spanish, actually,' called a voice from the back of the post office.

'None of us speak Spanish either so it's a moot point.'

'So what theories do you have?' Sam asked, inhaling a bag of Monster Munch with such gusto that the maize monster shapes barely touched the sides of the bag on their way out.

'Let's see,' Nigel replied. 'There's a few people who think this
is some kind of divine act. The Rapture, in fact, but since that
means we're the sinful ones, it's not a terribly popular opinion.
There's a school of thought that this is some colossal government
something-or-other that's gone wrong.'

'And you?' Jen asked.

'Ah,' he replied, pleased to have the floor. 'Let me ask you something. Would any of you care for a cigarette?'

'God yes,' Jen replied. Both Sam and Mira nodded, Sam struggling to get his affirmation through a mouth glued up with Monster
Munch.

'Nigel!' exclaimed two of the women in unison. There were looks
of consternation from the assembled elderly.

'Hey, if I'm right, it's smoking that saved these kids' lives.'

'What?' Jen said.

'Every single survivor we've met so far is a smoker. Everyone in
this village here, and everyone any of us have come across since the
storm. Now you three.

'The most recent statistics suggest that as little as ten per cent of
the population of the United Kingdom are smokers now, so one
would expect to see roughly the same percentage in the survivors,
but instead we have seen a hit rate of one hundred percent, albeit
from a relatively small sample pool. Nonetheless, it's a remarkable
point.'

'So wait,' Sam said. 'Do you have any cigarettes or not?'

Nigel chuckled and tossed Sam a pack.

'How do you know all this?' Jen asked.

'I work – or, sorry, I used to work – for the national advisory
board for the NHS's anti-smoking initiatives.'

'I thought you said the survivors are smokers?' Mira said.

'I work for the board, but I'll admit I've not been particularly
effective in advising myself to kick the habit. Now I'm rather glad
I didn't.'

Jen tried to take it in. She ran through every person they'd encountered since the storm hit and tried to remember if they'd been smokers, but in her head they all seemed to be smoking pipes in some bizarre trick of the mind.

'Of course,' Nigel continued, 'it could be I'm as wrong as Gladys and her insistence that this is the Rapture. Or maybe it's the work of our new Martian overlords preparing for an invasion, as Mr Stokes seems so convinced is the case.'

'Wait,' Jen said, trying to wrap her head around the concept, which felt both ridiculous and plausible. 'So we're all smokers. Say that's true, it still doesn't answer the question as to what the hell has actually happened to everyone else. It's not like every non-smoker in the world upped and died on their own.'

'True. And I can say from experience that not every smoker made it through the storm. I have no idea what caused the storm, or any of this. All I can say is from a purely rational standpoint cigarette addiction must be one of the factors as to why we survived.'

Silence fell over the post office. Jen looked around and saw the crowd had thinned somewhat. Perhaps they'd heard this theory too many times, perhaps they'd seen enough of the newcomers.

'It's an interesting theory,' she said. 'Listen, we're pretty tired, we could do with a wash and a rest. I'm not sure what kind of capacity you have for new people, but do you have anywhere for us to get washed up?'

Joan stepped forward, smiling.

'Of course there is, dear. You three follow me and we'll get you set up, don't worry.'

Joan led them to a little row of cottages behind the main street. The sun set behind the fields, and smoke rose from the chimneys.

'You'll have to do without electricity, I'm afraid,' Joan said. She opened the front door to one of the cottage. She pocketed the key, rather than handing it over to Jen. 'No creature comforts, either, but the fire works. We'll bring you some wood shortly. There's no running hot water, but the taps and the gas stove work for now, so you can fill up a bath from the kettle.'

Jen nodded.

'The bedrooms are upstairs. There's only two I'm afraid, so I imagine one of you will be on the sofa?'

The question came loaded with a sense of what would be an appropriate response, but before Jen could answer, Sam jumped in.

'That'll be me,' he said. 'Don't worry, I've had a lot worse. Sofa actually looks pretty comfortable.'

Joan looked placated by his response, and gave a terse little smile.

'We'll sort you out some duvets and stuff, Sam, thanks for being a gentleman,' Jen said.

'Not a problem,' he said with a smile, and went off into the house to explore.

'Now, dear,' Joan said, addressing Jen. 'I don't know what your plans are, we will leave that to you to discuss among yourselves, but perhaps tomorrow we can sit down and talk about what you want to do?'

Jen nodded, and Joan left, without handing over the key. Jen bolted the door.

The next few hours were a bliss of silence, baths, comfortable beds and thoughts of what might be. Jen even found a bookcase in her room that wasn't entirely without merit in its composition, and lay on her bed flicking through the pages of a well-thumbed copy of *The Secret History* by candlelight. She contemplated not even leaving her room, but Mira, hair still wet from her own bath and clothes thrown back on, appeared at her door, two bottles of wine in hand.

'Look what I found.'

Downstairs, Sam was busy setting up a private area for himself. As soon as they both appeared he took the filled kettle up for his own bath. Jen caught a longing look in Mira's eyes as she watched her boyfriend take the stairs.

'You realise you two are going to have to be a lot more subtle if we stay here, don't you?' Jen said.

'What do you mean?'

'You know I trust you two to be sensible, but we're in the land of the old people now. You saw how they reacted to the idea of you two smoking. They're not likely to be that happy about an underage, unmarried couple shacking up in a cottage with only a young woman of questionable values to chaperone them.'

'I...' Mira stammered.

Jen poured the wine. 'They'd probably disapprove of you drinking, too.'

'Jesus,' Mira said. 'Don't they know it's the apocalypse?'

'This is why we need to decide if we're going to stay here.'

'You don't want to?' Mira asked.

Jen considered the candlelit cottage, the wine, the bookcase. 'It's not that I don't want to,' she said. 'It's just... I've not decided if I think it's safe yet.'

'I know what you mean,' Mira said. 'That Nigel guy gives me the creeps.'

'Really?'

'He keeps eyeing you up. It's creepy, he's old enough to be your granddad.'

Jen laughed. 'What did you make of his theory?' she asked, taking out a crumpled pack of cigarettes from her jeans as a reflex. She handed one to Mira.

'I don't know. It kind of makes sense, I guess. But, that doesn't mean anything. I mean, if he worked at NASA I'm sure he'd be able to convince you it was aliens. Until someone comes up with some kind of official explanation, I don't know. And honestly, I don't care.'

'You don't care?'

'What does it matter? How does knowing what happened have any impact on how we get through tomorrow, or the next day? Unless knowing means we can somehow undo it, bring everyone back, bring my parents back, and your boyfriend, and all my friends, I don't care. This is the world we live in now, it's more important that we work out what that means.'

Jen stared at Mira in shock, which made Mira revert to her standard defence position, knees drawn up and hair over her face.

'I dunno, maybe it does matter and I'm being a brat,' she mumbled.

Jen smiled, and reached forward to brush the hair from Mira's face. 'I was thinking that was the most sensible, grown-up thing I've heard anyone say about anything since the storm.'

Mira smiled, her cheeks flushed red.

Jen raised her glass and they clinked a silent toast.

'You know, when I picked you two up I thought I was making the most insane mistake of my life. But I don't know what I'd have done without you both.' A smile spread across Mira's face, and Jen's heart swelled.

'You might want to reserve judgement on that,' came a voice from the stairwell. Jen turned to see Sam pulling on a jumper and running down the stairs. 'Look out the window.'

Jen put down her wine and moved to the window.

'What is it?' Mira asked.

Jen peered out.

The sight of the residents of the village staring at the cottage in the low night light was unnerving, to say the least. She backed away from the window. 'Jesus,' she said.

'Are they actually carrying torches?' Sam asked.

Jen scanned the crowd, stretched out in a line, staring towards the house with hate in their eyes, lit by the glow of torches.

'What do we do?' Sam asked.

'What? What is it?' Mira asked again.

'Shit,' was all Jen could think to say.

'The whole village is stood out there staring at our house like zombies,' Sam said. 'I can't tell if they have pitchforks, but it's freaking me out.'

'Right, everyone, go and collect your stuff together,' Jen said, before heading upstairs to do the same. Her room faced the back garden and the fields behind it, but it was total darkness out there. Besides, their car was on the main street.

What the fuck do I do?

She stuffed her bag full again and rushed back downstairs. Mira was behind her. Sam was back at the windows, peering out at the crowd staring back at them.

'Are they doing anything?' Jen asked.

'Talking amongst themselves. I think they're trying to work out how to get in. It's still freaking me out.'

'You got your stuff together?'

'Yep.'

Jen took a deep breath. 'Either we stay put and see out the night, or we make a run for it out the back and try and double back for the car.'

'Or we could go out there and talk to them,' Mira said.

I really don't want to do that.

'Or we could do that, yes. What do we think?'

The three of them stood in silence for a moment.

'Oh fuck this,' Sam said, grabbing the door. 'They're old people. We just need to move around them at a vaguely accelerated pace.'

He unbolted the door and threw it open, striding out into the night.

Jen and Mira followed.

'What the hell is going on out here?' Sam shouted at the crowd, who looked taken aback. Nigel was at the front, so Sam strode up to him, hands balled into fists at his sides. Jen thought he might actually swing for the older man.

Jen and Mira caught up.

'Nigel, if this is your idea of hospitality, it seems to have missed its mark,' Jen said.

'What did you do to Joan?' Nigel asked. Tears streamed down his face.

'What do you mean?' Jen replied.

'What did you do with her?' he shouted.

'Murderers!' came another voice, further back.

'What?' Mira asked, in a small voice.

'Seriously,' Jen said, taking a step back. 'What the fuck is going on here?'

'As if you don't know!' Nigel shouted. He held his arm up and pointed behind them. Instinctively Jen turned around.

'Oh shit!' Sam said, beside her.

There, beside their house, suspended between two trees, was the eviscerated and disembowelled corpse of Joan.

Chapter Sixteen
Get Real, Get Right

By the time the van finally stopped moving Tom didn't much care if he lived or died anymore. There were great dollops of searing pain where his legs used to be. His vision blurred. His head pounded.

They stopped long enough for Tom to realise he might finally have reached his death, when the doors opened. The brightness of the outside world obscured his vision, and he pulled at the fresh blast of air with all the gusto his lungs could manage.

He tapped Leon's leg, but got no response. Perhaps his friend was already dead. Perhaps he was playing dead. Tom hoped it was the latter. He couldn't face this world without Leon.

Two figures climbed into the truck. Tom closed his eyes and waited. Hands grabbed onto him roughly, and he felt himself lifted up.

'Fucking hell, he stinks,' said a voice next to his ear. He went limp. If he was being led to his death, then so be it.

If this is the best the new world has to offer you can stick it right up your arse, thank you very much.

As someone carried him out of the truck, he heard a grunt from Leon. Someone handed Tom down to someone else. A new set of hands, or two sets of hands, he couldn't quite focus to see. He felt ground beneath him, and a cold wet cloth wiped over his face. The pain was easing, and once his eyes were clean he blinked the world back into focus. A woman was leaning over him. Her clothes were marked and dirty, her hair hastily put up. A bruise covered one cheek. She smiled at him.

'Hi,' he said, trying and failing to sit up.

'Hi,' she replied. 'You thought you were a goner, didn't you?'

'Um, yeah, pretty much. Am I not?'

'I think you should be safe for a little while.'

'Oh, well that's good.'

She turned her attention to Leon. Tom managed to prop himself up.

The moment the mystery woman touched Leon's leg, he woke with a start and a yelp, before sitting up and casting his eyes about.

'Welcome back,' Tom said. 'Glad to see you're not dead.'

Leon rubbed his head.

'Jury's still out on that one,' he said, his voice little more than a croak. 'What's going on?'

'I have no idea,' Tom said, looking back to the woman. 'Perhaps you could enlighten us?'

'Gladly,' she said. 'But not now, okay?' She glanced off behind them.

Tom and Leon nodded.

'I need to get your leg in a splint,' she said to Leon, who nodded. She left them alone.

'You reckon we could make a break for it?' Leon asked, before laughing at his own joke, which in turn became a racking cough.

The woman soon came back with a rudimentary splint cobbled together from a bit of wood and the contents of a first aid box, accompanied by one of Baxter's men.

'They gonna be alright?' he asked, in a tone of voice that suggested he didn't give two fucks one way or the other.

'They should be,' the woman replied. 'So long as we can find somewhere to rest up for a few days.'

'Fine,' the man grunted. He stormed off.

The woman gave them a smile, finished the splint, and was off again, leaving the two of them half sat up in the grass by the side of the road.

There were houses not too far away, and if Tom craned around the side of the van he could see the rest of the convoy. The faces looked as anxious as before. One of Baxter's men helped them back onto a minibus, offering nothing by way of apology or explanation. The woman who put Leon's leg into a splint had gone, but Tom couldn't see Oak or Baxter, either.

They drove until they came to another hamlet. The convoy pulled up, and everyone started to get out. Tom supported Leon on his shoulder, trying not to knock his own bruises as he did so.

The woman found them again, and led them into one of the houses. Everyone seemed to be setting up shop in the village. Baxter's men were busy clearing the streets of the dead, while everyone else was bustling around looking busy. Tom and Leon were on the receiving end of some half smiles and nods from their fellow hostages, and cold stares from Baxter's men. Tom saw no sign of Oak, but Wiry gave them a glare that left Tom under no illusion as to how well this change in circumstances had gone down with Baxter's men.

The house was a basic suburban semi, but the beds inside were corpse free and clean enough. Tom had to make his own way up, while the woman helped Leon. She helped him into the main bedroom and Tom followed, desperate to find out what was going on.

He fell into an armchair, his legs aching from the effort, while she helped his friend into the bed.

'So,' she said, sitting down on the end of the bed. 'You may have noticed a few changes.'

'Yeah,' they replied in unison.

'Well,' she said, looking around her to ensure they were alone. 'We seem to have reached a kind of truce. But I wouldn't get too comfortable, I doubt it'll last for long.'

'What happened?' Leon asked.

'After you two got, well...'

'Stomped?' Tom offered.

'Yes, well, we all saw what happened, with that poor girl, with you. It was too much. When they carried you away, we thought you were dead. We confronted Baxter.'

'Jesus,' Tom said.

'We asked him exactly what he was planning for us. Without his goons around him he was a bit off guard. He wasn't going to take us all on.

'He started going on about starting a new utopia, new society, making Britain strong again. Stupid little prick, he thought he could take us somewhere, we'd all become his slaves and he'd have his own little kingdom.'

'That sounds like him,' Leon said.

'Anyway, we talked things through with him. He's an intimidating man, but he's not that smart. It didn't take us long to make him see how idiotic he was being. We told him we could make a fresh start, how we needed strong leadership, but using this as the basis for anything was never going to work.'

'How did he take that?' Tom asked.

'He didn't like it, but we flattered him enough to keep him on side. Told him we'd support him as leader, we'd follow him in his quest as long as nobody else got hurt, and so long as he kept his men in check.'

'You made him leader?' Tom said, incredulous.

'Keep your voice down,' she hissed. 'Of course we did. If we hadn't, you two would be dead by now.'

She fixed him with a furious glare and he bowed his head in agreement.

'Sorry,' he said. 'It's just...'

'I know, and I'm with you, okay? We all are. Baxter is the enemy, but he's stronger than us. We have to bide our time. In the meantime he'll be reticent to step out of line in case we turn on him. If that happens we'll overpower him, or more likely all end up dead, neither of which he wants to see.'

'You sure he won't just kill us and start again?' Leon asked, wincing as he pulled himself up a bit on the bed.

'If he kills us, he's the tin pot king of fuck all,' Tom said. 'Well done. You did a lot better than we did.'

'If you hadn't acted, I'm not sure any of us would have had the courage,' she replied.

'I didn't catch your name, by the way,' Tom said.

'Susan,' she replied. 'You're Tom and Leon, right?'

They nodded.

'So we've formed the insurgency, I guess?' Tom said.

'Looks that way,' Susan replied.

They sat in silence for a moment, Tom thinking how absurd it was that he'd gone from stoner slacker to insurgent warrior in only a few days. All he'd done to achieve this new status was get beaten up.

'What happened to the girl?' Tom asked.

'That was the other condition. I treated her face, where that meathead had punched her, and she told me what happened. When we spoke to Baxter we made him let her go. I explained to him she was liable to kill one of his men in his sleep if she stayed, and her presence would be a reminder to us all that he couldn't keep his men in check. He let her go. We watched her leave, to be sure.'

They sat in silence for a few moments more.

'So we keep quiet and let him be in charge?' Leon asked, uncomfortable with the concept.

'For now,' Susan replied.

'Then what?' Leon asked.

'Then we kill him,' Tom replied. 'Him, and all his men.'

The next few days passed with a mix of horror and boredom. Tom and Leon sat in their rooms, the aches and pains of their collective beatings lessening with time. Tom found himself with little else to do except read, eat, and watch the comings and goings of the people outside.

The tension was clear to see, even from the first floor window of his cottage. Baxter's men wanted to throw their weight around, wanted to regain control, but they were sticking to the terms of the truce. Their former hostages, on the other hand, all looked like they'd like to turn heels and run in the opposite direction. Tom guessed that the moment anyone took that option Baxter's men would use it an excuse to reassert their dominance.

He and Leon had a steady stream of visitors, but none from Baxter's men. Susan was their most frequent visitor, coming to tend to her patients. After the first few days, Tom noticed her bedside manner seemed more pronounced when she tended to Leon than to him. Tom was glad. This was the longest Leon had been without a girl in his life, so it was nice to see his friend's mojo had survived the apocalypse.

The rest of the survivors all came to see him, in drips and drabs. They seemed to mistake his futile gesture as some kind of bold move which made him somehow worthy of their adulation. His insistence to the contrary only seemed to strengthen their resolve.

Maybe they needed someone to rally around, someone to look up to, but he was sure as shit that person wasn't him, or Leon for that matter. So he smiled and nodded when people told him how much they admired him for 'taking a stand'. They would leave, and he'd go back to burying himself in a book or staring out the window.

He missed music. He hadn't heard a song in days, and he ached to fill this idle time with sound. He would kill for some pretentious post-rock, or math-metal, or some breakneck jazz. Christ, he'd settle for boy bands and Disney songs right now.

He looked at the books on the bookcase. Who would write stories now? Would anyone ever record an album again? Ten thousand years of civilisation behind them; was this the end of it? There might never be another play, or movie, or medical miracle. No more Children in Need or FA Cup finals or regenerations of *Doctor Who*. Every band he had ever dreamed of seeing live, every comic book that went unresolved, the perpetual basket of ironing which sat in his parents' house. What the hell was left for the survivors? Scrambling around over the scraps until they all died?

At the end of the third day the supplies in the village ran short. People rushed around talking to each other, and Tom listened as they came and asked him what they should do, as if he had some miraculous access to information they didn't.

The food shortage had come about because nobody had bothered with the fresh produce while it was still edible, ploughing their way instead through the longer-shelf-life food, but as soon as that ran out they had realised the fresh goods had rotted. Things started getting tetchy, until Baxter's men went and procured some food from a nearby village. Nobody seemed overly concerned how they had managed it.

The more Tom saw, the less he wanted to be there. He wanted to grab Leon and sneak out one night, as soon as they were up to it. Tom felt better now, but Leon still struggled to walk. Tom's face was still bruised and tender, as were most of his ribs.

Evening was falling on the fourth day when Leon hobbled into his room. 'Fancy a J?' he asked, brandishing a giant conical spliff.

'Fucking hell dude, how have you still got any weed?'

'This is the last of it, so we may as well enjoy it. It's medicinal, after all.'

'True.'

'So how are you feeling?' Leon asked.

'Like I want to get out of here,' Tom replied.

'Me too.'

They sat and smoked.

'We can't though, can we?' Leon asked.

Tom shook his head.

They smoked in silence, and when the spliff went out Leon went back to his room. Tom lay down on his bed in the dull candlelight and let the room spin around him.

The next morning, Tom and Leon were trying to cobble together some semblance of breakfast from the disparate contents of their kitchen, when Susan stomped into the house, slamming down a bag of supplies on the table and muttering under her breath.

'What's up, Suze?' Leon asked, as Tom started to pick through the carrier bag.

'His Lordship has decided to start throwing his weight around again. He heard that Pat and Phil sneaked away. He's sent two men after them. Thank God he doesn't seem to realise they left two nights ago and went in the completely opposite direction to his men, so they should be fine. But now he's saying it means he should never have loosened his grip on us.'

'What's he doing?' Tom asked.

'He's instructed everyone to meet outside this afternoon, says it's not optional. He told me to pass it on to both of you. He said he doesn't care if you're at death's door, attendance is mandatory. Well, he didn't use those exact words. I'm not convinced he'd know the word mandatory.'

'Any idea what he's planning?'

'Who knows?' she replied, throwing her hands up in exasperation. 'He wants to reassert his dominance. Could be he means to take you both out. I say we either turn up and cross our fingers, or we try to get away. Now.'

Tom went to the window and looked out. People were bustling about sharing anxious glances with each other, and Baxter's men had gone back into full on prowl mode.

'That's not going to work,' Tom said. 'Whatever he's got planned, we need to prepare ourselves. We can hear him out, but we need to be ready to act if he tries to pull any shit with us.'

'Act how?' Leon asked.

Tom turned to Susan. 'Can you get word around to everyone?'

'I think so.'

'Okay, good. Tell people to be ready. If it goes wrong, you take down the closest bastard to you.'

'How?' Susan asked.

'However you can. Kick them in the shins; punch them on the nose; or, fuck, stab them with a kitchen knife if you have to.'

'This is ridiculous,' Leon said. 'They'll kill us all.'

'Killed now, or killed later, I'm not sure I see the difference,' Susan said.

Leon shook his head.

'What about a signal?' Susan asked.

'Well I imagine if it goes down, it'll go down fast, but I dunno. Let's say "crossroads". If they hear me say that, they act first.'

'"Crossroads"?'

'I dunno, first thing that came into my head.'

'It's a bit Bon Jovi, but, fine,' she said.

'Pass it around, but, needless to say, it can't get back to Baxter and his men. Tell people if they can bring a weapon then do it.'

Susan nodded, gave them both a hug and left. The door closed and Leon and Tom exchanged a look. Tom's heart pounded, and he had a sudden and inescapable feeling of buyer's remorse.

'You sure this is a good idea?' Leon asked.

'Not even remotely.'

The crowd started to filter into the village square, such as it was. Tom wondered how far the word had gotten round. If Susan hadn't spread it far he was walking towards an epic suicide bid. He fingered the hilt of the small kitchen knife wedged into his waistband.

After days cooped up in the house, Tom was glad of the fresh air on his face, although his heart hammered too fast to appreciate it.

Tom and Leon split up, positioning themselves as strategically as they could. Tom stood near the centre of the small square, Leon near one of the exits, next to one of Baxter's men. Tom looked around for Oak, and saw him standing guard against one of the exit points from the square. He saw Tom watching and gave him a wry smile. Tom's stomach flipped.

The other hostages were wearing the same startled expressions they had worn before the service station. A murmur made its way through the crowd.

Baxter appeared from one of the houses, and strode past Leon, his perma-tan fading in this post-tanning-bed world. He headed straight for the centre of the park, and Tom thought for one horrible second that he was striding right up to kill him. He fought the urge to turn and sprint in the opposite direction.

'So good to see you back on your feet, mate,' he said as he passed Tom, a self-satisfied smirk playing across his face. Baxter reached the small centre of the square and climbed up onto the modest war memorial that stood there.

'Evening, ladies and gentlemen,' he said, his voice cutting through the murmured chatter. 'You may be wondering why I've asked you all to come and listen to me.' He turned and stared straight at Tom. 'It's just, I think we're at a bit of a... crossroad.'

Hands grabbed Tom roughly about the shoulders, stopping him from finally indulging his instinct to bolt. Hands forced him to his knees. There was no response from the crowd other than stunned shock, which wasn't of great use to Tom at that moment.

He could try to get the knife from his waistband, but that would just hasten the arrival of his imminent demise. He thought about shouting 'Crossroads!' at the top of his lungs, but what the hell would be the point? The moment had gone, and soon he would be too.

A boot smashed into his side, sending him sprawling to the ground. His head thumped against the cold tarmac. More blows rained on his body. All Tom could do was curl up into a ball as a flurry of kicks and stamps rained down.

Through the soft thuds of shoe on rib he could hear commotion and noise around him. The feet stopped for a moment, and Tom seized the opportunity to pull himself forward. His ribcage protested at the movement, but he carried on. He chanced a look up. Arguments and scuffles surrounded him.

There was damp somewhere around his waist. He remembered the knife in his waistband and reasoned it must be cutting into him. He reached down and pulled it into his hand.

He inched himself up into a sitting position. Nobody stopped him, although people were pressing against him. Through the crowd he made out Baxter, still stood on his little plinth, surveying the scene before him with the same wry smile plastered across his face.

Tom stood, his ribs trying their best to stop him on the way up. He gripped the knife handle, holding the blade up his arm to hide it. He focused on Baxter and began to walk forward. He moved quickly enough that Baxter barely had time to tear his gaze from the crowd before it was too late.

The knife was already hilt deep in Baxter's torso by the time Tom even felt any resistance. He locked eyes with him, watched his wry smile replaced by a look of total panic.

Tom thought back to the girl in the service station, to the kicking he'd received at the hands of this man, and to the ride in the lorry. He gripped the handle with both hands and pulled upwards with all his strength, spilling blood and innards all over both of them.

Warm blood gushed over him, soaking his jeans, and by the time the knife hit Baxter's ribcage and came to a halt, the panic had gone from his eyes. The body slid off the blade and fell to the floor.

Everyone stood silent, all eyes on him. He dropped the knife, which clattered on the ground. He looked down at his feet, covered in intestinal waste, then up at the shocked crowd.

It was as though someone had hit the pause button on a particularly unbalanced action scene. Fists were raised and held in mid-air, necks were held by the scruff, but all faces pointed towards him.

'What do we do now?' he called out, to nobody in particular.

The crowd looked around at each other but stood silent, until finally Oak dropped Leon to the floor, and started to stride toward Tom.

He only made it a few paces before Susan appeared from out of nowhere, pipe in hand, and swung it at the back of Oak's head with such ferocity that his face hit the floor with a sickening crunch before the rest of his oversized body did.

'Holy shit!' Susan said. Her nurse's instinct kicked in and she fell to her knees to try and save the man she had killed.

Tom looked around at the rest of Baxter's men, who as one dropped their weapons and raised their hands in surrender.

Tom laughed.

'Job done then,' he said, before fainting.

Chapter Seventeen
To Carry the Flame

Burnett forced the seat back as far as it would go, slipped off his boots and put his feet up on the dashboard. It had taken him two days to return to Cottingthorpe, one of which had been by foot, until, stumbling and beaten, he'd come across a farmhouse and a car that worked. One night there and he'd made his way back here, like it was a beacon. His leg still ached like a bastard, but he'd at least patched it up and cleaned the wound. He'd acquired a week's worth of junk food and energy drinks, and set himself up here, down the street from the sanctuary.

The stench of his own feet was unbearable, so he rolled down the window.

He had returned, but hadn't been able to face going in. He had pulled up outside when he arrived and seen the comings and goings. They'd evidently gotten along fine without him.

He waited. At some point or another, his killer would come back this way, and when he did, Burnett would be ready.

It was nothing to do with him being a coward.

No sir.

A one-man stakeout was unsustainable, but here he was attempting it anyway. Now he was here, he knew full well that the minute he went to go and have a shower, or tried to sleep, he would miss something. If he missed something, he would miss everything. So he sat, and he watched.

And watched.

He'd been awake for four straight days since his return, and the effects of severe sleep deprivation were taking their toll. He couldn't shake the idea that the killer was playing with him somehow, that he was out there, maybe even watching him, waiting for him to give up his vigil so he could strike again.

Or was that his sleep deprived paranoia? Maybe there was nothing to see here after all.

Move along folks, the show's over.

Maybe he'd spotted Burnett's vigil and decided better of it? No, that didn't fit. Here was a man utterly unafraid of the world, who'd killed dozens and walked free from a police station amidst an apocalypse only he seemed to have had forewarning of. It seemed unlikely he'd be put off by a dishevelled man sitting in a car.

His eyes stung. He was down to his last bottle of water now, so he poured a tiny amount into his hands and rubbed it on his face. He took a swig, cricked his neck and put the seat back up. Soon he'd be washing in Red Bull.

Tana and the priest seemed to be making a decent fist of their enterprise. The last few days had seen a fair bit of movement, especially. Tana and the priest had taken it in turns to go out and gather survivors, and they had been arriving in fits and starts each day, some looking close to the point of total exhaustion. Tana and the priest took each one in.

Burnett was glad for them, and pleased Tana had turned his back on the world of police work. He wasn't exactly detective material, given he hadn't even noticed their new haven had been under surveillance for four straight days. Or maybe he had seen Burnett out there and decided to ignore him. Burnett could hardly blame him.

What the fuck am I even doing out here?

He wasn't looking for a killer, he was sat becoming increasingly ripe for no good reason. He wasn't doing anything more valuable than sitting in the discarded packaging of processed snack foods, which now contributed to the fog of toxic stench Burnett had brewing.

'Oh, fuck this,' he said to the empty car, and opened the door.

His knees popped loudly as he stretched his legs out. He looked over at the hotel that served as a rudimentary refuge. The call of a comfortable bed was too strong. Should his psychotic murderer turn up in his room, Burnett might just let the man be done with him, so long as he didn't have to get out of his bed to die.

He entered the reception of the hotel, the gloom in sharp contrast to the sunshine outside. Candles were lit along one wall, their flickering light showing the priest sat behind the reception desk.

'Ah, Detective,' he said.

Burnett squinted through his sleep-deprived eyes. The priest wore his own dog-collared uniform. 'Your Holiness,' he answered.

'It's Father, actually,' he replied. If Burnett's slight had any impact on him he was gracious enough to ignore it.

'Sorry.'

'So, you've decided to give up your vigil, have you?'

'You saw me then?'

'I did. Very noble of you.'

'Hmm. Well it looks to be safe out there for now, and I could do with a wash,'

'I can imagine. Well there are some rooms free on the third and fourth floor. There's no hot water, but I can have someone bring you up some from the kitchen if you like?'

'Thanks,' Burnett replied. 'Give me a room on the fourth floor, facing the front, will you?'

'Of course,' the priest replied, and fished out a key.

'Thanks,' Burnett said, and started up the stairs.

In the past, Burnett would have called his room desperate, but his need transformed its wire frame bed and lumpy mattress into the height of opulence. He hadn't planned to sleep, but sleep came nonetheless.

He awoke to darkness and a rising panic. He sat up on the bed and saw a crack of gloom issuing through the curtains. He became aware of his own stench. It had reached a point where it was even making himself gag, so he could only imagine how bad it must be. He went to the bathroom but could only get cold from the tap. Remembering the priest's words he put his shoes on and left the room.

All was silent until he neared the ground floor, when he started to hear snatches of voices, allaying the fears that had festered in the silence. He opened the stairwell and walked straight into Tana, who gave a decidedly un-rugby-player whelp of surprise.

'Christ, Detective,' he big man said. 'You proper put the shits up me. Reverend mentioned you'd left the car. Feeling better?'

'Um, yeah, much,' Burnett mumbled.

'Not surprising, nap you've had.'

'How long was I up there?'

'Over a day,' Tana said. 'Don't you worry, I've been keeping an eye out. No sign of our man. You did miss all the excitement though.'

'What excitement?'

'Busload came in yesterday afternoon. Pretty shook up, too. I tried to question some of them, but they didn't want to talk about it. I figured they'd be best off talking to you.'

'Right,' Burnett said.

'Maybe after you've had a chance to clean up a bit though, eh?'

'That bad?'

'I'm surprised I didn't smell you coming. But, good news, we've got a working water heater now. It's not powerful enough to reach the rooms yet, but we've got hot water in the kitchens, and the showers in the changing rooms are working.'

'How did you manage that?' Burnett asked.

'Another new arrival this morning; a couple, actually. Turns out he's a plumber. Came in his van and everything. He hooked it up no bother. He said pretty much everything got knocked out in the storm, but he reckons anything not dependent on electricity or computers can be coaxed back to life, as long as there's gas in the pipes.'

'Good work,' Burnett said, impressed. 'How's it going other than that?'

'Not too bad. We're starting to get a few people who know what they're doing. We're low on food already though, and there's so many rumours and theories flying about you don't know who to believe.'

'Any problems?' Burnett asked. 'Fights, anything?'

'A few scuffles,' Tana replied. 'Nothing I couldn't handle. At the moment we've just about got enough to go around. For the most part people are happy to find a safe place. I get the impression it's pretty bad out there.'

'Well,' Burnett replied, 'it might be okay now, but wait until you run out of food or water, or rooms even. Once things get scarce, you might find the spirit of camaraderie only goes so far.'

Tana flashed him a dirty look. 'It beats not trying at all.'

He walked away. Burnett immediately regretted his words.

'Tana,' he called after him, 'I didn't mean...' but Tana was gone.

'For fuck's sake,' Burnett said to the empty corridor.

He trudged off in search of the shower block. There seemed to be a queue, but one look at the dishevelled detective and the crowd parted, until he found himself at the front. Burnett wondered if it was pity or self-interest, and settled on a mix of both. He wasn't about to complain, however, and soon he'd left his filthy clothes in a crumpled pile, picked up a towel and stepped into a cubicle. The shower was tepid and barely functioning, but at least the water was clean.

It took three tiny soaps before he started to feel halfway clean, and he lathered away until the stench abated. There was no shampoo for his matted hair or his bearded face, so he rubbed them with mini soaps, too, until finally he stood there, scrubbed red raw but clean.

He left the cubicle like a man taking his first steps. His dirty clothes had disappeared, replaced by a neat pile of clean underwear, jeans, a T-shirt, and a jumper.

The Reverend waited for him outside. 'Detective Burnett, I hardly recognise you!' he said, clasping Burnett round the shoulder.

'Your doing, I presume?' Burnett replied, holding up the jumper.

'I could call it divine provenance, but that might be over-egging it a bit. Don't think I've forgotten that you saved my life, Detective. Anyway, we've started pooling a collective clothing store for newcomers. So many of them are in a bad state when they get here.'

'It's much appreciated,' Burnett said.

'You're welcome, Detective, but in return I'd like a favour.'

'Oh?' Burnett said, trying to dislodge the water from his ears as he walked.

'Yes, it's nothing big. It's just, Tony told me about your, well, conversation.'

'Tony?' Burnett asked, confused.

'PC Tana,' the priest replied.

'That Tony. Right.'

'I wanted to say that I understand your concerns, I do. I share them too. But what we have here is quite fragile as it is, so...'

'So you'd rather I didn't walk the corridors spreading ill cheer and pessimism?'

'Exactly.'

'Don't worry, Father, I'll be the model of cooperative engagement.'

'Excellent. Now I understand you'll be wanting to talk to our new arrivals?'

'If that's okay?' Burnett asked.

'Of course. I'd like to know what happened to them myself, but it seems few of them are comforted by the sight of the clergy, so I think it'd be best in your hands.'

Burnett almost said something about perhaps not dressing in full priest get up, but looked into the priest's eyes and saw the tiredness in them.

'Maybe the police, or what passes for it now, will have better luck,' he said, offering a smile.

'I hope so,' the priest replied.

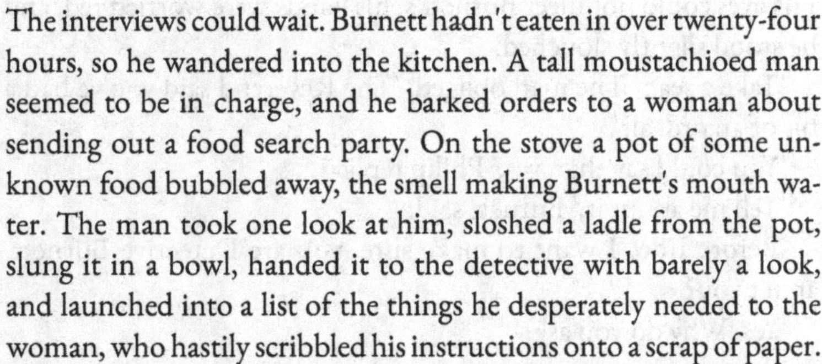

The interviews could wait. Burnett hadn't eaten in over twenty-four hours, so he wandered into the kitchen. A tall moustachioed man seemed to be in charge, and he barked orders to a woman about sending out a food search party. On the stove a pot of some unknown food bubbled away, the smell making Burnett's mouth water. The man took one look at him, sloshed a ladle from the pot, slung it in a bowl, handed it to the detective with barely a look, and launched into a list of the things he desperately needed to the woman, who hastily scribbled his instructions onto a scrap of paper.

He made his way into the restaurant, which was half-full of people sitting in little clusters, talking to each other in whispers, or sitting in silence. Burnett found a table to himself and sat. The food was an odd mix of different vegetables, tinned goods and potatoes, but it was hearty and tasty, and Burnett felt it warm him through with every spoonful. He finished it and pushed the bowl away. He leaned back in the chair and put his feet up on the one opposite. He felt the anger starting to subside, and wondered again whether the priest and Tana didn't have the right end of things, after all.

He was one man, an ex-copper for a force that no longer existed, chasing another man who may or may not even still be alive. Looking for what? Justice? What gave him the right? Wouldn't he be better off looking to make a positive impact in this fucked up situation?

He closed his eyes and thought. Somewhere along the train of thought he started drifting off to sleep, until he became aware of someone standing over him. The killer's face floated before his closed eyes for a second.

He sat bolt upright. It wasn't the killer, but rather a rotund bearded man, looking as startled by Burnett's sudden movement as he was.

'Detective?' he asked.

'Excuse me,' Burnett replied, embarrassed. 'Yes?'

'Hi, I'm Philip. I came in on the bus yesterday.'

Burnett looked him over. Experience told him this was a victim. His eyes could not meet Burnett's, his hands were worried red, and he stood slightly slouched.

'Take a seat.' The man obliged. 'The Reverend said you've had a bit of an ordeal?'

'You could say that, yes,' Philip replied.

'Tell me about it,' Burnett said.

'Before I do, I want to make sure, you are Detective Burnett, aren't you?'

'Yes. Why do you ask?'

'Because I have a message for you.'

Philip stood, and pulled a small pistol from his pocket. He raised it at Burnett, who only had a split second to react. The bang was so loud that Burnett was sure he must be dead, and he fell backwards from his chair, knocking the table sideways as he went. His ears seemed to implode and everything following the bang was a whistle.

He didn't hear the scream of the man who shot him, but as he hit the ground he saw the man's face twisted in hatred and pain. He raised the gun again and pointed it at Burnett's head.

Burnett kicked up, instinctively, knocking the gun upward. He didn't hear it go off, but saw the flare of the barrel as the man's second shot went up into the ceiling. The gun flew out of his attacker's hand, but it didn't deter him for a second. Philip fell on Burnett, his hands clasping around Burnett's neck.

Something knocked the big man sideways. Tana wrestled his attacker to the ground. Burnett scurried away like a wounded animal, watching as his partner knocked Philip unconscious with his elbow. Burnett clasped at his neck struggling for air. What the fuck could lead a man he'd never met before to try to kill him?

Chapter Eighteen
Aimless Arrow

A few weeks ago Jen might have looked at this well-tailored basement with a degree of envy, bedecked as it was with rock and roll memorabilia, an old fashioned jukebox and two sofas. Now it was nothing more than an elaborately furnished prison, the only light coming through a tiny window which showed nothing more than a dull echo of the room it once was.

Despite their many protestations to the contrary, the three of them were herded into this place for their supposed part in the defenestration of an old lady. Sam nearly managed to break free of the assembled mob of pensioners, but not quite, and so they had been hastily bundled into this cellar, from which they had listened to the barricades being erected. Since then there had been silence.

That was three days ago. They had discovered a well-stocked bar, but save for a few packets of salted peanuts and a fridge with a few bottles of pop, they had nothing tangible to survive on. The booze had kept them well entertained for the first night, but they had paid for it the next day.

At least once a day, Sam would try to escape, but the door remained locked. The window was both too high to reach and too small for even Mira to squeeze through.

Panic had set in at first, then given way to weary resignation and frustration.

'Fuck's sake, I'm hungry,' Mira moaned from the other sofa.

'I know,' Jen said.

'You think they've forgotten about us down here?' Sam asked.

'Sam, they think we're psychotic murderers capable of butchering a little old lady,' Mira replied. 'They're not going to be in much of a hurry to come down here and give us food.'

'There's always the chance that whoever killed Joan killed the rest of them and now we're stuck down here until we die of starvation,' Jen said.

'Great,' Sam said.

These three days had been awful. There was no toilet, so they had set up a bucket in one corner and covered it with a rudimentary lid so as not to stink out their prison, but to no avail. The stench of their own filth, sweat, and fear was now so strong it burnt Jen's nostrils.

Jen stared at the door again, willing it to open. She still had no clue what had happened out there, but became ever more accustomed to the idea she was going to die in this basement. Knowing it didn't make the prospect any less terrifying.

Upstairs, a floorboard creaked.

Jen sat bolt upright. They'd not heard a sound in days.

Another creak. A muffled voice.

They screamed at the top of their lungs.

'Help! Down here!'

Jen screamed until her throat hurt. They stopped as one and stared at the door. Jen thought she could hear muffled voices from the other side, but over the hammering of her heart, it was hard to tell.

There was a scraping sound, wood dragged across floorboards, and the sound of a key turning in a lock.

They had no way to defend themselves against whatever might come through the door, but Jen was so desperate to get out of the basement that she was willing to accept the devil himself as her liberator.

The door opened, and a face edged through the doorway. He was dark skinned, in his forties, Jen thought. His hair was thin, and the area under his eyes was several notches darker than the rest of his face. He wore the hangdog wearied look of a broken man, and his didn't strike her as a face she ought to fear.

The smell hit his nostrils and his face wrinkled. He saw the three of them and his face fell.

'Jesus,' he said. 'What happened to you lot?'

They made no answer, but trudged up the steps, not taking their eyes off the man, who in turn stepped back from them with a look of uncertainty. At the top of the stairs they stepped into the corridor, where a woman stood, looking even more anxious than her partner. Jen guessed she was the one arguing not to open the cellar door. She couldn't blame her, although she was glad the bitch had lost the argument.

'You guys must be starving,' the man said, trying to feign a cheerful hospitality.

'Water,' Jen said. The man scurried off and came back with tall glasses of tap water. Jen gulped hers down, her companions doing the same.

'Thanks,' she said to the man.

'What were you doing down there?' the woman asked.

'Do you mean what did we do to get barricaded in a cellar?' Jen replied, unable to hide the annoyance at the woman's tone from her voice. 'Absolutely nothing. Where is everyone else?'

'There's nobody else here,' the man replied. 'The village is deserted.'

'What about the body?' Mira asked.

'What body?' the woman asked.

'There was a body outside,' Sam said. 'It was... not in a good way.'

'We didn't see any bodies,' the man said. 'In fact, we were remarking on how this seemed to be the cleanest place we've seen so far.'

Jen nodded. 'There were people here before. Good people. We came here a few days back and they welcomed us with open arms. Something terrible happened to one of them, and with us being the newcomers, they assumed it was us. That's why they locked us down here.'

'They must have taken Joan down and buried her, then left,' Mira said.

Jen nodded.

'I need something to eat,' Sam said, and went into the kitchen.

Jen looked them over. They looked like a couple, like the kind of people who seem to morph into one entity when they start seeing each other, with their matching generic clothes.

'So what about you two?' she asked.

'What about us?' the woman replied, curtly.

'I'm Nadim, this is Tanuja,' the man said, uncomfortable with the tension in the air.

Either that or he's used to having to cover up for his wife's bullshit.

'Hi,' she said. 'I'm Jen, this is Mira, and that's Sam in there.' She offered her hand out. Nadim took it enthusiastically, Tanuja gave as derisory a handshake as possible. She looked over Mira with a questioning look, but said nothing.

'We've had a tough few days of it too,' Nadim said. 'Maybe not as bad as you three. We were on a coach a few days ago, but it came under siege from looters. It was, well, it wasn't nice. We decided to go it alone after that.'

'You two married?' Jen asked.

Nadim nodded. Tanuja ratcheted her glare up a notch.

Are you jealous because this stuck-up cow got to keep her man when the storm left yours dead against a radiator?

'Well I think we'd better be on our way,' Tanuja said.

Nadim nodded.

'Thanks for letting us out,' Mira said.

The woman gave her a half smile and headed for the front door. She was halfway into the street when the arrow struck through her left eye, sending her flying backwards through the open doorway and back into the house.

Mira and Jen froze, but Nadim reacted with a wail and rushed towards his wife before her lifeless body had even hit the ground. Jen saw the back of the arrow protruding from Tanuja's skull and knew there was no hope.

Nadim reached his wife. He barely had time to lift her torso to cradle her head when the second arrow came through the open doorway and pierced his neck, cutting off his wracking sobs.

Mira screamed.

Jen burst forward. She slammed the door shut, as a third arrow hit it, wedging itself in the splintered woodwork.

'Get down,' she screamed to Sam, who was entering from the kitchen carrying a big bag of Kettle Chips.

He fell to the ground as the window beside him exploded in a shower of glass. A fourth arrow lodged in the far wall. Mira stopped screaming and hugged the wall. Jen joined her.

'What the fuck is going on?' Sam shouted, scrabbling to get up and away from the window. Glass fell from his hair and clothes as he moved.

Silence fell. They stayed as still as they could, listening for any sign of a further attack. Sam edged his face to the window and peered out.

'Someone's moving out there,' he whispered.

'Do you think it's the same person who killed Joan?' Mira said.

'Could be someone who followed those two,' Sam said, motioning to the two fresh corpses.

Jen watched the door. If someone was going to come in it would be through there. She wondered if she might get to the arrow lodged in it, but it was too risky.

'Sam,' she hissed, and the boy's eyes stopped searching for an escape long enough to meet hers. 'Any knives in the kitchen?'

He shook his head. 'All gone.'

'Fuck,' Jen muttered. She ducked down and went over to Nadim's corpse. The arrow was embedded deep into his neck. She grabbed the feathered end and started to pull. The arrowhead pulled past bones and sinew and Jen fought back her gag reflex as the arrow worked its way free into her hands, the shaft and head smeared with blood.

She crawled over to the front door and stood beside it, grasping the arrow. She might not have a bow, but if the door opened she was going to jam the arrow into the person who came through it with as much force as she could muster.

There was a soft muffle of footsteps outside, and her grip intensified. The noise stopped, and the arrow wedged in the door was yanked back out.

'I'm getting all my arrows back you know,' came a voice on the other side of the door. It was nasal, and full of a sing-song joy.

She didn't respond, and after a moment she heard footsteps retreating from the house. She hardly dared trust it, but this was as good an opportunity as any to run. Mira and Sam hugged the wall like terrified statues.

'Go!' she hissed.

They darted to the back of the house. Jen found the back door unlocked and they ran into the rear garden. The gate at the far end looked unlocked, and they sprinted to it. Beyond the gate was nothing but serene English fields and hills.

They ran. The tree line seemed an eternity away. With every footfall Jen expected the silent thud of an arrow hitting her back. They ran past the point of exhaustion, past the tree line and into the woods, never once looking back. They ran until Jen thought her chest would burst.

Finally Sam stopped, holding up an arm to signal he could go no further. Mira collapsed to the ground, wheezing. Jen leaned against an uprooted tree trunk, her breath returning in hungry, rasping gulps. Each of them said nothing, trying to regain their breaths. Sam stood bent double, his hands on his knees.

'Do you think he followed us?' Mira said.

'No,' Jen replied.

'Why not?'

'Because we're still alive.'

'She's right,' Sam said. 'We were out in the open too long, and he's a good shot. If he'd been following us he could have taken us down in a second.'

'So he let us go?' Mira asked.

'Let's hope so,' Jen replied. 'Come on, let's get moving.'

'Can't we stay here?' Mira asked, moaning. 'I'm exhausted.'

'We have no supplies, no food, no clothes. We need to find somewhere to shelter.'

Mira nodded, and they moved forward. They'd been walking a few minutes when a loud crack rang out somewhere to their right. Sam caught Jen's eye, and motioned that they should move in the opposite direction. She nodded.

They walked on, careful not to make any sounds. Jen's heart had started to beat normally when another crack rang out in the trees ahead of them, followed by a high whistling sound.

'What the fuck?' she said under her breath.

Sam wheeled around, looking in every direction. 'I don't think he let us go,' he said.

'What do you mean?' Jen asked.

'We're being hunted. He's moving us in the direction he wants us.'

He let that sink in a second.

'Think about it. He's a skilled marksman. He hit his first two targets perfectly. I think he's a hunter. He's driving us into a killing zone.'

'What do you suggest?'

'Well he's going to know roughly where we are, but not exactly. If he could see us, he'd take us out. We need to change direction, find a road, get a car and get far away from here. Whatever we do, we don't fall into his trap.'

Jen was impressed. 'Who are you and what have you done with Sam?'

'You spend as much time playing *Assassins Creed* online against homicidal pre-teens as I have, you learn a thing or two.' He smiled. 'And to think, my mum always told me I was wasting my time.'

Another crack resounded, closer this time.

Sam looked around. 'This way.'

They moved as quickly and silently as they could, no longer attempting to run. The woods they were heading into were deep and getting darker, although that could be the gathering clouds Jen glimpsed through the canopy above. Every now and again Sam would bring them to a halt, look around, and head off in a completely different direction to before. Jen was completely disorientated. She hoped her guide knew what he was doing.

The first drops of rain were starting to filter through the leaves above them when Sam signalled to stop.

'We can wait here for a minute,' he said. 'I want to get a sense of whether he's still following us.'

Jen nodded. Mira sunk to the ground and looked sullen.

'So, survival man,' Jen said, 'you have any idea what we can and can't eat around here?'

'Not unless there's a Greggs hidden around this last corner,' he replied.

'We should try and get out of these woods. Which way do we head?'

'I don't know,' Sam said. 'I'm pretty sure that whoever is tracking us is probably in that direction.' He motioned with his arm towards a tall birch tree. 'I think he was forcing us down towards the valley beyond it. I don't know if he's worked out that we're not doing what he wants. I hope not.'

'Can we stay here?' Mira asked. Her complexion looked to be turning a worrying grey.

'No,' Sam said, going over and giving her a hug. 'Don't worry,' he said. 'I'll get you out of this.'

Jen couldn't help but crack a smile. Boys and their need to play the hero.

'We need to find food though, and water.'

Sam nodded. 'Let's head in this direction. We're not going back on ourselves that way. Who knows, maybe we'll find a farm or something.'

They set off. The way was darker now, and Jen stumbled more often on upturned roots. The rain intensified, but their cover kept them dry.

Just as Jen started to forget about their hunter, another loud crack rang out in the woods. They stopped, looking around, but there was no sign of any movement they could make out in the ever darkening gloom.

They moved again, with more urgency now. Jen wasn't sure if it was the adrenaline, but she felt eyes on her. She pictured their attacker, straight out of a redneck horror movie, waiting for them to stop and rest up so he could make his move.

She wanted to scream, but kept moving forward. There seemed no end to these woods, they were climbing higher and higher, the rain pounding harder above them. They were pretty well soaked now, and she made sure to keep Mira in front of her, lest the weakened girl should fall behind. The incline steepened again, their footing starting to get less and less sure in the muddy ground underfoot.

'I can't,' Mira cried out, and fell to her knees.

Sam came back and put his arm around her, helping her to stand. Jen stopped, her breath shorter than she'd realised. The trees above were thinning, the sky above entirely black.

'This isn't going to let up,' she called out. 'We need to stop.'

'Where?' Sam asked, incredulous.

Jen thought about the camping gear they had so gaily abandoned.

'Great fucking direction you chose,' Mira spat in Sam's direction.

'Better wet than dead,' Jen said.

Sam looked crestfallen at Mira's slight.

'This is fucking hopeless,' Sam said. 'There's no shelter, nothing to keep us dry, or warm, no food. We can't stop here.'

'Well I can't fucking go on!' Mira shouted. She slipped to the ground, squelching into the mud.

'We stop for half an hour, catch our breath, okay?' Jen said.

Sam nodded.

Jen knew Mira wouldn't want to sit in the middle of a deluge for long, and so it proved. After ten minutes she rose, mumbled an apology to Sam, and they were on their way again. Jen wished they hadn't stopped. After even a brief rest, her muscles were tight, screaming in protest at every movement.

The rain got worse. Within ten minutes it was like they were walking through sheer panes of water. There was lightning in the skies now, and deep rumbles which seemed to spring up from the ground rather than emanate from the sky. Her two companions eyed the heavens with utter terror. She didn't remember the first storm, but they had been there and watching the end of the world, or so she assumed. They'd spent so much time trying to survive that she'd never thought to ask them about the night of the first storm.

Is this it? Is this the world's end coming to finish the job it only half achieved last time out? Is this where I die, scrabbling up some pissing hill in the middle of fuck knows where?

Jen reached the top of the slope. There was an open field on the other side, and suddenly they could see the storm in all its ferocious glory. Light danced through the dark clouds, illuminating them like some veined, living being. The water coming off of them looked like stacked waterfalls.

'Oh my,' was all she could say.

'It's so beautiful,' Mira said.

'Look!' Sam shouted.

He wasn't looking at the storm any longer. He pointed down the hill. At the bottom, lit by bursts of lightning, stood a farmhouse.

Mira and Jen both issued squeals of joy and relief. They half ran, half fell, down the hill. Jen's calves chaffed painfully against her sodden clothing as she went, but she hardly cared.

The farmhouse was steeped in darkness as they approached, slowing down as they got closer. They peered in through the windows, but there was no sign of anything moving within. Sam tried to force the front door, but it was locked. Mira picked up a brick and slammed it against the glass pane in the heavy wood. It broke noisily. Jen reached in and opened the door.

After the colossal sound of the storm the silence was almost oppressive, but it was the pitch dark and the stench of decay which set Jen's hackles up more than the quiet. Not for the first time today she wished she had a weapon.

They moved through the rooms, checking first the living room, then the kitchen. There was a dark hole which looked to be some kind of pantry. Jen hoped it was well stocked. There was another dark room, but again no signs of life.

The stench intensified as they moved upstairs. Mira and Sam waited in the hallway while she investigated the first of the bedrooms. Two corpses looked to be entangled under the window, their dying act to watch the end of the world together. For a moment she stood and envied them, until a scream from the corridor brought her running back out of the room.

Mira had opened the second door, where she had discovered the bodies of two children, rotting in their beds. She stood staring at them, sobbing. Jen took her by the shoulder, trying to hold back her own tears, and guided Mira out of the room. She closed the door.

They went downstairs, where Sam busied himself lighting a fire. Mira sat on the sofa, tears still streaming down her face. Jen sat next to her and held her. Sam got the fire going, bathing the room in warmth and light, although none of them rejoiced in it much. They dried themselves in sullen silence.

'This is how it's going to be now, isn't it?' Mira said eventually.

'What do you mean?' Jen replied.

'Always running, always finding places full of dead bodies. Dead babies...'

'I don't know,' Jen replied. 'All this time I've been expecting we'd turn a corner and there'd be the army, or the government, or something. Someone to come and tell us it's going to be okay. Tell us what to do.'

She sat for a moment, staring into the fire.

'But I think we're past that now.'

'So what do we do?' Sam asked.

'Simple,' she said. 'We stay alive.'

Chapter Nineteen
Rise Up and Fight

Tom awoke to muffled voices. His entire body hurt.

He seemed to be on a bed. He scrambled to remember the last thing that had happened to him, and got a flash image of Baxter's guts all over his shoes. He tried to focus. Leon sat beside him, talking.

'...getting fairly ridiculous now, what with the endless fainting, collapsing, getting beaten up, knocked unconscious. You're starting to make me look bad. I mean, I've been injured just as many times as you have, but you faint and get practically carried here on the shoulders of adoring crowds. I had to hobble back up here. Nobody brings me chocolates. And if you don't wake up soon, I'm going to go ahead and eat your chocolates for you.'

'Hands off them, you filthy bastard,' he croaked as best he could. He looked over to Leon, who grinned at him, and returned whatever he could muster in the direction of a smile. He felt as though every inch of him had been tenderised.

'Fair enough, as long as you promise to share them with me,' Leon said.

Tom's throat burned, and he fumbled for a glass of water by his side, his arm barely up to the task of movement.

'How long have I been out this time?'

'A day or so. I swear, you must be the most well-rested man still alive.'

'What did I miss?' The memories of his victory over Baxter were coming back to him now, making his stomach turn.

'Not a lot. Most of Baxter's men pegged it pretty sharpish. A few of them have stuck around, but they're not the most popular people in the village. Oh, and there's a monster fucking storm outside as well.'

Leon caught the look of panic on his friend's face, and laughed. 'Not that kind of storm. The proper kind, with rain and that.' He stood and went over to the window, pulling open the curtains to reveal rain pounding on the pane.

Tom inched up a bit in the bed, his ribs protesting at the movement. 'So what's everyone saying?' he asked, wondering whether he was now the hero of the hour who brought down a tyrant, or the crazy man who carved someone up in a pretty brutal fashion. He hazarded a guess at somewhere in between.

'Nobody's going to be crying over Baxter, if that's what you're worried about. I think everyone is sizing up their next move, and waiting to see what you say about it. I don't think anyone will be planning to leave tonight, but maybe tomorrow everyone will want to put this behind them and move on. Or they'll decide that sticking together is the best idea. Who knows?'

'What do you think?' Tom asked.

'That it's time for me to go to bed,' he replied, standing up. 'I'm glad you're okay. Get some rest.'

He left. Tom lay staring at the window, trying to get to grips with the fact that he was a killer now. The rain was hypnotic, and after a while he struggled out of bed, went to the window and sat in the same chair he'd recovered in when he'd last had the crap beaten out of him. Before he'd killed a man.

He took the covers off the bed and wrapped them around him to ward off the cold. The rain beat down as he tried to work out what might happen tomorrow. Part of him wanted to grab Leon and run, far away.

When he woke, the rain had died down, but dark clouds hung portentously in the sky. His back ached from both the kicking he'd received and the ill-judged choice of a wooden chair as a bed. He was able to stand more freely now, though. He searched for a cigarette, but had to make do with the painkillers which had been left by his bedside table.

He had been dressed in boxers and a T-shirt, so he started to look for clothes. He presumed his old clothes had been removed, soiled as they were with bits of Baxter, so he searched the wardrobes. The results were not great. A pair of corduroy trousers and a shirt at least one size too small on him were the best he could manage from the geriatric stylings of the room's previous occupant.

He wondered if he'd have better luck in Leon's room and made his way out into the corridor. He entered without knocking and was confronted by the sight of his best friend enjoying an early morning romp with an unknown woman. He was halfway into the room and about to call out before his brain processed what was happening, at which point he found himself stranded too far into the room to go unnoticed.

'Jesus!' called the woman, who Tom realised was Susan, their one-time rescuer and nurse. She leapt from astride his friend, pulling the covers over herself so vigorously that Leon was exposed in all his morning glory.

Leon stared at Tom with a look of surprise.

Tom felt his face redden and heard a bizarre sound come out of his own mouth, like a squawk. 'Um, sorry,' he said. 'Not quite what I expected to see.'

He shut the door to the cacophonous sounds of laughter on the other side. He stood dumbfounded in the corridor, until the sounds of amorous activity resumed and he felt the need to move far away.

Downstairs, he scoured the kitchen for food. It was well-stocked with cereals, herbs, jams, and other food that was of zero use without fresh bread, milk, meat, or vegetables to accompany them. He found a few tins lurking at the back of a cupboard which would suffice. He also found Leon's tobacco pouch and a functioning lighter, so he smoked a cigarette, before making himself breakfast.

By the time Leon resurfaced from upstairs, Tom was enjoying a bowl of beans with tiny sausages, a cup of coffee and his third cigarette.

'Morning,' Tom said jauntily as Leon appeared, a sheepish grin on his face.

'Morning to you,' Leon replied. 'Sorry about that,' he added, without even a hint of remorse in his voice.

'Well this is the longest I've known you to go without the love of a good woman. I was beginning to wonder if you'd lost your touch,'

'Well I was a little busy with the apocalypse.'

'Fair enough.'

'You sleep okay?'

'In a chair,' Tom replied. 'But I slept. I feel like I've done nothing else recently.'

'You mean apart from the whole "become a revolutionary" thing?'

'Yes, aside from that. Insurgency and sleep, the only two things I'm good for these days.'

It hit him that he had awoken to a world without Baxter. They were free. No more beatings, no more living in terror. Today was a whole new world.

'So what's the plan today?' Leon asked.

'Oh you know, have a mooch about town, hit up the comic store, cinema, joint in the car park. Usual Saturday.'

'Sounds good, except how do you know it's Saturday?'

'Do you know, I have no idea what day it is,' Tom said.

'Well, spending most of your days unconscious will do that to you,' Leon said, easing himself into a chair. 'Funny how soon something as concrete as the days of the week ceases to matter. Do you know what I'm really starting to miss though?'

'What?' Tom asked, easing himself into his chair.

'Music. I haven't heard any in days. Longer, maybe.'

'I know what you mean.'

'All my favourite bands are dead.'

'But so are all the shit ones.'

'Good point.'

'The end of the world is a small price to pay for no more Nickleback albums.'

It felt so good to be talking bollocks with his friend that Tom hardly dared burst the bubble, but he knew he had to some time. 'I had a thought last night,' he said.

'Do tell.'

'Well, as much as he was a total fucking lunatic, Baxter was on to something.'

'Please tell me we're not going to start abducting people?'

'No,' Tom said. 'But the idea of starting to gather people together, growing a community out of whatever the fuck this world is now, perhaps isn't the craziest idea. We could head for an army barracks, or a hospital, or a fuck off big hotel. Shit, maybe even a whole town.' He sat forward. 'When Baxter and his men were in control of this village, they ran out of food in days, and people just milled about, terrified. What we need is to give people a sense of purpose, ensure we're invested in rebuilding what we had before. We're going to need to learn about farming, about medicine, about how to govern. We're going to need to elect councils and find a way we can survive this, whatever this is.'

Leon sat back. 'I don't disagree, I don't. But are we seriously the ones to do it?'

'What's the alternative? If we don't start to rebuild, are we going to spend the next few years scrabbling around trying to eke out a basic survival? For what?'

'What happens the next time we run into another Baxter? There's going to be an endless supply of people out there who are going to want to take power, run things themselves.'

'Of course there is, but people like that need a vacuum to operate in. They can pick people off one by one, but if they come across a determined group who are willing to stand up for themselves, for their freedom, it's a different story.'

'The only thing necessary for the triumph of evil is that good men do nothing,' Leon said. He looked up and chuckled. 'Sorry, must be a random bit of my education there that I haven't smoked out yet. Edmund Burke.'

'Wasn't he the founder of conservatism?'

'It's still a good quote.'

Leon rolled two cigarettes for them both, and they sat smoking in silence. Tom watched his friend trying to find a counter argument.

'Someone has to make a stand. I get that. Total agreement. But why us two? Two hapless fucking stoners who couldn't pull together the wherewithal to pay their own electricity bill, who were about to embark upon the most ill-advised road trip in history until the apocalypse interrupted us.'

'I'd go with you.'

They hadn't noticed Susan's appearance. She sat halfway down the staircase, watching them, her hair wet. Tom felt a pang of annoyance, not for the first time in his life, that Leon was the good-looking one of the two of them.

'You would?' Tom asked her.

'You're right, both of you. We need to rebuild, and we need to do it together. As one. Leon, you wonder if you are the right people to pull this together, to lead us from now on? I don't know. I mean,

I know you get beat up a lot, but the fact you are even reticent to take the job means you're a damn sight more qualified already than Baxter was. So I'm in. I'm not saying I'll follow you, but I'd like to help you.'

Tom flashed her a smile of gratitude. Leon sank back in his chair, frowning.

'Listen,' Tom said. 'This could be entirely academic. We might float the idea to that lot out there and they stick their fingers up at us and we go our separate ways. All I'm saying is we gather everyone together and see if there's actually an appetite for this idea.'

Leon nodded. Susan moved from the stairs and sat on Leon's knee, putting her arms around him. She gave him a kiss. Tom mumbled his apologies, took his cigarette, and headed out of the house for some air.

It didn't take long to gather together the remaining members of the group. A few had collected their things that morning and left. Tom could hardly blame them. Once the group was together it numbered thirteen in total. Not the most auspicious of starts, perhaps. What was worse was that Tom couldn't remember any of their names, and felt it was too late now to start asking. The curse of the English. He wondered if they all felt the same. Thirteen apocalyptic survivors referring to each other as 'mate' out of politeness.

Two of Baxter's men remained, shuffling about at the edges, trying to avoid eye contact with the rest of them, who, in turn, ignored their existence.

So there was Tom, Leon, and Susan, two of Baxter's men and eight others. Not perhaps the numbers needed to recolonise the world, Tom thought, but a start. If they bought into it.

Into him.

He stood in front of them, rubbing his hands together until the skin was raw, waiting for people to turn their attention to him. Finally, he started to speak. He ran through a repeat of the conversation he'd had with Leon and Susan, and saw that his audience seemed at least vaguely responsive.

'What makes you qualified to be in charge?' a man called out, a great big bear of a man.

'Tom's not saying he's in charge, Petr,' Susan said from beside him. 'That's the whole point. We move forward as one group, but Tom's the one who has stood up for us in the past. He rescued us from Baxter, I think he's earned the right to be heard.'

Petr nodded.

'Susan's right,' Tom said. 'But for now, until we get set up somewhere, if you're happy for me to take the lead, it's going to be easier. That doesn't mean you can't challenge me, or leave if you disagree with me. But in the interests of getting stuff done...'

'What about them?' a woman cut across him, pointing towards Baxter's men. 'Are they welcome?'

'That depends,' Tom said.

'On what?' one of the two men replied. Both of them were looking up now.

'On whether you want to come with us, on whether you did anything to personally hurt anyone who was here, whether we will take you, and whether you can make yourselves useful.'

Tom knew this would be a pivotal moment. His standing in the group would last exactly as long as his first wrong decision, and he may well have just made it, but he had no memory of these two doing anything other than witness the violence. They had still been parties to it, though, happy to go along with Baxter and his madness.

'Do you want to stay with us?' he asked.

The two men looked at each other and nodded. 'If you'll have us,' the first one said, his voice marked by a heavy Yorkshire accent. 'I can understand why you wouldn't. We've got no excuses for what we've done, but we're military men, used to following orders, like. I know that don't make it right, but there ain't one of you here can say we've hurt you ourselves.'

'Okay,' Tom said. 'Are you willing to do your bit?'

They nodded.

'I guess it's down to you all,' Tom said, and looked out to the rest of the group.

Susan nodded first, followed by Leon, who gave more of a disinterested shrug than a nod, to Tom's mild annoyance. Slowly everyone indicated their agreement until, finally, the lady who had raised the question nodded a hesitant assent.

'They get one chance with me,' she said, grudgingly.

'They get one chance with all of us,' Tom replied. He looked over to Baxter's men and they nodded. He blew out a deep breath, and smiled. He had a feeling that down the line having two men with military training could come in useful.

'I propose we leave here. Today.'

'Why can't we stay here?' asked another from the group.

Tom realised he was going to have to learn everyone's names at some point. 'Because a lot of Baxter's men ran, and they might come back,' he replied, which brought an end to the discussion. 'Go back to your houses, pack up anything you think is useful. Clothes, food especially. Meet back here in an hour.'

With that, the group broke.

Tom grabbed the arm of one of Baxter's men. 'I put my neck out for you both there,' he said, in a low voice. 'You're not going to make me regret it, are you?'

The man shook his head.

Tom felt dizzy. He'd done it. Or at least he'd done the first part of it.

On their way back to their house, Tom eyed Leon, who seemed deep in thought. 'You kept pretty quiet back there,' he said.

'You seemed to have it under control,' Leon said, flatly.

'You still think this is a bad idea?'

'I guess we'll find out soon enough,' Leon replied, as they got inside. Without another word he bounded upstairs and into his room, leaving Tom alone in the living room with his duelling relief and fear.

Chapter Twenty
The Bug

Burnett's throat burned as he sipped the water the priest had given him. It'd been an hour at least since Tana had saved him from the grip of the madman, but he could still feel Philip's fingers pressing on his windpipe.

He wanted to know what was going on in the next room. It took all his self-restraint not to pull open the door, stride past Tana and beat the living shit out of the man who had attacked him. But he would wait. Whatever reason Philip had for wanting to kill him, the last person who should be interrogating the man was himself.

All the same, he wished he could be in there. No offence to Tana, Burnett thought he seemed like a nice guy, but he was a street bobby and not a detective. He didn't even know if Tana had handled an interrogation before.

At least in this case his partner wasn't bound by the rule of law. Which wasn't to say Burnett was one of those officers who bitched and moaned about civil liberties and the Human Rights Act and all that. He'd spent half his career having to listen to officers whining about how they had to let someone go free because of 'civil liberties'. Burnett was of the mind that a civilised society was civilised to all and if you couldn't make a collar within the rules either you didn't try hard enough or the collar couldn't be made. But in this case, with his throat stinging and rage swelling in his chest, he was bloody glad there wouldn't be a busybody desk clerk interrupting the interrogation to say time was up.

Finally the door opened and out stepped Tana, his face ashen.

Burnett's stomach lurched. 'So?' he asked.

'You can go in. He wants to talk to you. He'll tell you everything. Better you hear it from him.'

Burnett stood up.

As he walked past, Tana stopped him. 'Go easy on him, he's had a far worse time of it than you.'

Burnett stepped past him and into the room. The dank smell of sweat hung heavy in the air, and his assailant sat in a chair on the other side of the table. Gone was the taut ball of nervous energy who'd wrapped his hands so forcefully around Burnett's throat. The man before him now was a shell, his top soaked with sweat.

He looked up as Burnett entered, his eyes red and swollen.

'Hello again, Philip,' Burnett said.

'Detective,' he replied, leaning forward and holding his bound hands up to Burnett. 'I'm so sorry; you have to believe me, he told me you were the one, and I believed him. I wanted to believe him, even after everything.'

'Slow down,' Burnett said, holding his own hands up. He took a seat opposite Philip.

'Sorry,' Philip said again, and took a breath. His hands were trembling.

'Okay,' Burnett said. 'If I take that off your wrists, you're not going to try and hurt me again, are you?'

Philip shook his head. Burnett leaned forward and worked the knot loose. Philip issued a deep sigh of relief and sat back in the chair. Burnett saw tears beginning to well up in the man's eyes.

'Why don't you tell me what happened? Start from the beginning.'

'From the storm?'

'If you like.'

Philip nodded.

'We were at home, my wife Carol, our two...'

He hesitated for a second.

'Our boys, Aiden and Drew. I was doing the bedtime routines, when Carol called down to me that I should come see the sky. The boys love a storm, so we ran downstairs and into the street. It was full of people, staring up at the sky. It was so strange. The stillness in the sky; it felt like everything became charged. The boys were staring up excited, but I got a splitting headache. I looked at Carol and she was clutching her head. I looked at the boys and they were already on the floor. They were convulsing, but before I could reach out to them, everything went black.

'I woke up and it was morning. I was so confused at first, but then I remembered the storm and the boys. I sat up, and there was Carol, cradling their...'

He stopped, and his eyes welled up again. Burnett knew better than to interrupt.

'We stayed that way, surrounded by dead bodies, cradling our boys. We didn't say anything to each other. We couldn't. We took the... the bodies back into the house and put them in their beds. We couldn't speak to each other. I wanted us to comfort each other, but Carol couldn't even look at me. I don't know if she blamed me somehow, or what. But she slept in the boys' room that night, and I fell asleep on the sofa downstairs. When I woke up the next morning she was gone. She left me a note.'

He fished into his pocket, pulled out a scrap of paper and handed to Burnett. It said, 'I'm sorry, I can't, Carol.'

Burnett handed it back. 'Jesus,' he said.

'I was so angry at her, but I was so scared. I didn't want to lose her as well. So I started looking for her. I didn't know where she might go, so I went to her friends' houses. I checked her work. She'd gone. Clearly she didn't want me to find her, but I kept looking anyway.

I went two days without seeing anyone else. When I did, the first thing I asked was if they'd seen her. I had no idea what direction she'd gone in.

'It was a tough few days. I got attacked by a man who stole my supplies, and there was a lot of looting and other... unpleasantness. I found bodies in the street that were from after the storm. I gave up hope. Carol didn't want to be found. I started to think maybe she'd changed her mind and gone back to the house for me and I'd gone. I went back, but the whole street had burned down. My poor babies. I never got to bury them.'

He sat in silence for a moment. Burnett looked across at the pitiful wreck in front of him and wondered what kept a person going after so much trauma.

'I was in a supermarket trying to find something to eat, a few days after, and there was a man there. We got talking. He had some pretty crazy theories about what the storm was, but he seemed like a decent enough man. He was heading off to find some family, he said, and so I told him about Carol. I described her to him and he said he couldn't be sure, but that he might have seen her. I was asking out of habit more than anything else. I didn't think I'd actually find her. But here was a man offering me exactly that. Until he'd said he'd seen her with another man.'

'Let me guess,' Burnett said. 'A policeman.'

'Exactly. Detective Burnett.'

A surge of anger within the man seemed to focus him a little, and he sat up straight in his chair before continuing.

'The man's name was Ewen. He was... unassuming. Geeky, student type. He said he'd had a run in with a detective. He said he'd been trying to get food one day when this guy had come up and robbed him at gunpoint, waving his police badge around. He had a woman with him, and they seemed... close. He'd left them. He promised to take me to where he'd last seen them, he said it wasn't too far.'

'And did he?'

'He did,' Philip replied. 'It took us a few hours to walk there, and I had no idea what to expect. Even if it was Carol this boy had seen, what could I expect to do? She had moved on, seemingly, with a guy who would likely kill me if I tried to take her away. But I had to be sure. What if she regretted leaving?

'He showed me to an industrial estate, said he wasn't sure if they'd still be there, but they had looked like they might be settling in. It was worth a look, he said. He led me to a small warehouse and showed me inside.'

Philip stopped, his eyes welling up. Burnett waited for him. He needed to know.

'What did you find?' he asked.

Philip's face crumpled.

'Carol,' he said, trying to hold back his tears. 'She'd been... I couldn't take it. I couldn't understand what was in front of me. She'd been... carved up.'

'How did Ewen react?'

'He gave me a gun.'

Burnett nodded. 'How did you find me?'

'He took me away from the warehouse. Said to stay put, he'd go find food and come back. When he came back he said he'd spoken to people who had heard a policeman was gathering people together at some hotel somewhere. From their description it sounded like you. He goaded me on. He spent a day talking about what he would do in my position, how he'd kill the person who put someone he loved through so much pain. He talked about what might happen to the people you were pretending to be a Good Samaritan to.'

'And so you came in search of me?'

'Yes.'

'Why didn't Ewen join you?'

'He said he still had to look for his family.'

'So you don't know where he went?'

'Last time I saw him he was at the warehouse.'

Burnett nodded. 'How did you hook up with the minibus?' he asked.

'I can't remember. I was going to walk the whole way, but they pulled over and let me in. They had their own horror stories, but I barely listened to them. How could anything they'd been through compare to what I'd suffered?

'When we got here I half expected to find a slaughterhouse. I figured I was walking into my own death, taking a whole minibus full of people with me, no less, but I knew I was going to take you down.'

'I can't blame you for that, Philip,' Burnett said. 'You know it was him, don't you?'

Philip nodded.

Burnett leaned forward. 'I'm going to make him pay for what he took from you, Philip. I promise that.'

Philip nodded again, his face crumpling into sobs.

Burnett stood and left the room. As he closed the door he heard a moan of anguish from the other side of it. Tana and the priest were sat in the hallway.

'Whatever that man needs, you give it to him,' Burnett said to the priest.

'What are you going to do?' Tana asked.

'What do you think?'

He looked at the priest expecting a protestation, but there was none forthcoming. He looked at Tana.

'Are you going to help me?'

The question hung in the air for a second, and Burnett half regretted asking, but eventually Tana shrugged. 'Fuck it,' he said. 'Sorry, Father, but I'm needed elsewhere.'

Burnett's car remained a rank testament to the power of human odour, so they scouted around for an alternative, which was difficult seeing as so many of the cars had rotting corpses in situ. They settled on a big old Jaguar three streets away from the hotel, whose owner had been kind enough to get out of his car before dying on the ground next to it.

'At some point we're going to have to deal with these corpses lying about the place,' Tana said as he got into the passenger seat.

'I know,' Burnett replied. He started the car and pulled away, crunching some part of its previous owner under one of the wheels as they went.

'It's so sad,' Tana said. 'All these people who'll never get a proper burial, never be mourned, never have people eulogising them.'

'I think St Peter will still let them through the gates without a funeral,' Burnett said, as he looked at the road signs and tried to determine where he needed to go.

'I never took you for a church type,' Tana said.

'I'm not,' he replied. 'I was being sarcastic.'

'Your sarcastic voice sounds pretty much the same as your normal one.'

'It's been said before,' Burnett replied. 'You have any fucking idea where we're going?'

'Um, yeah, that way I think,' Tana said, pointing back at a turnoff they'd just passed.

Burnett cursed and swung the car round. 'Did Philip give us any more useful information on our guy?' he asked.

'Not really,' Tana replied. 'We don't even know if Ewen is his real name. Philip said he'd told him he'd been a scientist before the storm, and Philip didn't get the sense he was local. He told Philip was he was looking to find his family, and naturally Philip was too preoccupied with the murder of his wife to take a particular interest in his companion.'

Burnett nodded, his head full of his own preoccupations.

'Imagine finding out you'd spent days with the person who'd butchered your wife without even realising it,' Tana said.

'I know,' Burnett replied.

'Do you reckon we'll find him there?'

'I dunno. You'd have to think he'd scarper as soon as Philip went on his way. He might even have followed to watch the aftermath. But something about this seems like a provocation rather than a full on assassination attempt. He seems too focused on me to have someone else kill me.'

'That's a cheery thought,' Tana replied. 'So we're playing his game, by his rules, and going to his turf to do it?'

'Yes,' Burnett said.

The rest of the journey passed in silence, and Burnett could feel the tension building in him as he got closer to the industrial estate. Over the years he'd learnt to channel the anticipation of a crime scene into something nearing a zen process, allowing the adrenaline to focus his mind without overriding his common sense. He was already clicking back into the old mental routine, running through check lists of things to look for, processes to follow.

Next to him Tana didn't seem to be undergoing the same process, his partner fidgeting with increasing intensity the closer they got.

As they reached the outskirts of the town a column of smoke rose into the air.

'What do you reckon?' Tana asked.

'I'd say someone has left us a great big arrow saying "come here",' he replied.

'Yeah, come here and be killed,' Tana said.

'Let's make sure it doesn't come to that.'

They drove slowly through the streets, looking for any kind of movement, but all was still and calm. The dead littered the pavements as usual, but none showed signs of being anything other than the storm's dead.

The smoke grew ever closer, and the surroundings changed from residential houses to industrial estates. Burnett supposed any of them might hold Susan's corpse or Burnett's killer, but he felt sure the column of smoke was the real pointer.

They rounded a corner and there it was, in front of them. Outside a large pair of old warehouses sat a pile of burning tyres, thick black smoke billowing from the fire burning at its heart.

'Here we go,' Burnett said. Tana shifted next to him and pulled out a gun in anticipation.

'Remember, if you see this wanker, you shoot him as hard and as much as you can. No hesitation, right?' Burnett said.

Tana nodded. They parked and Burnett pulled out his own gun. They sat in the car for a second, waiting for any sign of movement. The thick odour of burning rubber filled the vehicle.

'Let's go,' he said.

The large metal door to the first warehouse creaked open, announcing their arrival to anyone within earshot. The reek of putrefaction escaped like a blast of hot air and they stepped back.

'What I wouldn't give for full riot police get-up right now,' Tana said.

'Or a SWAT team,' Burnett replied. He held up his weapon and moved inside.

The warehouse was dark, but there were shafts of light creeping in from somewhere ahead. It was practically empty, save for some abandoned rusting equipment and discarded boxes. Burnett assumed whatever business had once occupied this place had been a victim of one of the country's many recessions. He thought about every news report of natural disasters, which seemed to come with a monetary cost attached, as though that were people's only meaningful frame of reference. He wondered what the monetary cost of this particular apocalypse would be. He pictured some poor researcher in the bowels of a major newsroom, ignoring the world's collapse as he frantically tried to calculate the financials.

The cavernous room was silent, except for the echo of distant water dripping onto metal. Burnett tightened his finger on the trigger, expecting something or someone to leap out at him at any moment. He tried to remind himself that this was only one man, at least as far as he knew. Not a monster, or a mythical being, or a vengeful god. Simply a man. Or so he hoped.

Without a word, he and Tana split the room in two and moved forward, Burnett taking the left. He headed toward the dripping sound, when a noise ahead of him made him stop. The shadows at the far side of the room shifted.

He fired, over and above the moving object. The moving thing paused for a second, turned and retreated. It wasn't a man, Burnett thought. An animal of some kind, presumably attracted by the prospect of meat.

He followed the movement. As it passed under a shaft of dull light, Burnett made out a large black dog. It reached the far end of the room and stopped. It turned towards Burnett and bared its teeth. Burnett looked into its eyes and saw that any remnants of domesticity had gone.

Burnett hated dogs, as a lot of policemen who had once been the first ones through the door did. Too many half-arsed drug dealers who thought an abused Staffie was as good as having a bodyguard. He was twice bitten, thrice shy. He looked at the dog in front of him and saw nothing but aggression in its eyes. He dared not take his eyes off it, but out of the corner of his eye he saw Tana moving forward, his own gun raised.

'It's okay,' Burnett called. 'I've got this one.'

'It's not that one I'm worried about,' Tana replied.

Burnett glanced around him. He'd been so focused on the one, he hadn't seen the other five. They were completely surrounded. 'Clever girl,' he muttered under his breath.

'So. Count of three?' Tana asked.

'Okay,' Burnett replied. He decided the dog in front of him had to be his first target.

'Three, two, one,' Tana counted down.

As one, their two guns fired, the shots ringing around the empty room. Burnett's bullet caught the first dog in the head and it collapsed, but if he'd hoped the shots might put the others off, he was mistaken. All four survivors started towards him at the same time.

He swung to his right towards a large Doberman, which bore down on him when another jumped at his outstretched arm and sunk its jaws into his forearm. Burnett nearly dropped his gun in pain and surprise, but managed to whip the gun round in his other hand and fire a shot point blank at the dog's head. Its jaws went slack as the dead dog fell to the floor.

Blood showered over Burnett, and the blast knocked his senses for six, deafening him. For a few seconds he stood in silent confusion, until he remembered the other dogs. 'Fuck!' he shouted to nobody in particular, and swung the gun round to where the other Doberman had been a second ago, but there was a canine corpse there instead. Tana must have got it.

He looked over at Tana, who had climbed up on a box and was waving his presumably empty gun at the last of the dogs, which was snarling at him and sizing up if it could make the leap itself.

Burnett didn't give it the chance. He raised his gun and put the dog down.

'Thanks,' Tana said, jumping down from his box. 'You okay?'

Burnett looked down at his arm. Deep gouges were visible in the flesh of his forearm, and blood flowed freely down to his hand. The sight of it made him feel faint.

'Not really,' he said.

'Sit down,' Tana said.

'Ah shit,' Burnett said, lowering himself down while trying to keep his arm raised.

Tana took off his shirt and tore it into strips and tied them around Burnett's arm. 'We need to find a doctor to look at this,' he said. 'This is going to get infected.'

'I don't think we'll find many GP surgeries still open,' Burnett replied, getting to his feet. 'Let's worry about that later, shall we?'

The six dead dogs lay still on the ground, and Burnett felt a wave of guilt about having had to kill them. 'We'd better check the rest of the place,' he said. 'Fucker could still be around here somewhere and we still need to find the body.'

It didn't take long. In a room adjoining to the main hall they found it, barely recognisable as a human corpse. The malevolence meted out to it in death had been compounded by the dogs that had feasted on the torn and broken flesh.

Neither of them wanted to linger long, but they both went into forensic mode, examining every inch of the room. Satisfied there was nothing of use to them, Burnett carried on through to the next room. There were no signs anyone was using it as a base, or even that anyone had been there at all.

'Nothing,' Burnett said finally.

'At least we know Philip was telling the truth,' Tana replied.

'Doesn't exactly help us though, does it?'

They walked through the main building and its assortment of dead dogs.

'What now?' Tana asked.

'I'm done,' Burnett replied, his voice cracking.

'What do you mean?'

'I mean I'm done. Let this fucker come and find me if he wants to. I'm done walking into his traps.'

'What about Philip?'

'What about him?'

'You made him a promise.'

Burnett frowned. Curse Tana and his memory. He stared at the floor. 'I'll break it. I can't bring his wife back.' He looked up, and fixed Tana with a determined look. 'The only time we've gotten close to this mother fucker is when he's wanted us to. I'm sick of playing his games.'

'Listen,' Tana said. 'I used to think you were mad, chasing this guy down. But we can't let this guy go on killing and torturing people.'

'Why not?' Burnett said. 'It's not like anybody is paying us to catch him.'

'You don't honestly mean that?'

Burnett sighed. 'No. Of course not.'

'We have to keep going.'

'Fine.'

'Good. So what do we do now?'

'Don't ask me, you're the one who wants...' Burnett stopped. He looked around him. 'Son of a bitch,' he said.

'We have no idea where this guy is right now,' Tana said, oblivious. 'He could be back at the hotel carving them into pieces. He was here, what, three days ago?'

Burnett turned round to face him. Tana looked at him with a vexed expression.

'We know he's close by,' Burnett said.

'How?'

'Turn around.'

Tana looked about, but saw nothing, and turned back, shrugging his shoulders. Burnett raised his eyebrows and Tana turned around again. This time he saw it.

'Bastard,' he said quietly.

The bodies of the six dogs had been gutted, their entrails spread out across the floor. Tana went over to a pile of boxes and climbed up.

'Does it say what I think it says?' Burnett asked.

'It says "missed me".'

'Anything else?'

'A smiley face.'

Burnett nodded. His arm stung as he raised it to rub his eyes.

'So we carry on?' Tana asked.

'We carry on.'

Chapter Twenty-One
The Sun Smells Too Loud

Tom loaded his supplies into the minibus, the back half of which was laden with various boxes of tins, pasta, suitcases full of clothing, and various other things which people had considered of importance. Someone had wedged in a small bookcase full of books. Others had also gone to the trouble of giving the minibus a clean, which Tom made a mental note to thank them for if he ever worked out who they were.

He watched as they milled about, getting organised. The minibus could hold nine, including the driver, and they had Baxter's old Land Rover as the lead vehicle. He wondered which he should ride in.

One of Baxter's men came over. 'Tom,' he called. He was the one who had done the talking at the meeting. He was tall and there was a lot of him.

'Yes,' Tom replied.

'We've got these for you.' He gestured to his companion, the quieter one, who held a large duffel bag. The other one held the bag open, revealing guns. Lots of guns, and ammunition too.

'Oh,' Tom said.

'We figured you should have them.'

'Okay. Thanks.'

'Listen, I know you said you wanted us to pitch in, so, we're both drivers, Ralph and me. We drove convoys in Afghanistan and Iraq. Hostile areas and that. We'd be more than happy to be your drivers.'

'I'll have to... talk it over.' Tom said.

'I'm Patch, by the way. Listen, if you'd be happier with us sitting in the back, that's fine. Wanted to make the offer.'

Tom shook the man's outstretched hand. He took the bag from Ralph, its weight taking him by surprise, almost sending him toppling over.

'What was that about?' Leon asked, coming over as soon as the two men were gone.

'They gave me a big bag of guns and asked if they could drive for us.'

'Fuck,' Leon replied. 'Wait, you're not actually entertaining the idea, are you?'

'Well, they're trained military drivers. They know what they're doing, and they'll be the best ones to react if we come under fire.'

'Do you think that's a good idea, putting our lives into their hands?' Leon asked, his tone moving from friendly to aghast.

'I don't know! They gave us the bloody guns, didn't they?'

'No, you don't fucking know!' Leon replied, his voice raised now to the level where people around them started watching. 'You have no idea if anything you've decided is a good idea, and yet you keep blindingly doing it anyway!'

'Well, I tell you what, if you come up with any better ideas than standing there and bitching and moaning at me you feel free to step up,' Tom shouted back. He turned his back on his friend, feeling the heat in his face and the eyes on his back.

He was glad he hadn't told Leon he'd already considered giving Patch and Ralph guns, too. Leon could be right, of course. If those men got into a fire fight with their old comrades, who knew where their allegiances would fall? They could be setting him up to lead them all straight into an ambush to pay him back for what he did to their boss. He felt stupid for losing his temper, but was still too annoyed at Leon to go to make peace.

Leon got into the minibus, and, after a frown, Susan joined him. Tom guessed he would be in the front car, after all. He climbed into the front passenger seat of the Land Rover wondering if he could do this without Leon. Did he even want to, if that was the cost? If anything should bind tighter the bonds of friendship, he'd thought the apocalypse would.

There was a tap on the window. Leon and Susan stood by the car, Leon looking sheepish. Susan motioned to wind down the window. Tom obliged.

'Listen, if I'm going to have to play marriage counsellor every ten minutes with you two it's going to get pretty boring,' Susan said. She opened the rear door and jumped in behind Tom.

'Sorry, mate,' Leon said.

'Me too,' Tom replied.

'It was supposed to be me and you against the world.'

'That's what I want; I can't do this without you.'

'Fucking hell,' Susan said from the back. 'If you want I can leave you two alone to have a cuddle?'

'Yeah, alright,' Leon said, and joined Susan in the back. As soon as he pulled the door closed, Patch appeared.

'Alright, am I driving or what?'

Tom looked behind him, and Leon rolled his eyes before giving a curt nod. Patch smiled and got in the driver seat.

'Good lads. Now, where are we going?'

'Christ, I've no idea,' Tom said.

'Not really thought this far ahead eh?' Patch asked.

'Where are we now?'

'Um,' Patch said, straining to read a road sign so far away you could barely make out it was a road sign, let alone read it.

'We're in Brompton,' Susan said, from the back seat. 'It's near Northallerton. If we head roughly south we'll get to York. But whatever you do, don't head east or we'll spend days driving aimlessly round the moors.'

'South it is,' Patch said. 'Aye, aye, Cap'n.'

They started off, the minibus staying close behind them. Tom glanced in the mirror and saw it wasn't Ralph behind the wheel, but the burly Petr, so he guessed that was something.

It turned out Susan knew the area pretty well from her affinity for rambling, which had taken her onto the moors countless times. Tom had thought rambling was something old people did in cagoules, but Susan assured him otherwise. She guided them away from Northallerton, where she said any survivors were likely to be of a less than savoury nature.

Patch turned out to be quite the entertaining driver. He regaled them with amusing anecdotes from Afghanistan and Iraq that were more horrifying than funny, but he had a way of telling them.

'So you guys didn't get any warning before the storm or information about it afterwards?' Susan asked him.

'Nah,' he replied, 'at least nobody told me anything. Baxter was never one to share his intel though. He could be a good CO at times, but he was a bit of a dick really.' He looked around his passengers. 'But you probably worked that out already.'

'So, Patch,' Leon said. 'Say you're in charge, what would you do?'

'Me? I'm not cut out for command.'

'Say you were on your own.'

'Well, I suppose I'd head for an army base. Either there'll be a unit operational there, or you'd find yourself a pretty good place to secure and hunker down in. Most barracks tend to be pretty well stocked with rations and weapons. Plus fuck off great big walls.'

Tom thought about this. The notion wasn't without merit.

'There's plenty of them around here, too,' Susan said. 'Mostly air force bases. RAF Leeming, RAF Topcliffe.'

'Yeah, but the problem is if we get to these places and find they're already taken, we could find ourselves fairly quickly up shit creek,' Leon said.

'Aye, you would at that,' Patch said, chuckling.

'Well, we're not far from York,' Susan said. 'There's barracks around there, but there's likely to be more survivors around. We could try and make the convoy a bit bigger, or we might even find a decent rescue effort going on there.'

'What about a holiday village?' Leon said.

'What, like a caravan park?' Patch asked.

'Not a bad idea,' Tom said. 'Everyone gets their own place, but with central facilities we can try and coordinate from.'

'You'd have hard work trying to defend that, if it came to it,' Patch said.

They rode on in silence for a bit.

'I think we should head toward York,' Tom said. 'See what the lay of the land is. I think we see what people want to do, but I think the holiday park idea is a winner.'

'York it is,' Patch said.

'We should make it to Thirsk pretty soon if the going isn't too rough,' Susan said.

Almost as soon as the words left her lips they came across their first major wreck: a multi-car spectacular that had burned so fiercely it had melted the tarmac and left charred bodies strewn about. The wreckage was nigh on impassable. Patch said he'd be able to take the Land Rover round it, but the minibus would have no chance. They wasted an hour trying anyway, until eventually they reversed back and headed back to the same village they had left. They sized up their options.

'I reckon the back roads will be our best bet,' Patch said. 'Less likely to have been many on the roads when the storm hit.'

Tom nodded, and Susan shrugged her shoulders. 'Let's take this one and see if we can't work our way south that way,' she said.

It was a good plan, for half an hour or so at least, but when they rounded a steep corner an overturned lorry blocked the narrow country road.

'Shit,' Tom said, as Patch pulled off an impressive emergency stop.

'Hang on,' Leon said. 'What does that lorry say down the side?'

'Umm,' Patch replied, straining to see round the back of the lorry. 'I think it's a Tesco lorry.'

Leon got out, and the others followed.

'What?' Tom said.

'This is a supply truck,' Leon said. 'If we're lucky, it'll be full of food.'

Tom was so wrapped up in the journey that he'd not given any thought to food. Leon went to the overturned rig and started fiddling with the rear doors.

'Chances are it'll be mixed goods,' he said. 'If it's fresh produce it'll have been baking in the back of here since the storm and this'll reek a bit.'

He started with the lock on the back of the lorry and soon had the massive latch open. Tom shot him a puzzled look.

'Back in college I worked for Tesco as a shelf stacker over the summer,' he said.

'You never mentioned it,' Tom said, surprised.

'Yeah, because it's the kind of thing you brag about,' Leon replied, as he swung open the massive door.

He had to leap back as a cage of breakfast cereal boxes came tumbling down, breaking open and spilling Cheerios over the road.

There was a huge cheer. The minibus had pulled up behind them and everyone piled out. The question of food had been weighing more on their minds than it had Tom's.

Leon pulled the cage clear of the doors and climbed up. As soon as he was in Tom heard a disgusted 'ugh' from inside.

'You okay?' he called.

'Yeah,' Leon shouted from inside. 'Something's definitely rotten in here though.'

There was silence for a moment, the gathered crowd watching the back of the lorry expectantly, until Leon appeared back at the door, holding a case of tinned sweetcorn. He held it aloft, and everyone cheered.

'We've hit the tinned food jackpot,' Leon announced, to yet more cheers.

Tom turned to Patch. 'Do you think we can get this up and running again?'

Patch replied with the eternal sigh of the plumber readying themselves to tell someone they need a completely new set of pipes. 'Dunno,' he said. 'Doubt it. You'd need a tractor to right it. I don't see one nearby.'

'Well, we can take as much as we can with us now, and keep an eye out for a farm. Can we at least get past it?'

'Aye, I reckon.'

The members of the group took turns heading into the lorry and returning with wrinkled faces and armfuls of supplies, ranging from tinned goods to powdered milk to toiletries. When Tom's turn came he climbed up and into the darkness. He held his sleeve up to his mouth and fought back his gag reflex as the stench of fetid spoiled food hit him in the back of the throat

Even in the dull light from the back door he could see it was an impressive haul, with whole cages full of mixed goods. Most of what they brought out was from one cage by the looks of it, but there were rows more of them, stacked along both sides of the truck. He delved into the cage and brought out a pack of nappies. He looked at it, and wondered how long it might be before anyone needed them. He'd yet to see a single child survivor of the storm, come to think of it.

That's a depressing thought.

He tossed the nappies and reached in again, pulling out a box of toothpaste and another of toothbrushes. He headed back out into the light. There was a lot less of that now. Night wasn't too far away. He placed his toiletries on the pile in the road.

'I think we need to get moving,' he said to the crowd. 'Find somewhere to bed in for the night. Let's load up and get on the road. If we manage to find a farmhouse or a tractor along the way, we'll come back tomorrow.'

It took the minibus a few attempts to go round the lorry, resorting to wheel-spinning through the muddy verge, but soon they were on the road again.

'How's the petrol looking?' Susan asked Patch after a few miles.

'Not great,' he replied. 'I've got a yellow light saying I'm about empty. Fuck knows how they're doing in the minibus.'

'Next time we see somewhere we can stop we'll take it,' Tom said.

'There was a hamlet a mile or so back,' Susan said. 'If we keep going in this direction we could end up getting stuck out on the moors.'

'Sold.' Tom said.

Patch signalled the minibus and swung back around. As they reached the hamlet, the minibus spluttered to a halt behind them. They congregated on the centre of a street, surrounded on either side by houses and the increasing evening gloom.

'We're out of petrol,' said Petr.

'That could be a problem,' Leon said.

'Couldn't we take petrol out of the cars left on the side of the road?' asked one enterprising sort.

'Depends,' Ralph said. 'Could be we end up mixing diesel and regular and then we're fucked.'

'Let's worry about it in the morning,' Tom said, too tired to deal with another crisis. 'Listen, I know we've not made it very far today, and we've not found any other survivors, but we've got some supplies, and there are more not far away. We'll deal with tomorrow, tomorrow. In the meantime, I can see enough houses for everyone, if people don't mind bunking up with each other.'

'We should clear the houses, make sure they're empty,' Patch said.

Tom nodded. 'Can you and Ralph manage it?'

'Gladly,' Patch said, a big smile lighting up his face. The two men headed into the first house.

'You trust them to do that?' Petr asked.

'At some point we'll have to start trusting them,' Tom replied. 'In the meantime, let's start sorting out care packages for everyone to get them through tonight.'

The sun had almost set by the time the two men returned to say the coast was clear. They also provided a breakdown of each house's capacity and which ones had rotting surprises contained within, one of which they ruled out due to the two corpses in the living room. They locked that one up.

The group divided itself up, with Tom, Leon and Susan taking one house. Patch and Ralph stood alone, with nobody willing to take them in.

'Patch, you can bunk in with us,' Tom said. 'Ralph?'

'We've got a spare bedroom,' called a woman at the back, earning herself a glare from her new housemate.

'Cheers,' Ralph said, giving both a weak smile.

Their bungalow was a two bedroom, but Tom assumed Leon and Susan would be sharing.

'I'll take the couch,' Patch said, before Tom could offer. 'I'm used to a lot worse, trust me.'

'Cheers,' Tom said.

He was starting to enjoy the company of the gruff former adversary. Patch was a big jolly bear of a man with a past that seemed to have happened more by accident than design. He spoke of his military career with some pride, but a persistent knee injury had ended his service to Her Majesty, so he'd found himself in the service of Baxter instead. His former employer had been a typical mercenary leader, he said, he'd never had too many complaints about his leadership when they'd been abroad. Indeed, Baxter had saved the lives of his troops in Helmand, which was why, when he'd gone full despot in the wake of the storm, none of them felt able to challenge him. He spoke about the events of the past week with a mix of bewilderment and shame, and seemed pleased with the prospect of a new life, where his skills might actually be put to good use.

'What's in the care package?' Leon asked.

'Um,' Susan replied, picking through its contents, 'We've got toiletries, some tins of beef ravioli and spaghetti hoops, and some instant coffee sachets.'

'Party time,' Leon replied. 'Give me the tins and I'll rustle us up a feast.'

'Good plan, Batman,' Susan replied, and squeezed Leon's behind as he went.

'You two, eh?' Patch said.

'Looks that way,' Susan replied.

'Holy shit,' came a call from the kitchen.

The three of them sprang up at once and ran into the other room. Leon held up two wine cases, replete with bottles.

'Wahey!' called Patch.

'There's more too,' Leon said.

'We should share it with the others,' Susan said.

Tom nodded.

It felt good to be going door to door with pleasant news, and every door which opened to them precipitated a big smile at the sight of wine. There was enough for two bottles per house. He and Patch became the good wine fairies, dispensing mirth and joy as they went.

'There's no answer at the last house,' Patch said as he returned with an empty box. 'I left it by the door for them.'

'Nice one,' Tom said. 'Hopefully Leon's finished with the grub by now.'

They went back in the house, which was now lit by candlelight. Susan and Leon were in the kitchen.

'Honey, we're home,' Tom called.

'Hiya,' Susan replied. 'We've got good news and bad news.'

'Good news first.'

'Good news is the stove is gas, the bad news is that the gas cut out, so the food is lukewarm at best. Oh, and the chimney is blocked, so there's no way to have a fire. But dinner is served.'

Tom was too hungry to care what it was, and wolfed his bowlful of lukewarm tinned pasta down. Once the sounds of hastily consumed food had abated and the wine had been poured, the four of them sank into their respective sofas.

'I've missed wine,' Susan said.

'You had wine a few days ago,' Leon said.

'Yes, and I've missed it ever since.'

'I miss telly,' Patch said. 'DVD box sets.'

'I tell you what I don't miss,' Susan said. 'Getting up at four in the morning for a double shift.'

'I don't miss the news,' Tom said. 'You worry and fret and care about everything that's going on in the world, until the world is reduced to what you can see, hear, and touch.'

'I dunno, I'd be pretty comforted by a newspaper right now, telling me what's going on,' Leon said.

'What good would it do?' Tom asked. 'We have no idea what caused this, or how widespread it is. We have no idea if it's the whole wide world or the North of England, and none of it matters right now because I've had a tin of processed ravioli that somehow managed to be the tastiest thing I've ever eaten in my life.'

'You know,' Susan said, 'I look back to before the storm, how I lived my life, and it's like all I did was fill time. Going to work, living for the weekend. Passing time between sleeps. Sometimes I'd feel noble going to work, contributing to society, or when I read a classic novel. Sometimes it'd be trying to watch an entire season of *24* in less than a weekend, but either way, I was just... filling time. Now it feels like the complete opposite. Everything I do now is about survival. Even sitting here with you three, it feels vital somehow.'

They continued in this vein well past the point at which the wine had ended, until Tom remembered they were camped out in Patch's bedroom. The big man's eyes were starting to droop, so Tom made his excuses and headed upstairs, followed by Leon and Susan, who were already giggling between the sheets by the time Tom crawled between his own.

It was refreshing to wake the next morning without the litany of aches and pains that had become a staple of Tom's waking moments for the last few weeks, although there was the stomach churn and dull headache from the wine to contend with. He dressed without a creeping sense of dread for once, and he had started to entertain feelings of positivity as he went downstairs in search of something halfway edible for breakfast.

'Morning,' he said to the stirring Patch on the sofa.

'Aye,' he replied, sitting up and stretching.

Patch was topless, and Tom noticed that the man had a hell of a physique, albeit one with its fair share of battle scars. A long, angry red line stretched up his back where it met a mess of other scar tissue. Tom gave the man a smile and went through to the kitchen, where he found a packet of bacon flavoured crisps. He reasoned it was close enough to a breakfast to count. He was about to munch down when he heard a scream from outside.

'What was that?' Patch asked.

'No idea,' Tom replied. He headed to the door and opened it, but outside everything was calm.

'Did you hear something?' Susan asked, appearing from the stairs with Leon behind her.

Tom walked into the crisp morning air. He looked around, but all he could see were the inhabitants of the other houses checking their windows. A few doors opened and people stepped out.

At the far end of the street another door opened and out ran a woman, her clothes red with blood. She started to scream, caterwauling inhuman sounds of utter terror. She ran towards the centre of the street. Someone managed to catch her before she went sprawling.

Patch appeared alongside him and they both ran toward the empty doorway, Tom's heart pounding. He should have stopped for a weapon, he realised, but carried on running regardless. He reached the door at the same time as half a dozen others, and had to barge his way to the front. Nobody seemed to want to take the first step in. Nor did Tom, for that matter. Patch tapped him on the shoulder and the two of them went in together.

The beige carpet of the hallway was dotted with bloody footprints: a single pair, headed to the door. The screaming woman, possibly. Tom took a step into the lounge. It was dark, the curtains pulled tightly closed, and there was no real light in the room. Even so, Tom could make out the two decapitated corpses sat upright on the sofas, crude carvings visible in their chests under a sheen of wet blood. In the centre of the room were two poles that displayed the heads.

'Holy shit,' Patch said, beside him.

Tom couldn't move, completely unable to process the scene before him. His eyes adjusted to the dull light, and more horrifying details became visible. Their eyes were gone. Empty sockets remained. Their mouths were sewn shut.

He tried to say something, to do anything other than stare at them, but he couldn't. It felt like his head was shutting itself down.

The taste of bile rising in his mouth was enough to get him moving again, and he turned towards the door, but not quick enough. He emptied his breakfast over the carpet.

'Let's go,' Patch said.

They headed back down the corridor, a wave of numbness spreading over Tom. A crowd had gathered by the door, and Tom had to fight past their questions to get outside where he could take great deep lungful's of air. People pushed him, trying to find out what was going on. He looked over at Patch, but the big man stared at the floor, colour drained from his face. Voices chattered around him and he felt his head spinning until Leon's voice cut through the others.

'Alright, for fuck's sake, give the man some room!'

People backed away from him.

'Nobody go in there,' Tom said.

'Why?' someone asked. He tried to focus on the floor to stop the spinning.

'Butchered,' he replied, his voice struggling to make it out of his mouth.

There were gasps around him. He noticed blood on the soles of his shoes and vomit on his jeans.

'Who has?' Susan asked.

Tom shook his head. Enough questions.

'Where are they?' came another voice. Petr headed towards him, fists clenched by his side, double chin wobbling with rage.

'Who?' he asked.

'Baxter's men,' he replied. 'Where the fuck are they?'

'You don't think?' Tom asked.

'Of course I fucking well think,' Petr yelled. 'You'd have to be a complete fucking idiot not to think it. They wanted payback.'

'Now, wait a second,' came another voice. It was Patch. It was as though everyone suddenly realised he was there. The crowd around him dispersed. 'I didn't fucking well...'

'You fucking liar!' a woman yelled.

'Wait a fucking second,' Leon said behind him. 'Patch was with us last night, and the other one,'

'Ralph,' said the angry woman, her eyes full of hate.

'He was in one of the other houses, right?'

Tom tried to remember who Ralph had gone off with last night, and to see if he could see any of them in the crowd. Everyone was casting about looking for them.

'Oh, Jesus,' someone said to nobody in particular. Tom tried to count up who was there, but there was too much noise in his head. Had he made a terrible mistake? He looked over to the doorway of the house where they'd found the bodies, his stomach tying itself in knots. Sure enough, there were two bottles of wine outside the door.

He tried to remember when he and Patch had given out the wines. Tom had stopped to speak to quite a few people along the way, could Patch have had time to go in and commit such awful atrocities? He was a professional soldier, God knew what he could do given such a short window of time.

Another door opened and everyone turned. Ralph and two women emerged from the house at the far end of the street, each wearing a confused expression. They were still walking over when Petr turned to Patch.

'What did you do?' he asked, getting right up to Patch, who held his hands up to indicate he didn't want any trouble.

'Nothing,' Patch replied. 'I drank wine and went to sleep.'

'Is everyone accounted for?' Susan asked, but nobody answered her. They were too busy glaring at either Patch or Ralph, who'd arrived with the two women and seemed to be cottoning on that something bad was happening.

'What's going on?' one of the women asked.

Before Tom could reply, Petr lunged forward at Patch, catching the soldier unawares. Patch fell back awkwardly, with Petr following him down. They hit the ground and Petr started punching Patch, delivering furious blows to his head and body. Patch was trying to defend himself but evidently didn't want to retaliate, his arms trying to block the blows, but not returning fire.

Tom and Leon leapt forward and tried to grab Petr's shoulders, but he shrugged them off, before winding back one of his arms and throwing his not insubstantial weight behind another punch. Patch managed to throw an arm up to block it, and having had enough, threw a punch of his own, which sent Petr sprawling.

Patch sprung up, his face covered in blood, an ugly cut above one of his eyes. He loomed over Petr, who was struggling to regain his composure.

'Stay the fuck down,' Patch bellowed, and the man complied.

Everyone stood rigid, waiting for the next move.

'Look,' Tom said, his arms outstretched. 'Patch was with us last night, evidently Ralph was in his house. We need to calm down a second.'

'Just because you three have forgiven these bastards doesn't mean the rest of us have,' a woman called out.

'Just because you haven't forgiven them doesn't mean they did anything,' Susan replied.

'Sorry,' Ralph said, 'what's happened? What am I supposed to have done?'

'There's been a murder,' Tom said.

'Who?' Ralph asked.

'Stacey and Neil,' a woman said. 'We think, anyway.'

Tom's stomach turned. Two more dead on his account, two more whose names he hadn't known. 'There are two bodies,' he said, and the woman who had called out the names sobbed.

'Where were you last night?' the angry woman asked Ralph.

Ralph opened his mouth to answer, but nothing came out. The reverberated crack of a rifle shot echoed through the street. There was a gaping hole where Ralph's throat had been, and blood splattered over everyone stood around him.

There was a moment of stunned silence, until another shot punctured it.

Somebody screamed.
Everybody scattered.

Chapter Twenty-Two
As Each End Looms and Subsides

The sound of birdsong brought Jen out of her sleep. She opened her eyes and saw a ray of bright morning light bursting through the crack in the curtains. She wasn't fooled for a second. Outside the window there might be birdsong and sunshine, but there was also death, misery, hardship, and pain.

Every bit of her ached as she stretched her muscles and sat up from the sofa. She looked on the floor at her two companions. They'd started off separately in makeshift beds on the floor, but sometime in the night Mira had crawled in with Sam, the two of them curled up together.

For the first time in days, she thought of Daniel. She missed waking up next to him and wondered if she'd ever wake up next to someone again. Daniel seemed like a lifetime ago now, but still she reproached herself for not having thought of him more.

Her two charges stirred and woke as one, and Sam looked surprised to have Mira nestled in with him.

'Good morning,' the young girl said. She smiled.

Jen felt like an intruder on their intimacy. She started to get up, intending to leave them alone, but then Sam remembered she was there and sat up, his face flushed with embarrassment.

'Morning,' Jen said. 'Don't get up. I'm going to see what the breakfast options look like.'

She gathered her discarded jeans and pulled them on, which served only to heighten Sam's embarrassment. He looked away, his cheeks reddening. She stood, flashed them both a smile and went through to the kitchen, shaking out her limbs as she went.

The smell in the hallway was still pretty bad, but the broken window in the front door had at least allowed a little bit of fresh air to mingle with the stale.

The cupboards they had picked bare the night before had not magically replenished themselves in the night, but she looked anyway, hopeful the daylight might illuminate some hitherto unseen treasure trove of food. No such luck was forthcoming. The best the cupboards yielded was a tin of pine nuts and half a bag of flour.

'Isn't it infuriating when people don't stock up for the apocalypse?' said a voice behind her, making her jump.

She whirled around. Behind her, perched on the counter with the bravado of a man holding a crossbow, was a man holding a crossbow. The arrow contained within pointed at her chest. He was curiously anonymous looking, bedecked in as bland a jumper as Jen could recall ever seeing. A smirk of satisfaction played across his face.

Stay calm.

Instinctively her hand went to the knife drawer, but before she even got halfway to it he raised the crossbow slightly to let her know the error in judgement she was about to make.

Well, he hasn't killed me yet. That's a start.

'What do you want?' she asked, trying to keep as even a tone as she could.

'Me?' he replied, laughing. 'Nothing. Well and truly nothing. I have the whole world. Seems enough to me. Sit.'

He motioned to a chair. Jen moved slowly over to it and sat, never taking her eye off the bolt in the crossbow.

'Good girl,' he affirmed.

'Okay,' she said, trying to keep the battle between fear and anger internalised, as well as an irritation over the good girl comment. 'So, why are you chasing my friends and I across the countryside with a crossbow?'

He smiled.

'My friends and I? Bravo! I was beginning to think there was nobody else who appreciated the English language.'

'You're killing people because you're a grammar Nazi?' she replied.

The smile left his face. 'A man must have a hobby,' he said.

I don't like those eyes.

He smiled again, but there was nothing happy behind it.

'You see,' he continued, 'the end of the world has given me the opportunity to finally pursue my life's dream. I like killing people. Well, I always assumed I'd like it. All that trying to live in the world got in the way, but ever since I knew the end was nigh, I've been getting stuck in. It's a lot of fun, I have to tell you.'

The smirk was back. Jen's stomach turned. She willed Mira and Sam to stay in the lounge, but at the same time she knew the only way she was going to survive this conversation was to keep it going as long as possible.

'Why?' she asked.

'That's a good question. What's your name, by the way?'

'Jen.'

'Well, Jennifer, I'm not sure exactly. From a biological standpoint, I assume I have some kind of chemical imbalance, the figurative "screw loose" in my head. Whether it's born of some kind of genetic disorder, emotional trauma, or a good old-fashioned blunt force to the head as a child, who knows? The long and short of it is that I get an immense satisfaction from watching others in pain.'

Jen's stomach lurched again.

'Of course, before the storm I could only dream of indulging my fantasies. I tortured the odd animal, but nothing more severe than that, save for a predilection for a certain shade of adult entertainment. But once I knew what was coming, I was free.'

'What do you mean "once you knew what was coming"?' Jen asked.

'Ah, you caught my little baited hook there did you?'

A wide, smug grin spread across his face, and Jen became so furious at him she forgot for a second he was a murderous psychopath and not just some odious little toad.

'Oh, you mean I picked up on the blatant fishing for a question that you dangled in front of me? Yes, as a matter of fact I did, you little prick. Now are you going to tell me what you meant?'

The grin disappeared.

'I'd be careful if I were you, Jennifer. I've killed people for a lot less.'

They stared at each other for a second, his dark eyes holding hers like a tractor beam. Her heart pounded until finally he broke off contact and smiled.

'What do you know about coronal mass ejections?'

Jen recalled something from a documentary she'd seen last year that had talked about solar flares, but she figured the man in front of her wasn't expecting her to know anything about it, so she shrugged.

'Solar flares, in the more common parlance,' he said. 'You see, before the storm I was a physicist, not too far away from here. My job was to watch the sun, looking for solar storms. They can really fuck with electrical systems you see.

'In 1989 a solar storm wiped out power to Quebec. The power station there got overloaded. As you can imagine, the more dependent on technology we became, the more paranoid governments were about solar storms. Our planet has been battered by solar storms for its entire existence, but most of the time we barely notice, unless you happen to be watching the Northern Lights.

'I was part of a team at the University of York trying to find ways of predicting solar storms, which, I can tell you, was fascinating. But two days before the storm I started to see something... unprecedented. The ancient Chinese astronomers a thousand years ago reported sun spots far in excess of what we've seen in recent years, but not even they saw anything on this scale. Usually a sun spot you'd see on the surface would be massive in our terms, between five and ten times the size of Earth. Not all of these become solar storms, but some do. You can imagine my surprise when I saw a sun spot which would register as around a thousand times the size of Earth. If you had known about it, you could have walked outside and seen it with your naked eye, although you would have gone blind if you looked too hard.

'As you can imagine, the scientific community went into meltdown. It was building to a coronal mass ejection of unprecedented scale, and if it came to Earth, who knew what havoc it would cause? People were talking in hushed tones of a return to the Stone Age, but I knew it would be even more severe than that.

'I saw my chance. Once the CME burst out and it was clear it was coming, I knew I had one chance to, well, shall we say, "live the life I was meant to live". What would it matter in the long run, anyway? Everyone was almost certainly going to die.'

He laughed.

'How could you know that?' Jen asked.

'Call it instinct. I went to go and speak to a priest about it, but, well, he annoyed me. I figured I had around twenty four hours to indulge my fantasies, and I tried every dark whim that had ever taken me.

'In the process I felt a power, an incredible feeling that all this, everything that was about to happen, was for me. I felt like the butterfly breaking out of his chrysalis, except it was the whole world that broke apart to allow my rebirth. In that case, how could I be killed? I knew I was to be spared.

'As the storm came and people dropped like flies around me, I survived. Once the storm had passed, the Lord saw fit to give me back just enough people to keep myself entertained.'

He leaned in, his eyes sparkling with life now.

'You see, this is my world now.'

A shiver ran down Jennifer's back.

You're about to die.

'I didn't catch your name,' she asked.

'Ewen.'

'Do you smoke, Ewen?' she asked. He looked puzzled for a second.

'I...'

'Do you smoke?' she asked again.

'What does that have to do with anything?'

'Do you?'

'I... yes, as a matter of fact I do.'

Jen gave a little laugh.

'You weren't chosen by God, Ewen. You smoke. Everyone who has survived so far is a smoker. You survived the storm by sheer coincidence.'

Ewen stepped back and looked at her in horror. She felt sure she'd feel the weight of his rage any second. She hoped Mira and Sam would make a run for it and get away from this lunatic. Instead of pulling the trigger, he gave a hollow little laugh.

'Well done, Jennifer,' he said. 'You've solved the final part of the puzzle.'

'Good for me,' she replied.

He ignored the sass. 'Those of us who knew the storm was imminent were entranced by what would happen when it did. There were so many crazy theories from rational scientists that it was as though the whole scientific community started sounding like the crazy people you'd hear on the bus.

'Some said the seas would boil, some said the atmosphere would burn clean off the planet and we'd suffocate. Nobody envisioned what actually happened, but you've made sense of it.

'Human beings are electrical systems at our core, and the storm acted like a giant electromagnetic pulse, blowing every single electrical appliance in the world working at that moment. But, as I suspected, it also overloaded the electrical system that is the human brain.

'I couldn't work out why anyone had survived at all, but it was the smokers who survived. Addiction, especially nicotine addiction, alters the pathways of the brain. It alters the way your brain works, and it meant the storm gave us headaches and not much more.'

He gave another little empty laugh.

'I don't know which the greater tragedy is,' Jen said. 'The fact you're killing people with impunity, or that you're arguably the one person who could solve the mystery for everyone out there who has survived, and lead us out of this nightmare to start to rebuild. But instead, you're pissing it away so you can live out the idiotic fantasies of a killer.'

A darkness crossed his face and he moved forward, getting close to her.

One step closer and maybe I'll try to take that crossbow off you.

'Rebuild?' he snarled. 'Rebuild what? The decaying bloated civilisation of man? The world of cruelty and pain and loneliness every single one of us had to struggle through every day of our wretched lives? The civilisation hell-bent on destroying the planet we inhabited with no thought to the billions of other species forced to share an existence with the most perverse, greed-ridden plague?'

He leaned in again, and Jen realised the point of the crossbow bolt was inches away from her throat. She looked into his eyes and saw nothing behind them.

'Have you noticed how much of the animal kingdom survived the storm, Jennifer? This was no random attack of chance. This is the second great flood, and I'm Noah.'

'Which is it, Ewen? Is it divine providence, or the electrical network peculiar to the human brain?'

'God moves in mysterious ways.'

The door to Jen's right burst open. Sam stepped into the kitchen. His eyes went wide at the scene before him. He'd no doubt heard raised voices and had rushed in, but before he could even take a step into the room, and before she could start to form a warning in her throat, Ewen turned to Sam.

There was a flash of movement.

Sam stopped. He looked down at the shaft protruding from his chest. His eyes filled with panic.

His body slumped to the ground.

'Sam!' she screamed.

Jen whirled around, but Ewen was already gone, the back door closing behind him. Rage exploded through her veins. She wanted to give chase, to find him and beat the life out of him until it ran red over the field, but instead she turned to Sam, fell to her knees and held his body.

She felt for a pulse, but there was nothing.

Mira appeared at the door, still dressed in the pyjamas she'd slept in. At the sight of Sam's body in Jen's arms, she let out a noise somewhere between a scream and a howl. Jen ignored her as she tried to shake Sam into staying with her, trying to meet his eyes as he faded away.

It was too late. She looked up at Mira.

'He's gone,' she said.

'No,' Mira moaned.

Jen stood and pulled the girl into a hug, hoisting her away from the body, feeling her top sticking to her where Sam's blood had seeped through it.

What the fuck are you going to do now?

'We have to move,' she said to Mira, but Mira didn't respond. She stared at the body laid on the floor, mouth open. She started to hold a hand out to touch Sam's face, but pulled it back.

Jen caught the smell of smoke before the first tendrils made their way under the frame of the door Ewen had left through.

He's trying to burn you out.

She hauled Mira up, the young girl giving another moan of despair as she did so. Jen had no doubt she would choose to stay here and die with Sam given half the chance, but she was not about to lose them both. She didn't think she could take that. Half-carrying the girl under her arm, she barged back into the hallway.

The fire had been set at the rear of the house, and as she threw open the front door, into the trap she knew had been set for her. The first arrow buried itself into the doorframe an inch from her face, but the second one made contact, grazing her side. The burst of pain told her it had hit home, but she didn't have time to think about it. The arrows brought Mira around, and her sobbing stopped.

She pulled them back into the doorway. The house behind them filled with smoke. They needed to make a move, and make it fast. Jen chanced a poke of her head out and saw a septic tank, walled in with concrete barriers. It sat, nestled at the foot of a hill, on the far side of the house from which she presumed the arrows were coming from. Getting there would mean running into the open, but they were shit out of other options.

'Go,' she hissed, and the two of them ran along the wall. Jen expected another hit at any second, but she hauled herself and Mira behind the low concrete wall.

'You're hurt,' Mira said, panting.

Jen looked down at her side, where her blood soaked her top now and mingled with Sam's. There was a deep gouge below her ribcage, but it didn't look too bad. She just needed to make it stop bleeding.

Sam.

She thought of his body, laid out on the kitchen floor, looking so much more a child in death than he had in life. Now his body was likely burning in the fire set by his murderer. The flames were nearing the point of consuming the whole structure. She couldn't stay here. She looked around again, trying to work out a possible escape route. There was no sign of Ewen.

He's out there somewhere, scrambling for higher ground, trying to get the advantage.

There were hills around them and a long flat valley behind them. She guessed he'd want them in the hills, so he could play out his hunter stalker fantasies.

What I need is a car.

Those dead bodies upstairs hadn't lived in the middle of nowhere without the means to get about. On the far side of the burning building she made out what looked like the front end of a car, barely visible through the heat haze of the fire.

That'll do.

'Mira,' she said, grabbing the girl by the shoulders and staring deep into her eyes. 'I'm going to run for that car, okay?'

Mira stared back, dumbfounded, and Jen guessed she'd gone into shock.

'Stay here,' Jen shouted.

She took a deep breath, stood and started to run.

Her side shot bursts of pain with every step, and she hadn't gone more than a few feet when she saw an arrow flash in front of her. It came from her left, so instinctively she ran closer to the wall and the flames licking out of every pore of the house, hoping the smoke and heat would obscure his view of her.

The car was a large Land Rover, de rigueur for the country life and sturdy enough for her needs, but as she neared it she realised she'd made a huge mistake.

She had no keys.

The likelihood was that the keys were smouldering in the hallway of the burning house right now, perhaps in a little ceramic bowl that had shattered in the heat. She closed her eyes and put her hand on the handle and gave a tug.

Her heart leapt as the door swung open, and she dived into the driver seat. An arrow glanced off the window, not even chipping the glass, and a burst of triumph soared through her.

She looked down, and her heart soared further. The keys were in the ignition. She looked over to where the arrows seemed to have come from, and sure enough there was Ewen standing at the top of a small hill, smirking at her. Their eyes locked for a second; his smile widened and he turned away, back toward the front of the house, the way she had come.

Mira.

Quite forgetting she couldn't drive, she threw the car into gear and sped forward, then stalled the engine.

For fuck's sake, Jen.

She turned the ignition and eased the pedals, and this time she moved forward. She put her foot on the gas and spun it round, pointing past the flames and back toward the only thing in the world she now cared about.

She saw movement to her right as she cleared the house. He was ahead of her. She peered through the windscreen and the smoke and saw Mira, sat, knees tucked up to her face.

He's going to get there first.

She honked the horn, and pulled every lever she thought might do something. The wipers went on, trying to clear water that wasn't there, but so too did the headlights, full beam.

The horn and the lights did the trick, and Mira looked up, dazed. Jen screamed at her to move. To her left, Ewen ran at full pelt. His crossbow was slung over his shoulder now, and he had a large knife in his hand, a serrated army-style job that caught the sun and glinted through the heat haze. He bore down on Mira, a fierce grimace locked across his face.

She stepped on the gas and saw Mira's eyes widen in horror, not at the approaching maniac, but the accelerating Land Rover. Jen waited until the last second, not knowing if it was going to work, knowing that if it didn't, there'd soon be two more bodies to be cremated in the house.

She yanked the handbrake up, ignoring the mechanical howl that accompanied it, hit the brake and spun the wheel.

Ewen realised at the last second what was happening, but too late. Jen watched the fall of his face with great satisfaction. He tried to jump away, but the side of the Land Rover smashed into him, sending him into the air and toward the burning house.

Her head smashed into the steering wheel as the car came to a final stop. Her vision danced with stars. A sharp pain erupted in her neck, but she didn't have the luxury of doing anything more than make note of it.

Add it to the list.

She leaned over and opened the passenger seat and screamed: 'Get in!'

Mira leapt into the seat.

'You fucking got him!' she yelled.

Jen smiled, even as the first trickle of blood from a gash on her forehead crawled across her skin. She didn't look back, she put the car into gear and went.

They rode on for a few miles in silence, both of them alone with their thoughts for the first time. Jen tried to focus on the road, but all she kept seeing was Sam's body lying there on the floor of the kitchen, the crossbow bolt sticking out of his chest. Next to her, Mira stared out of the window, tears streaming down her face.

Jen didn't know what she was doing with the car. She must have done some damage back at the farmhouse, because soon it started making a wrenching clank. A moment later smoke appeared under the bonnet, and power started to drain away.

'Shit it!' Jen shouted, pulling the Land Rover over to the side of the road. She hit the steering wheel a few times. She checked the rear-view mirror, half-expecting Ewen to be standing right behind them, but it was empty tarmac.

It was early afternoon, the sun high overhead, the storm of the previous night replaced by clear skies and burning heat.

'We should probably get out,' Jen said.

Mira nodded, but neither of them moved.

'Jen?' Mira said quietly.

'Yeah?'

'Thanks,' she said and flashed Jen a smile.

Jen's heart broke. Mira got out and Jen did the same. They looked at each other, Mira still dressed in pyjamas that were unrecognisable under soot and blood. Mira's hair looked like a fright wig, and Jen could only imagine what a mess her own face was now. Neither of them had a single possession left in the world. Mira burst out laughing, and Jen followed suit.

'Good morning, by the way,' Jen said. 'I don't think I've actually said that yet.'

'Good morning to you, too,' Mira said, and did a little curtsy.

'What do you want to do today, Mira?'

'Oh, I dunno. Let's have a girly day.'

'Deal.' Jen said, and pulled Mira into an embrace. 'Just me and you now, kid.'

Mira nodded, and when she pulled away she blinked back tears. Jen looked around. The area was completely deserted.

'Come on,' she said. 'Let's go find us some houses and a change of clothes. Food too.'

They walked for a good hour without seeing anything. Jen was starting to worry about their lack of food and water, when they saw a few houses by the side of the road up ahead. It took them a further half an hour to reach them, by which point Jen felt faint.

It was a small hamlet that looked like it had stood unmolested since the storm. The first house was locked up good and tight, but the door to the second swung open.

The now familiar stench hit them as they entered, but they were too tired and hungry to care. They walked past the two rotting corpses in pastel easy chairs and went into the kitchen, where they closed the door to attempt to block out the stench, somewhat unsuccessfully.

The cupboards were well stocked, and amongst the rotting produce in the dead refrigerator were a few bottles of water. They guzzled them down and set about making a functional and quick meal in silence.

Once they'd finished they made their way upstairs and into the bedrooms, where the wardrobe of the woman decomposing in the living room provided them both with clothes that more or less fit them. They emptied the man's gym bag and stuffed more jeans, tops, trainers and hiking boots into it. Jen cleaned the blood from her face and examined the wound at her side. She had been lucky; the crossbow bolt had opened a heavy gash underneath her ribs, but not done any more damage. Mira found a first aid box and they dressed the wound the best they could, before throwing the rest of the kit into the bag.

'Classy stuff, this,' Mira said.

'Yeah,' Jen replied, still not quite at peace with the grave-robbing element of her ongoing survival.

Mira went to the window and stared out.

'Do you think he's dead?' she asked.

Jen didn't answer. A distant rumble from the road had appeared at the periphery of her senses, and her heart leapt into her mouth. She moved to the window and peered out, trying to keep herself hidden from view. A few minutes later two vehicles came into view; another Land Rover and a minibus. Both looked full.

Don't stop.

The thought came unbidden, and Jen wondered if her trust in people was now utterly broken. All she knew was she wanted the convoy to keep rolling by.

The Land Rover in the front slowed down as it went through the hamlet, but as it cleared the last house, it sped back up. Jen let out a breath she hadn't even realised she'd been holding. She looked back at Mira, who hugged the wall, terrified.

'They're gone,' she said quietly.

'What if they come back?' she asked, peering down at the now empty street.

'Well, we can't stay here, anyway. We need to get moving again. Let's raid the cupboards and get out.'

Ten minutes later they were out the door again, carefully this time. The sun wasn't so high in the sky any more, and Jen realised that wherever they headed, they needed to find somewhere to sleep tonight. She looked along the road. It was either follow the convoy, or back along the road to the farmhouse. No option really. She hoisted the bag onto her shoulder and headed in the same direction the Land Rover and minibus had gone. They'd look to deviate as soon as they could, just to be sure.

The bag was heavy, and Jen marvelled at how good at scavenging they'd become. They'd been in the house for two hours, maximum and they'd managed to wash, change, eat a meal, and strip the place of anything that might be of use to them. They had blankets, clothes, water, food, toilet roll, the first aid kit, and a box of medicine.

It's bloody heavy though.

They stuck to the shadows as they moved through the hamlet, Jen unable to shake the feeling they were being watched. She knew it was probably nothing more than paranoia, but given recent events, she was willing to give paranoia free reign.

They reached the end of the houses, beyond which lay empty road and rolling hills. The sun threatened to dip behind them, the evening approaching and the temperature starting to drop. They paused.

'What do you want to do?' Jen asked.

'Not stay here,' Mira replied.

They walked for half an hour with no sign of anything but farmland, seeing no movement beyond the occasional livestock. Fog started to creep over the hills. They moved off the road, walking along an old fence line, where the tall grass gave them an element of shelter from both visibility from the road and the growing chill in the air. The soft ends brushed Jen's cheeks as she walked. It was slower going, but they both felt safer.

They had walked the best part of a mile, by Jen's reckoning, when ahead of them there was a sound, like an engine struggling to turn over. They stopped and ducked into the grass. A few minutes later the convoy trundled past them again, back towards the hamlet. They waited until the tail lights were completely gone from view before moving. Mira stood first.

'Thank fuck we left, eh?' she said.

Jen stood up and hoisted the bag over her shoulder. She stared back the way the convoy had gone.

'Let's go,' she said, and turned away. 'We'll walk a bit further, and if we can't find anywhere soon, we'll sleep by the roadside. The grass will give us cover.'

There were no more houses. The road wound back and forth so many times Jen worried they must be heading back in the direction of the farm house. Soon they were walking in the light of a full moon, and eventually Mira asked to stop. They got out the blankets and some food, and were about to crack open a tin of spaghetti hoops when Jen felt the hairs on the back of her neck stand up.

Freeze.

She motioned to Mira to stay quiet and both of them moved silently to the ground, while Jen cleared half a view back to the road through the grass.

Footfalls came from the grass behind them, barely perceptible. They passed no more than twenty metres away from Jen's hiding place, until they reached the road. They stopped. Jen could hear her heart jack-hammering in her chest, but didn't dare lift her head to see. The footfalls started again, heading back up to the hamlet. As the walker moved into view Jen heard a sharp intake of breath from her companion and felt her own skin crawl.

Ewen.

He was no more than twenty metres away from them, on the road, the crossbow slung over his shoulder, rifle held by his side, and what looked a lot like a meat cleaver tucked into his waistband. He struggled, limping, his face set in a grimace. Jen wished she could take more pleasure in that. Beside her, Mira was perfectly still, her eyes trained on the road.

He stopped. For half a second, Jen expected the rifle to be raised and pointed at them. There was nothing she could do about it if he did. He cricked his neck, adjusted his weapons and hitched up his jeans, then he was on his way again.

They watched him until he was out of sight, then waited some more to be sure.

'He should be dead,' Mira said eventually, her voice little more than a whisper. 'He should be dead and burning up in that fire.' Her fists were clenched, shaking, by her side.

'He's gone now,' Jen said. 'Let's get as far away from here as we can.'

'What about those people?'

'We can't help them.'

'We have to.'

Jen grasped the young girl's shoulders. 'No. I feel bad for them, and I hope together they can stop him, but we don't know them. Who's to say they even stopped? Maybe they carried on going. Maybe they're like him. Maybe he's with them.' Her own hands were shaking now. 'I am not going to lose you too, Mira. If we go back there, we die.'

Mira nodded, and stood back up, dusting herself down. They headed up the road, Jen checking behind her every twenty steps or so to make sure they weren't being followed.

Chapter Twenty-Three
Break the Static

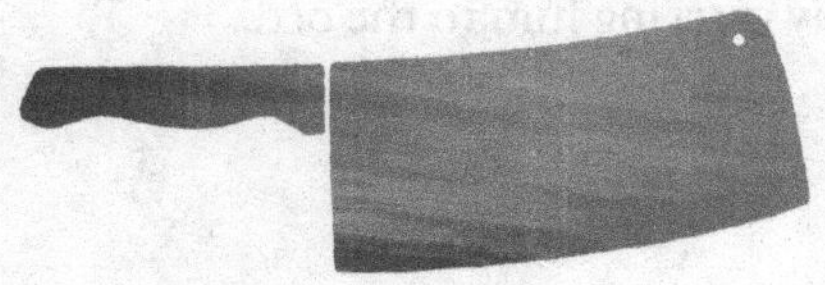

Hours of nothingness had tempered Burnett's rage, but only slightly. After Tana had helped him out to the car he'd vented for a few moments. He now sat in the passenger seat looking at the busted remnants of a side mirror.

They drove around the village until it got dark, and found an empty house to sleep in. They ate a wordless meal together and went back to their rooms. Burnett stared at the ceiling, anger coursing through him.

He woke the next morning barely able to move. He stumbled downstairs, where Tana was already preparing food.

'Jesus,' he said when he saw Burnett. 'You look terrible.'

Tana examined Burnett's wounds. Burnett watched the Samoan's face and gathered it must be pretty bad, but said nothing. He noted the big man's gentle hands on his skin in some distant part of his mind, but there was sharp pain and it was all he could do to keep hold of his consciousness.

'Sorry,' Tana said. 'It's pretty fucked up, Detective.'

Burnett nodded.

'I can rest up in the car,' he said. 'You're driving.'

'We're not going anywhere today.'

'We have to,' Burnett said. 'We have to find him.'

'How about this, you go back to bed and get a few more hours' sleep, and I'll get you up at lunchtime. I'll try to find a map and draw up a plan of where we should look for him. Okay?'

Burnett nodded. He hated the idea. He wanted to be out there, but what the hell was he going to do if he caught up with the killer in this state? He climbed the stairs, although Tana did most of the work, practically carrying him to the bed.

He wasn't surprised when he woke up to find the sun coming up on a new day. He cursed Tana, but knew the man had taken the right course of action, too. He felt much stronger. Once Tana stumbled downstairs and found Burnett fixing breakfast, he tried to apologise, but Burnett cut him off with a raised hand and a smile.

'Let's get on the road,' he said.

'We'll catch the bastard, don't you worry,' Tana said, as he drove on through hamlets and villages, looking for their quarry.

If nothing else, the events in the warehouse had hardened his partner's resolve. The jovial ex-rugby-playing bobby-on-the-beat who'd somehow survived the apocalypse trapped under his boss's corpse and preferred pies to police work was gone. His eyes never stopped searching, expecting their bogeyman to jump out at them at any second.

'You okay?' Tana asked.

'Me?' Burnett replied. 'Fine.'

'Well, if you start to feel weird or anything, you let me know.'

'Weird how?'

'Well, a dog bit you. Looked to me to have gone pretty feral, so if you start foaming at the mouth I might have to leave you by the side of the road to go and chase the other puppies.'

'Fair point,' Burnett replied. 'I feel fine.'

That wasn't true. He wasn't anywhere near as weak as he had been, but he couldn't feel much in his arm except a burning, and he could barely move his fingers. He didn't much care though. He was back on the hunt.

'Shit,' Tana said. 'Well we're back where we started again.'

Burnett looked out through the windscreen and sure enough, there was the warehouse.

'Pull up,' Burnett said. 'Maybe he doubled back.' He didn't much believe it but they went through the motions anyway, scouring the warehouse, which had accumulated the further stench of two extra days' decomposition, but Burnett could tell instantly that the killer hadn't returned.

They got back in their car.

'What now?'

'Let's try a different direction. We've not seen another person in days. We might have some more joy if we can find people to talk to. Maybe they've seen something. I dunno.' He was grasping at straws now, but didn't know what else to suggest.

Soon the industrial landscape gave way to scattered houses, then to endless greenery. Burnett wondered how long it would take for nature to reclaim total dominion over all humanity's creations. How long before the whole world looked like those eerie photos of abandoned towns and fairgrounds people had been so fond of sharing on Facebook? The total numbers of survivors, in this part of the world at any rate, seemed bafflingly small. How could any sense of civilisation, technology, or industry ever come to be again? He wondered if the world would ever again know the hum of a power station. Hundreds of years of progress wiped out in a few moments.

His eyes hurt. He was weak. Even now, closing his eyes in the passenger seat as his exhaustion threatened to overtake him, the face of the killer danced before him, and he snapped back to full alert.

Something caught his attention out of the corner of his eye.

'What was that?' he asked, sitting bolt upright.

'What was what?'

'I saw someone. Or people, I'm not sure.'

'Where?'

'Back there, on my side.' Burnett said. Tana started to slow down and check the rear-view mirror. 'No, don't stop, keep going until you find a place to pull up.'

'Was it him?'

'I don't think so.'

'You sure you saw something?'

'No.'

Tana pulled the car up at the side of the road. Burnett got out and stared back up the road. There was a petrol station maybe half a mile in the distance, barely perceptible through a light fog. Was that all he'd seen? He was sure he'd seen a head pop up.

'Shit,' he said to himself.

'Maybe you dreamed it,' Tana said, getting out of the driver's side and staring back up the road. 'Wishful thinking.'

'Maybe,' Burnett replied. 'I want to go back and look anyway.'

'You're the boss,' Tana replied, getting back in the car. 'At this point all I'm doing is driving around aimlessly anyway, so what's the harm?'

Tana turned the car round.

'Slowly,' Burnett said, and Tana obliged. 'We don't want to spook them.'

'Because stopping, turning around, and crawling back slowly looking for them is going to put them right at ease.'

Burnett didn't reply. He pulled his gun out, checked the magazine and the safety, and moved it into his good hand. Not that it was ever really his good hand. He was a shit shot at the best of times, as likely to shoot himself in the foot as find his target, but it felt bloody reassuring to hold.

He stared out the side window, inspecting the thick bushes for movement. Maybe he'd dreamt it. Fuck it, at least they could go to the petrol station up ahead to try to find some kind of food. He was sure Tana thought the same.

It took them ten minutes to crawl along the road to the Esso garage. There was no sign of any movement. Burnett cursed himself for falling asleep in the first place and for deluding himself.

'Maybe the pumps will be working,' Tana said as he pulled onto the empty forecourt.

'I doubt it,' Burnett replied. 'No electricity.'

Tana pulled up alongside one anyway, stared at the pump for a moment, tapped the side forlornly and gave up. Burnett looked around, but the only movement was the evening breeze through the trees.

The door to the shop was open, and the smell of death hit them right away. Its source was the decaying corpse sat behind the counter, dried up and feeding some full-looking bluebottles which arced lazily around him. Poor sod had spent his last night on earth sat in a no doubt uncomfortable chair selling fags and sweets to drunks, stoners, and lorry drivers. He hadn't even deserted his post for the apocalypse.

How long had it been, Burnett wondered, since that night? How long had he now been running around after one man, ignoring the apocalypse around him? Best not pick at that scab, he thought.

'Fucking hell, if there's a Ginsters stand in here I'm going to eat so much pastry that I'm going to burst,' Tana said.

'Given it'll have been sitting unrefrigerated in a hot room for a fortnight or so, swelling and bursting is not out of the question,' Burnett replied.

'I think you're underestimating the great Ginsters pastie,' Tana said. 'Ginsters remain edible for entire millennia. They aren't made of food, but some kind of immortal science sauce.'

Burnett surveyed the empty shelves. 'I don't think you have to worry about that anyway.'

'Oh, bollocks.'

The whole place had been stripped bare, the shelves bereft of goods, save for a few bits and pieces discarded by whomever had gotten here first. Burnett wondered if this was the work of a singular person of exceptional foresight, or an endless trail of hungry survivors who saw this lonely petrol station as a beacon of hope and crisps on an otherwise desolate road.

'Piss,' he said, half to himself. 'At least tell me there's some cigarettes left?'

'Let's have a look,' Tana replied. He wandered over to the kiosk, where the shutter was down on the cigarette cabinet. He leaned over, avoiding the corpse.

As he pulled the shutter up, a fist flew up from behind the counter, connecting with Tana's jaw and sending him flying backwards.

Burnett had his gun drawn and pointed at the counter before he even realised what was happening. Tana picked himself up, looking shocked, but otherwise fine. He fumbled for his own weapon.

'Hey!' Burnett called out. 'Who the fuck is back there? Come out now, with your hands up.'

'Really?' came a woman's voice from behind the counter, dripping with incredulity. 'That's what you're going with? Come out with your hands up?'

'Well, yeah,' Burnett replied.

'What, like you want us to believe you're police?'

'As a matter of fact...'

'Bullshit,' the woman countered. 'Look, you and your friend get back in your car and piss off, yeah?'

'Why exactly should we do that?' Burnett said.

'Well, because there's nothing here worth taking as you can already see, and we've got a shitload of paper towels, lighter fluid and matches back here.'

'Let's go,' Tana said, dusting himself down.

'In a second,' Burnett replied. 'Miss, we'll leave in a second. We mean you no harm, I promise. But before we go, we're looking for a man. Mid-thirties white male, brown hair, glasses. Anonymous seeming but with a serious nasty streak. Don't suppose you've met anyone like that on your travels?'

The question was met with silence, and after it hung in the air for a moment unanswered, he turned to leave.

'Wait,' the voice called.

Burnett stopped. There came the sound of muffled, heated discussions behind the counter. Evidently the woman behind the counter was not alone.

'Look, we're putting our guns down, okay?'

He laid his pistol on the ground and motioned for Tana to do the same. Burnett raised his hands. Two women appeared from behind the counter, armed with deodorants and lighters. One of them looked to be no older than fourteen.

'Hi,' he said.

Chapter Twenty-Four
Sorrow's End

Tom's teeth knocked together as he slammed into the cold road, and his mouth filled with the coppery taste of blood. There was another crack, a scream, another crack, and something exploded above him, showering him in glass. Feet ran in all directions. Bodies littered the floor. Ralph's exploded trachea oozed his life over the road.

Another crack.

He had to move. As soon as another crack reverberated he jumped up and ran. The shots seemed to be coming from the far end of the street, so he made for the nearest house. The murder house. He wasn't alone. Three others huddled in the hallway, not wanting to go further in to the house, but not wanting to walk into the line of fire, either.

'Who's shooting?' a woman asked behind him.

He shrugged.

'What's going on?' came another voice, and Tom saw one of the three was Petr, still holding his bloodied nose.

'I have exactly the same information as you,' Tom said.

He turned and looked back out into the street. It was clear now of all but the dead, everyone else had scarpered. There was no sign of Leon or Susan.

'The shots were coming from down there,' the woman said, pointing back to the other end of the hamlet. On cue, another crack came from that direction, the bullet shattering a window across the street. A howl of pain or surprise followed. Someone had thought a window would provide adequate shelter from a gunman and had had that preconception challenged.

'What do we do?' Petr asked.

Tom felt like shaking the man.

'We wait,' he replied instead.

'Wait for what?' Petr asked, evidently not satisfied with the response.

'Given that we don't have any weapons and someone out there is shooting at us, I guess we wait to see what his next move is.'

'Oh, great plan,' Petr replied, rolling his eyes.

Fuck it.

He grabbed Petr and slammed him against the wall.

'Right,' he shouted, his face getting right up to Petr's, 'I've had enough of you bitching and moaning. What do you think? Perhaps you'd like to go out there and ask him what he's up to? Or perhaps we could use you as a human shield while we charge for the minibus? Let me guess, you want to avoid making any decisions for yourself, but you're not happy with any of the decisions anyone else has made, right?'

Petr stammered something, but Tom didn't let him speak.

'I've fucking well had enough of it. You don't like the way I'm doing things? Well kindly fucking fuck off.'

He let go of the man. For a second he thought the bigger man might launch himself at Tom; he just looked indignant for a second, then ashamed. He said nothing.

Tom returned to the door frame.

Petr did have a point. Standing around waiting to be shot was hardly the world's best ever plan. He tried to think of ways out, but each plan in his head played out like the level of a computer game which ended with him lying on the floor in a pool of his own blood, with 'Game Over' or 'You Lose' hovering over his corpse in bright red lettering.

He poked his head out of the doorway a little. The crack came quickly and he pulled his head back, in time to see a chunk of brickwork behind him splinter and explode in a puff of smoke. His heart raced.

He looked around for Patch. The best course of action here was to turn to the battle-hardened veteran of Afghanistan. He chanced another look, and saw the splayed legs of the man whose company he'd enjoyed the previous evening in the street, his body face down on the tarmac.

'Could you see anything?' the woman asked.

Tom shook his head. The gunman could be on the first floor of one of the houses which stood on the bend, giving the shooter a perfect view of the whole street. Tom could perhaps try and work his way round the back of the houses and sneak up on whoever it was, but that didn't sound like something he'd actually want to do. If the gunman was alone, he might have a chance, but what were the odds of that?

He scoured the houses opposite, making sure his head never popped into the gunman's line of sight. His heart soared when he saw Leon and Susan, huddled in the doorway two down from the house opposite, their backs to the gunman. Leon waved a sarcastic little wave.

Relief flooded through him. He wasn't alone. If it weren't for the homicidal maniac, he could have run across the street and given his old friend a bear hug.

Leon started gesticulating manically at him, trying to convey his own plan, but Leon didn't know anything about hand signals and Tom knew even less about reading them. Their attacker sensed the communication and the wall next to Leon exploded as a bullet hit it, sending Leon reeling back in surprise and falling into Susan's arms.

Tom got the gist of it though: head round the back and take the shooter by surprise. He tried to signal an acceptance back to his friend, but Leon was too busy studying the chunk of brickwork that had once been right by his head.

'What's going on?' the woman beside him asked.

'I think we're going to try and ambush him round the back,' Tom replied.

None of his three hallway companions said anything. Petr looked intently at his shoes.

'Look,' Tom said. 'That's the plan. I'm going round one way, Leon and Susan will go round the other way, and maybe we can sneak up on the bastard. Maybe we'll get shot. If you want to join me, join me. If you want to stay here, stay here. If we die, get out of here as best you can and look after yourselves. Okay?'

Nobody stepped forward to offer their support, which was as much a blessing to him as it was to them.

'Good luck,' Petr said weakly.

Tom moved through to the back of the house, making sure not to linger over the sight in the living room. The kitchen led out onto a small, unkempt garden with a back fence. He stepped out into the garden, expecting a shot to ring out at any time. He couldn't see the street.

He moved through the garden and hopped the fence. After the carnage of the main street, the path behind the houses was eerily quiet. Beyond the path there was nothing but open fields and woodland, and Tom felt exposed. He realised he didn't have a weapon to defend himself with.

Good planning, idiot.

He moved on. He looked out at the fields almost wistfully, but remembered Leon would be waiting for him. No running off into the trees.

Every footfall sounded to him like a thundering herald of his approach, but no traps were sprung, no gun barrels appeared from windows. The path bent round and he slowed, not sure exactly which house he needed to go into.

Another crack rang out, but now it sounded muffled and distant. There was no movement near him, so he edged himself to the rear of the house he guessed held their assailant, his eyes never leaving the windows.

He saw movement out of the corner of his eye and froze. It was Leon and Susan making their way round with the same measured crawl he'd used. They locked eyes and raised eyebrows in acknowledgement. They too were bereft of weaponry, and Tom wondered exactly what it was they were expecting to achieve.

Susan signalled Leon and Tom to go in, while she stood guard at the gate.

They entered the back garden and moved to the door. Every instinct in his body screamed at him to turn and run away, but he stood mute as Leon put his hand on the handle and turned.

Inside, the house was silent and dark, but Tom could make out the outlines of a particularly nice kitchen. His first instinct was to find as big a knife as he could, and worry about bringing a knife to a gunfight later.

He stepped forward, but something moved in the shadows before him. It swung forward and connected with the side of his face. He fell back, his hand lashing out to grab anything. There was a counter, but he managed to do was slam into it, his side taking the brunt of the force. Pain flared up his ribs.

He tried to see who had attacked him, but his eyes weren't yet adjusted to the darkness. He heard movement. Leon was knocked back too, his head slamming into the wall. He crumpled to the floor.

Tom struggled to get to his feet, but he was barely able to get moving before their assailant was on him again. He pulled Tom to his feet and punched him in the stomach. He fell again, winded.

Their assailant moved into the light. Tom struggled to reconcile the brute force being meted out to them with the nerdy-looking bespectacled man wearing a woollen jumper who dispensed it. Leon tried to stand and lunge at the man, only to find their assailant much quicker. The man in the jumper brought his arm round in a chopping motion, the side of his hand met Leon's throat and Leon stumbled back again, his hands pulling at his neck, His face filled with panic as he struggled to breathe.

Tom tried to get to his feet again, but couldn't. He looked up and noted with not an inconsiderable amount of terror that the man now had a hammer in his hand and was making his way over to him. He fell to the floor and let out an involuntary whimper of fear.

The hammer came down.

Tom's knee erupted in pain. He scrambled back, each movement bringing fresh shards of pain and terror. He was lifted up and panic overtook him. He felt warmth spread throughout his crotch. The knowledge of his impending death did nothing to diminish its terror.

He was taken into another room and dumped roughly into a chair. He tried to get up, but his hands were bound with plastic that cut into his wrists. The man left for a moment, and returned with Leon, pulling him by his leg as his friend still fought for air through his bruised windpipe.

'What do you want?' Tom asked, but the man's only reply was a nasal chuckle.

He lifted Leon into a chair and tied his hands and legs as he had Tom's. Tom and Leon were now facing each other. Tom saw his own panic reflected in the eyes of his best friend, who started to take in air in deep, rasping breaths.

The man disappeared. Tom looked around him. The room was lit by three small candles, which flickered softly, revealing a spacious living room, almost identical to the one they had been in last night. There was nothing out of the ordinary, save for a duffel bag, out of which protruded the tip of a crossbow.

He pulled at the plastic ties, but that made them cut deeper. He looked down at his knee, but through his jeans it looked normal. He smelt his own urine and went back to panicking.

The man came back, carrying the knife block Tom had been so intent on finding when he entered the house. Leon let out a moan of despair.

'Okay, chaps,' the man said, his voice high and nasal. 'We're going to play a little game.'

He made a show of choosing a knife, holding it out for both to see.

'What do you want?' Tom asked again, his voice sounding far more desperate than he wanted it to.

'The good news,' the man replied, 'is that I'm not torturing you for information. By the looks of you, you'd have nothing to offer me. Unfortunately for you both, that doesn't mean I'm not going to torture you. But you can be safe in the knowledge there's nothing you can give me that'll stop me.'

He grinned. Tom's stomach turned.

'Why are you doing this?' Leon asked, his voice little more than a croak.

In a flash the man was on him, the blade of his knife held to Leon's eye.

'I haven't finished!' he roared, then stepped back. 'You two are going to torture each other, for my amusement. Whoever can present me with the face of his friend will live. Refuse, and you both die.'

He cut the ties binding them to their chairs, threw the knife to the ground and stepped back, pulling a pistol out of his waistband and brandishing it at them both.

Neither of them moved. Tom looked across at his friend and they both started to laugh. Tom couldn't help it, the laughs came thick and fast in his chest.

'You going to cut my face off, Tom?' Leon asked him.

'Er, nope. Not today, anyway. You?'

'Um, I dunno. Probably not though.'

They both laughed again. Tom tried to control the sudden onset of hysterical giggles, but it was like the time Leon had gotten him stupidly high, made him do poppers, and phone for a pizza. He couldn't control the waves of laughter, which turned to racking coughs.

'Mate,' Leon said, turning to their attacker, who still held his gun up at them both, but who'd lost a bit of his swagger. 'Look, you can do what you want to us, and I'm sure you will. I'd rather you didn't, obviously, but if you want us to turn on each other you're about three years too late.'

Their attacker continued to smile his rictus grin, but his eyes flickered between them, unsure.

'That man there,' Tom said, finally gaining control of himself, 'has had to physically carry me home when I was so drunk that I couldn't get a taxi because I'd been sick in my own hands. He's put up with me making him watch every single episode of *The West Wing*, twice, and since the apocalypse he's saved my life more than once. So you can go fuck yourself.'

The man laughed. 'So very cool, eh? Well if you don't want to play, so be it.'

He strode back between them both and picked up the knife. He raised it high and buried it in Leon's chest.

'Your loss,' he said to Tom.

He laughed, the sound mingling with Leon's dying howl and Tom's own screams.

Chapter Twenty-Five
Long Grass

After hours of walking along the same deserted country road, both Jen and Mira had run out of conversation, having long ago exhausted the topics of the pain in their feet, the gnawing in their stomachs and the dryness in their mouths. They'd drunk what water they had, and dumped the heavy bags, deciding they were too much to walk on with.

Jen didn't think it was possible to walk this far in England without seeing so much as a farm or a house, but here they were, trudging for mile after endless mile along a road whose surroundings alternated between light woodland and sparse farmland.

She looked back at Mira walking a few paces behind her. The young girl looked close to collapse, her expression fixed, eyes glazed and distant. Jen had to do something.

'You know what I miss?' she asked. 'Baths. Baths and books. I used to be able to lose an entire afternoon in a bath with a good book. Now I feel like I haven't washed in so long there might be things living actually on me. I may well have developed moss.'

Mira gave her a half smile. 'We'll find somewhere, won't we?'

She looked up at Jen with those great big dark eyes and Jen's heart sank. She stepped in and gave the girl a cuddle.

'Of course we will.'

A thin mist obscured the way ahead, but she was almost sure she could see a structure through it. She'd thought that a few times now, but every time they'd come within touching distance of whatever mythical building she thought she'd seen, it had turned out to be nothing.

'We'll be fine, honey.'

They walked on, and as they got closer, Jen could see it might be a real building. Five minutes later the Esso sign became a beacon, drawing them in. Mira even gave a startled giggle when she noticed it, and their footsteps quickened as much as they could, given the blisters on their feet.

They were so focused on the garage that the car was upon them before they even heard it, a sleek saloon that approached, at speed. They didn't have time to react to it, let alone get out of sight from the road. They stood dumbstruck, waiting for the car to pull up and some fresh hell to fall out of its doors.

It went straight past, paying them no heed.

'Holy shit,' Mira said.

'We should get off the road,' Jen said. She turned and watched the car as it carried on down the road towards the edge of visibility. She was about to let out a sigh of relief when, a mile or so away, the distance straining the limits of her eyesight, the glare of brake lights flared through the fog.

'Let's go,' she said. They moved away from the road, working their way through the rough grass. The going was rougher, but the renewed threat and the proximity of the petrol station spurred them forward. A few minutes later they were at the back of the building. Jen turned and looked back down the road. Sure enough she could make out the car working its way back to them, crawling along the road in search of them.

'Let's get in,' Mira said.

The door was open, and Jen's heart sank as they got into the shop. The shelves were mostly bare, aside for a few bottles of water. They grabbed a bottle each, pulled the top off and downed it.

'Chocolate!' Mira exclaimed, discovering a lower shelf of untouched confectionary. An entire Wispa magically disappeared before Jen's eyes. Mira smiled at her, her mouth full of chocolate. Jen looked at her goofy smile and remembered she was still a child.

'They'll be here soon,' she said.

She noticed the dead cashier sat at his post for the first time. The shutter to the cigarette stand was down.

'I've got an idea,' she said.

She jumped the counter and pulled up the shutter, being careful to avoid the dried out corpse. Whoever had ransacked the shop had taken their favourite brand, but most of it was still there, endless shiny packets of nicotine. More importantly, there were boxes of lighters, matches, and even lighter fluid.

'Ooh, do we have time for a fag, do you think?' Mira asked.

Jen laughed. 'Are there any toilet rolls or anything?' she asked.

'Um,' Mira replied, looking around. 'Oh, yes!' She threw a four pack of Andrex at Jen.

Jen looked out the window and saw the saloon pulling up outside.

'Shit,' she said. 'Get behind here, quick.'

Mira saw the car and jumped the counter. Jen grabbed a lighter and some fluid, pulled the shutter down and crouched down out of sight. Mira crouched down too. Jen grabbed her hand. The door opened, and Jen heard what sounded like two people enter.

'Fucking hell, if there's a Ginsters stand in here I'm going to eat so much pastry I'm going to burst,' came a first voice, deep and booming.

'Given it'll have been sitting unrefrigerated in a hot room for a fortnight or so, swelling and bursting is not out of the question,' another voice replied; another man's, quieter than the first. Neither of them sounded like the man who'd killed Sam.

'I think you're underestimating the great Ginsters pasty,' the first voice said, 'Ginsters remain edible for entire millennia. They aren't made of food, but some kind of immortal science sauce.'

'Yeah well,' the other voice replied. 'I don't think you have to worry about that anyway.'

'Oh, bollocks.'

Jen let out her held breath, as quietly as she could. They didn't seem to be looking for them, but how could she know? She tried to picture the two men, but all she could see were two Ewens, stood leering on the other side of the counter, waiting for her to show herself.

'Piss,' said the second voice, disappointed. 'At least tell me there's some cigarettes left?'

'Let's have a look.'

Every muscle in Jen's body tensed. One of the men moved closer. He leaned over the counter, his thick black jaw just visible, his hand stretching out to the shutter in front of her.

Without thinking, she summoned all the force she could muster and punched upward, her fist connecting with the man's chin. She felt his teeth knock together through her hand and he fell backward, out of sight. Mira was so shocked at Jen, she actually gave a startled laugh. Jen felt adrenaline coursing through her, and an instant regret. The sound of a gun cocking echoed in the room.

What the hell did you do that for?

'Hey!' one of the men called out. 'Who the fuck is back there? Come out now, with your hands up.'

'Really?' Jen replied, astonished anyone would actually say that, and still filled with the adrenaline that overrode her fear. 'That's what you're going with? Come out with your hands up?'

'Well, yeah,' the man replied.

'What, like you want us to believe you're police?'

'Well, as a matter of fact.'

Jen's heart soared.

Police! Real life actual police officers!

She looked at Mira, who shook her head.

Of course. Why the hell should I trust them? They could be in full-on bobby outfits and it wouldn't mean jack shit.

'Bullshit,' she replied. 'Look, you and your friend get back in your car and piss off, yeah?'

'Why exactly should we do that?' Burnett said.

Jen grabbed a roll of toilet paper and the lighter fluid. Mira pulled open a pack of deodorants stashed under the counter.

'Well, because there's nothing here worth taking as you can already see, and we've got a shitload of paper towels, lighter fluid, and matches back here.'

'Let's go,' the other voice said. He sounded pissed off.

'In a second,' the other man replied. 'Miss, we will leave in a second. We mean you no harm, I promise. But before we go, we're looking for a man. Mid-thirties white male, brown hair, glasses. Anonymous seeming but with a serious nasty streak. Don't suppose you've met anyone like that on your travels?'

The words dropped on her like an anvil. Was this real hope, or another trap? She looked at Mira, her face full of panic. She heard the men turning to leave.

Decision time, Jen.

'Wait,' she called.

'What are you doing?' Mira hissed

'Trust me,' Jen said.

'I do,' Mira replied. 'It's them I don't trust.'

'Look, we're putting our guns down, okay?' the man said.

Jen gave Mira and imploring look, and the young girl responded with a resigned shrug.

'Give me a deodorant,' she said, and Mira handed her one.

She stood up, holding a lighter and the spray can in front of her, and Mira did the same. Before them stood two men, a huge black guy rubbing his jaw, and a dishevelled-looking middle-aged white guy, who had his hands held aloft. A gun lay at each of their feet.

'Hi,' the second man said.

'Hi,' she replied.

'I'm Detective Burnett, and this is PC Tana,' he said, his hands still raised.

'You're sticking with that story, are you?' she asked.

'I have my ID somewhere if you don't believe me,' he said, although he made no motion with his hands to get it.

'Was it him you were you looking for?' Jen asked.

'What do you mean?'

'Back there, on the road,' she said. 'We were walking along the road when you drove past, and you turned round and came back. What were you looking for?'

'Yes,' he said. 'We've been looking for someone. There's a killer on the road.'

'Is his brain squirming like a toad?' Jen replied with a laugh. The faces of both the would-be policemen and her travelling companion showed their confusion. 'Not Doors fans? Never mind.'

'As I said,' Detective Burnett continued. 'There's a lunatic out there and we've been trying to find him. You know, like policemen do? You two are the first people we've seen in days, so we wanted to know if you knew anything.'

She paused. 'We know where he was last night,' she said.

The detective looked at his partner.

'Listen,' he said, lowering his hands. 'I'm not going to make you come with us, not if you don't trust us, or if you don't want to. But it would be a big help if you could show us exactly where you saw him.'

'We'll go with you,' Mira said immediately. 'On one condition.'

'What's that?' Burnett replied.

'When you catch him, you let us watch you kill him, or better yet we get to do it ourselves.'

Jen stared at her companion and felt her jaw go slack. Mira's face was set with a grim determination she'd not seen before.

'Fair enough,' Burnett replied. 'You ladies fancy a drive?'

Chapter Twenty-Six
Landmine Spring

Tears streamed down Tom's face, stinging the fresh cuts on his cheek.

'Please,' he said, his voice barely making it through burst lips and bleeding gums. 'Please just let me go.'

He had no idea how long he'd been there. The only thing he knew for sure was that he'd never understood the concept of pain before, not truly. Even in the weeks since the storm, he'd experienced nothing to compare with the slow raking of dull blades across his chest, the extraction of healthy teeth, or the sight of his best friend's corpse sat in front of him.

All these things and more he'd now experienced between blackouts, but whether they'd been over the course of hours or days he could no longer tell. He thought back again to the headless corpses they'd found in the house. He no longer feared that end. He just wanted an end.

'What was that?' the man replied.

Tom stared back with as much intensity as he could muster. Over these hours or days he'd learnt a fair amount about his attacker, beyond his obvious penchant for sadistic violence. His name was

Ewen, and he just loved to talk. Tom preferred the talking to the pain.

He'd heard speeches on how the world had ended, on how much Ewen liked to torture animals, on how many people he'd killed – even speeches on particle physics. He didn't care what Ewen talked about, those were the moments when he could gather his strength, apart from the one occasion when Ewen had delivered a rambling speech about his father's sexual predilections whilst cutting slices into Tom's arm.

'So what's next, Thomas?' Ewen asked. 'Maybe we could cut out your kidneys, eh?'

'Or maybe,' Tom said, 'you could just go fucking fuck yourself.'

That earned him a punch to the face. He closed his eyes for a second, and when they opened he was still staring at Leon's body across from him, a deeper wound inflicted than anything he'd endured since.

'How about this?' Tom continued. 'How about I tell you about the man you killed? A man who never so much as hurt a single person, who managed to survive the end of the world, only to be killed by an emotionally-stunted loser who's mad at his parents.'

Another punch, this time to the stomach. Another to the face, reopening an earlier cut and sending a fresh stream of hot blood into Tom's eye.

'Don't think for a second you can get me angry enough to cut short what's coming to you,' Ewen said, leaning forward.

'I have no intention of letting you kill me, you scabrous wound,' Tom replied, spitting blood from his mouth. 'I still fully intend to make you pay for what you did to my friend. I just haven't worked out how to do it yet.'

Hubris, perhaps, but it made him feel better.

If he was going to escape from this, he had no idea how. His hands were bound again. His solitary hope had been that the rest of his travelling companions would burst in en masse and overwhelm Leon's killer, but if that were going to happen, it would have happened a long time ago. More likely they'd taken the opportunity to flee, and who could blame them? Survival first. He just wished he'd thought of that.

'Do you think this is why you survived?' Tom asked. 'The end of the world rolls around and you decide that's your cue to whittle the numbers down even further?'

'Why not?' Ewen replied.

'Well, because it's bloody stupid, for one thing.'

Ewen snorted.

'What,' he sneered. 'You think I should be out there helping people? What people are these you think I should be helping? Braying idiots wandering around like headless chickens? People so stupid they'd actually put a wastrel like you in charge?'

He picked up a long blade and inspected its edge. 'You want to know what I've seen since the storm?' he asked.

Tom didn't, but he didn't much want him to use the knife on him either.

'These people, they weren't selected by a higher power to rebuild the world. They're idiots. Their first thoughts are to pillage and plunder and scramble around like rats, picking away at what's left of the world with no thought of the future. Do you know what's going to happen a year from now, once all the food reserves are gone? All these people will die. Not one of them will think to till the earth, grow food. Useless scavenging pigs, the lot of them, and they need to be put down like the filthy vermin they are.'

He leaned forward, grinning, wielding the blade.

'I call bullshit,' Tom said, and the grin disappeared. His strength was waning now, but he carried on. 'It's bullshit. You can try and dress it up however you want, but you and I know the real truth. You kill people because you like to kill people. You're a sick bastard, and you know it. You waited until the world of police and justice and prisons was gone, because as well as being a fucking lunatic, you're also a fucking coward.

'You think the people who survived won't make it? Fine, go and tell them what they need to do to survive. Be a leader. But don't pass off your own personal issues as some kind of noble act, because it just won't wash.'

He spat blood at Ewen's feet again to underline his point. He stared at the lunatic's dark eyes and saw his expression harden.

The knife slid into his shoulder. A jolt of pain unlike anything he'd ever felt coursed through him and the grin returned, inches from his face. He tried to struggle, but to no avail, the plastic ties cut deeper into his flesh. Every shake seemed to tear chasms in his shoulder muscles. He stopped, exhausted.

'Fuck!' he shouted. 'Just fucking stop it, will you!'

'Are you going to beg?' Ewen asked.

'Fuck you, yes, I'll beg if it makes any difference,' Tom said.

Ewen laughed. 'Not really, no.'

Tom felt the blade slide back out of him. Ewen moved away. Tom was spent, and the prospect of any more pain seemed more exhausting than terrifying. Somewhere in his head a switch went off, and all thought went out of him, all hope evaporating with the tears on his cheeks. He was going to die.

Ewen returned, a pair of pliers in his hand. He lifted Tom's head by the hair, his face so close Tom could smell his rancid breath.

'Come back to me, Thomas,' Ewen said.

Tom whipped his head forward and grabbed Ewen's nose in his teeth, biting down hard, teeth sinking into flesh. Blood filled his mouth and ran down his chin. He didn't stop.

The air filled with Ewen's blood-curdling roar, but Tom didn't let go, even when Ewen remembered he had pliers and started lashing out with them.

Ewen pulled away and there was a tearing sound. He stumbled backwards, his face a bloody, gaping wound.

Tom spat the contents of his mouth on the floor, and saw a disfigured lump of flesh land by his feet. He wasn't disgusted by it, he was proud. He could die now knowing he'd affected some small measure of revenge.

Ewen squealed, horrible sounds uttering from his nose as he tried to scream. From somewhere there was a crashing sound, and movement. Tom closed his eyes and waited to die.

Chapter Twenty-Seven
Stuck Pig

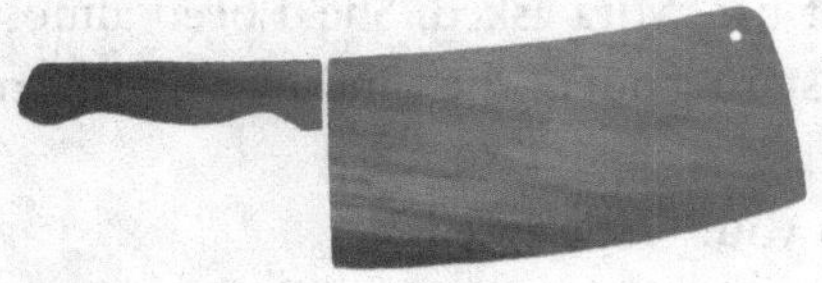

As the car pulled into the hamlet she couldn't see any movement, which wasn't to say nothing had happened since Jen and Mira had walked away from there. At least four dead bodies were in the street, and Jen knew for certain they hadn't been there the last time.

'They look new,' Tana said from the front seat, echoing her thoughts.

'You loaded?' Burnett said to his partner as he slowed his approach.

Tana nodded, pulling up a shotgun from a duffle bag at his feet.

In the twenty minutes since they'd met, they'd swapped potted histories of the man who had terrorised them since the storm. Jen told them everything he'd told her in the house, his theories about the storm, and what had happened to Sam. Tana detailed their chase around rural North Yorkshire for a man who killed for sport.

Somehow, the knowledge that Ewen's rampage had been so widespread was a comfort to Jen, although not as much of a comfort as the two policemen in the front of their car, or the duffel bag full of guns in their laps.

As they pulled into the hamlet, Burnett slowed.

Jen spotted movement in one of the houses. 'In there,' she said. 'People.'

Burnett pulled up outside the house. Through the front window, they saw a group of people in heated discussion. As one, they noticed the sudden appearance of the car and whatever discussion they were having tailed off.

'Shall we?' Burnett asked. He loaded his own gun.

'What about us?' Mira asked. She'd been almost silent for the entire journey, staring out of the window while the rest of them had caught up.

'What about you?' Tana asked.

'Don't we get a gun?'

The men both stared at Mira for a second, then looked at Jen.

'I'm with her,' she said.

'Do you know how to use one?' Burnett asked.

'I think I can work it out,' Mira said.

Burnett nodded to Tana, who pulled out two small pistols and checked they were both loaded.

'Here are the safety catches, okay?' he said, pointing to two small buttons on the guns. 'Press them and you're good to go. Just don't shoot us, okay? Or yourselves.'

Jen nodded and took one.

Mira took the other. 'Thanks,' she said, with a smile. It was the first one Jen had seen in a while.

They got out of the car. The people were still staring through the window like they'd landed from Mars. The sight of the guns seemed to stir them, and they started to scatter.

Burnett opened the front door and walked in. The rest of them followed. The front room was full of people trying to hide and realising they didn't have time. Jen scanned their faces and saw Ewen wasn't there.

'Who are you?' a woman asked. She alone had stood her ground.

'Police,' Burnett replied.

'Or, we used to be,' Tana added.

'What's going on?' Burnett asked.

'There was someone shooting,' the woman replied. 'Some friends of ours went in to try to stop it. They've not come back out.'

'She won't let us leave!' called another voice.

'She wants us to go after them!' called another.

'They risked their lives for you!' she screamed back at them.

'That was their choice!' called the first voice.

Burnett held his hands up and the room fell silent. Jen could see why he made a good police officer, he held the room completely.

'Where?' he asked.

'The far end of the street,' the woman said.

Her red eyes told Jen she wasn't ready to give up on her friends yet.

'How do you know he's still there?' Tana asked.

'There hasn't been shooting for hours, but we've heard...' Tears welled in her eyes.

'Why the hell didn't you go in there?' Jen asked the rest of the room.

This many people storming one person. It would have been easy. The first woman shook her head with anger, then shot Jen a look of shared frustration.

'Let's go,' Tana said to Burnett, and the four of them turned to leave.

'I'm coming with you,' the woman said.

The rest of the room fell silent. Most found something suddenly fascinating about the carpet below them.

'I'm Jen,' she said, holding her hand out.

'Susan,' the woman replied, taking it.

'I hope your friends are okay.'

'Me too.'

They went back into the street, the two policemen moving forward with their guns drawn, scouring the street for movement, working their way to the end houses.

'How long?' Jen asked Susan.

'Hours. I nearly went in on my own, but...'

Jen put her hand on the woman's shoulder, and tried to offer a reassuring smile. The woman took a deep breath, steeling herself for whatever was about to come.

As they reached the front door an unholy scream wrought the air, unlike anything Jen had ever heard before, and her stomach turned. Tana stepped forward, raised his leg and kicked the front door with all his might. It gave on the second attempt, bursting open in a hail of splinters. The sound of the scream increased. The reek of putrefaction hit them, but they ignored it and moved into the hallway. There was a closed door to their left. Burnett grabbed the handle. He twisted and pushed the door open.

The scene inside was dizzying in its lack of sense. A corpse sat in one chair, an ugly wound in its chest. Opposite him, another man sat strapped to another chair, the evidence of torture clear to see all over his body. Blood covered his face and his mouth twisted in a grimace of satisfaction.

In front of them, barely recognisable, was Sam's killer.

He wheeled around in a panic, unsure of his footing and falling to his knees. His face was a gaping wound. He, not the man tied to the chair, was the source of the inhuman howl.

Susan let out a wail from behind Jen. The gun fell to Jen's side. Burnett and Tana's did the same.

Mira's did no such thing.

Jen heard the catch of the young girl's gun as she strolled past her, raised the weapon and put it to the temple of the kneeling man. Without hesitation, she pulled the trigger, dashing Ewen's brains across the far wall.

The noise stopped immediately, leaving only the echo of the gunshot to ring out across the room. Ewen's body fell forward with a thud, and the five of them stood in stunned silence, staring at it, until a voice broke the quiet.

'If any of you feel like getting me out of this, I'd really appreciate it,' the man in the chair said, his voice muffled by the state of his mouth

They turned and stared at him.

'Seriously, I'd really appreciate it.'

The spell broke. They rushed forward to help him.

Chapter Twenty-Eight
The Doorway

The hospital was abandoned, save for the rotting corpses that filled most of the rooms, but the medicine and bandages were still there. Susan and the others had rushed Tom there in the back of a full car after a wispy angel had ended his torment with a bullet to Ewen's head.

Yet again, he found himself nursed by Susan. She was no longer the carefree spirit who had brought him back from the brink before. Now she alternated between caring for him, blaming herself for failing to rescue him, and weeping for Leon. He was with her on that last one, but as for blaming herself, he told her continually not to. She'd explained how she'd tried to convince the others to join her in rescuing them, but it had been hard enough getting them not to flee completely. She'd only managed that by convincing them they'd be shot as soon as they set foot outside.

He kept expecting Leon to breeze into his room, somehow unscathed, to start teasing him about being in a wheelchair, but it was never going to happen. It had taken him a few days to truly realise it.

Not that he was short of visitors. The rest of his group had been so fawningly apologetic for letting him rot in that room that they fussed endlessly, bringing him food and water and anything else they could scavenge up for him.

Then there were the two cops and the two women who had rescued him. The five of them spent most of their time together, common survivors of the man called Ewen. They spoke of the future, of Ewen's theories, of Jen's, but never of the things they'd been through. There was no need.

Over the weeks that would follow, their many visitors would bring word of the outside world, of other survivors found. They told of small communities, some desperate to protect their little slice of this new world, others open to all and eager to rebuild.

There were rumours of a new government forming in Birmingham from the ashes of the old one. There were others of London aflame. Tom barely listened. He was still trying to convince himself he wasn't tied to that chair.

Every now and again, though, the five of them would sit talking and he would get a small glimpse of a future not filled with pain – of a new camaraderie. He just wished he wasn't so alone now.

He sat up in his bed and stared out of the window. The storm clouds were gathering again, but in places the winter sun was breaking though, little shards of light to go along with his gossamer tendrils of hope.

KEEP READING

The story continues in
SLEEPWALK CITY

Surviving the end of the world was just the beginning
Now the battle for control has begun

SCAN ME

Leave a review

I really hope you've enjoyed reading *Blood on the Motorway*.

If you did, the nicest thing you could do for me right now is to leave a review, on this or any of the books you've enjoyed. Reviews are absolutely crucial to discoverability, and social proof. If you could take a second to rate and review this at the store of your choice, I'd hugely appreciate it.

Thanks,

Paul

Leave a review

JOIN THE HOLLOW STONE

Join my reader's group
and be the first on the planet
to hear about new releases,
and get exclusive content
you won't find anywhere else.

SCAN ME

Author's Note

Blood on the Motorway was my first book. Like most first books, it took the best part of a decade to write and resembles the initial idea about as closely as The X Factor resembles true artistic integrity.

The initial seed of an idea has remained throughout. I was a child raised on a steady diet of John Wyndham and Stephen King, and in later years I was hugely inspired by Robert Kirkman's The Walking Dead. Kirkman spoke in his intro to the first book about getting to the end of every zombie film ever made and wondering what happened next. I felt the same way about every end-of-the-world tome I ever came across.

With Blood on the Motorway and its sequels, I wanted to explore that same idea, except removing the zombies altogether. Come the end of the world, I wanted to know what would happen when the real threat to the survivors was their fellow man. So were born the stories of Tom, Jen and Burnett. Over the course of this novel and its sequels the driving force is that question: What happens next, for them and the wider world?

In terms of getting the book from that idea to the finished article, there are hundreds of people who have helped to nudge me in the right direction, but I'd like to call out just a few:

My wonderful wife, Ellen, who has to put up with a hell of a lot of abandonment, so I can lock myself in the utility room and tap away madly.

My editor, Ro Smith, who put pay to the myth that you can't polish a turd.

Then there's Will, Lydia and Libby, all of whom read through various drafts, made notes in the margins and offered helpful critiques.

Lastly, there's the people behind two podcasts: Johnny, Shaun and Dave of SPP; and Joanna from The Creative Penn. You've never met me, and you probably aren't reading this, but if it weren't for you all this would never have happened.

START THE CHRONICLES

Plague. Murder. Unrest. Humanity's future looks far from bright.
The year is 2115, and Earth is dying. For Wyn, Lois, and Judd,
that's the least of their problems.

Get the first episode in the monthly sci-fi horror
serial that's guaranteed to knock your socks off...

SCAN ME

About the Author

Paul Stephenson writes pulp fiction for the digital age. His first novel series – the apocalyptic *Blood on the Motorway* trilogy – has been an Amazon bestseller on both sides of the Atlantic. A former journalist, he has a diploma in Creative Writing from Oxford University.

His stories have been featured on the chart-topping horror podcasts, *The Other Stories* and *The Night's End*. His newest project, the ebook serial *The Sunset Chronicles*, is a dystopian sci-fi thriller that will delight and terrify fans of science fiction and horror alike. He is also the creator of the podcast *Bleakwood*, tales of terror from a mysterious English town, and one half of the *All Creatives Now* team, with fellow horror author, Kev Harrison.

He lives in England with his wife, two children, and one hellhound.

To keep up to date with his books, please visit his website PaulStephensonBooks.com

Also by Paul Stephenson

BLOOD ON THE MOTORWAY

Blood on the Motorway

An apocalyptic storm. A killer on the loose. The battle for humanity's survival starts here.

Sleepwalk City

The fight for control has begun. Who will prevail in the battle for humanity's future in the pulse-quickening sequel to Blood on the Motorway?

A Final Storm

The sky is full of lights once more, and the survivors will need more than luck to get them through the coming storm. Who will survive, and who will thrive, in this heart-pounding finale to the Blood on the Motorway saga?

SUNSET CHRONICLES

Plague. Murder. Unrest. Humanity's future looks far from bright.

The year is 2107, and Earth is dying. For Wyn, Lois, and Judd, that's the least of their problems. Each holds a key to Earth's cure and humanity's survival in The Sunset Chronicles, the new sci-fi horror thrill-ride from Paul Stephenson, author of the bestselling British horror saga, Blood on the Motorway.

BLEAKWOOD

Introducing Bleakwood, a horror podcast from the creator of Blood on the Motorway and the Sunset Chronicles.

In the years since the fall, many of us have tried to find out why. To find what lead us here. But with so much of the old world gone, there are more questions than answers.

What tore a hole in the world?

Can we ever get it back?

But I think I've found something. A binder in the rubble. Don't ask me where. Full of stories about a little town called Bleakwood, stories that seem to show a way that....

They're not in any order, really. And I might be wrong. They might not have the answer.

But I think it's in here.

A way back. To the before.

Listen, I'm just going to read them out, and you judge for yourself.

DARE YOU VENTURE INTO BLEAKWOOD?

WHAT TORE A HOLE IN THE WORLD?
CAN WE EVER GET IT BACK?

Find out in Bleakwood, the new horror podcast from the creator of Blood on the Motorway and The Sunset Chronicles

Created and narrated by Paul Stephenson and with stories by some of the most exciting voices in British modern Horror, subscribe to Bleakwood for a fresh story every month.

SCAN ME